A NOVEL BY A.S. FITZ

Cover Design by Brian Banash

Printed in the United States of America

First Printing, 2017

ISBN 978-1502570031

DEDICATION

To Angie, who isn't afraid

CHAPTER ONE

Paris. Summer, 2008

Before I became a monster, I fell in love with a girl named Celeste.

On the day we met I awoke drenched in sweat, the unrelenting heat wave that gripped Paris stretching into its 13th day. Eager to escape the stifling room I shared with Coco, a kindred spirit and wandering misfit from the Ivory Coast, I blindly sifted through a pile of clothes on the floor. Shrugging into a pair of shorts, I lost my balance in the darkness and fell back against the frame of the bunk bed. "*Beaucoup de Soleil*" he moaned in his sleep, as I slipped on my flip-flops and hurried past him. Stepping outside, I was met by a wall of dank air. The sun hadn't even risen and the air already held a palpable weight, promising yet another oppressive day of searing heat and humidity. Yet it felt good to be breathing the outside air, free of the confines of our modest hostel, the appropriately named *Maison des Hommes*. I felt a thin sheen of perspiration break out on my face, as I made for a nearby café whose doors were just opening to the street. With an effort I repressed a deep longing for a towering iced coffee, which they didn't serve anyway, and instead ordered a steaming espresso, relying on the bitter elixir to burn away the night's cobwebs.

Raising the child-sized teacup to my lips, an expansive yawn popped my jaw. I'd slept poorly once again, waking often and disoriented throughout the long night. A whimpering cry drew my attention to a table across the room. At the foot of a chair, a Yorkshire terrier lay fast asleep, pawing the air in the throes of a dream. An older man in a pressed linen shirt and cream colored bowtie paused from his newspaper to reach down and scratch its head. His mustachios were waxed and curled to an exquisite porcelain-like perfection. My father had been equally proud of his own wild and unruly cookie duster, although why I'll never know. It had squatted on his upper lip like a bloated caterpillar, as ill-tempered as he was himself. The dog whined again and I thought of my childhood dog, long dead these many years. The café was nearly empty, yet it felt crowded with the ghosts of my past. As I took another sip of espresso, a dream fragment from the night before came back to me.

I had been a boy again, enfolded in the plush velour of my mother's canary yellow love seat, knees tucked snugly under my pajama top. I waited in anticipation before the stout wood-paneled Zenith for my favorite show to start. A kind-looking man appeared on the screen, his hair a perfect snow-white like my grandpa, and announced the start of the program with a broad smile: *Mutual of Omaha's Wild Kingdom.* "Today my fellow adventurers, we will travel deep into the wilds of uncharted Africa," he proclaimed. His face grew serious, the smile diminishing. "On this journey, you must remember never to look into the eyes of a predator. They will consider it to be a direct challenge and attack!" The scene switched to a lioness tracking an endless herd of water buffalo as they lumbered across the open expanse of the savannah.

She lay hidden within the tall grasses, but the buffalo could clearly sense her presence, snorting and stamping their hooves in agitation, while she slid with a liquid grace through the concealing brush. I saw the fear reflected in the wide bulging eyes on the screen. The camera panned to a mother circling around her young calf. I feared for it, knowing she could not protect it from the lion.

"To survive, the calf must learn to read the hidden signs that warn of a predator's approach" said the man's voice. I knew the truth of this first-hand, having learned to recognize the forewarnings of my father's rages. The purple and orange blossoms coloring my arms and legs were reminders of the price for being careless. He too struck without warning. My senses had become attuned to the nuances of his anger. I remained on constant alert for the twitch of an eye, or a thinning of his lips, that like distant flashes in the African sky, foreshadowed the thunderclap of violence.

In spite of my usual vigilance, I had become so engrossed in the program, that I didn't hear him enter the room until it was too late. The wooden floors were creaky, but he knew where to step. His open hand flashed out in a blur, slapping me hard across the face.

"Devil's box!" He cursed, and angrily twisted the knob. The wilds of Africa shrank to a pinpoint of light as his heavy tread carried him out of the room. My cheek stung like a swarm of angry bees. I raised a hand to it and the breath hitched in my chest, my eyes welling with tears.

Don't cry.

I repeated it to myself until the clammy grasp of fear was replaced by the slow burn of anger. I hated him almost as much as the man who'd run over mommy with his truck. To my father, the only show not broadcast by Satan himself aired every Monday and Wednesday night on channel 77: *Hour of Power,* with Reverend Robert Tilton. My father would sit entranced, rapt with wonder, his prayer cloth clasped tight in trembling hands. The cheap square of white cotton had come in the mail one day in a large, oversized envelope, and he carried it everywhere with him. On the screen, Tilton's clean-shaven face erupted with divine joy one moment, only to crumble the next with sorrow for the world's countless sinners. I watched his eyes. They were flat and hungry, like the lion's. The Reverend mopped his brow with his own prayer cloth (which would later be auctioned off to the highest bidder in the television audience, can you say *Amen!*) and then he looked up, his eyes boring through the screen into my own. "All sinners can be saved if they accept the Lord Jesus Christ, but not you son." An evil smirk tugged at the corners of his mouth. "You're going to burn."

"*Burn.*" repeated my father, a feral hunger in his eyes. He lunged at me, lifting my small frame into the air with hands that had become claws, his jaws stretched wide.

"Monsieur?"

I jumped from my chair, upending the table with a crash. The commotion brought a ruffled *"Ahem"* from the mustachioed man, but failed to wake the dog. With a mumbled *desole* to the alarmed waiter, I fled from the café into the street, down one lane and then another not caring where my strides took me, until at last I stopped, gasping for breath. Looking around, I failed to recognize a single landmark or street name. I was in a part of the city wholly unfamiliar to me –much older with blackened cobblestone streets, lined by ornate gas lamps with brass finials. Open air markets were commonplace in Paris, and the street was flanked on either side by rows of tables displaying the usual tourist trinkets: mini-plaster statues of the Champs-Eleys and Mont Saint Michelle, postcards, bottle openers and "I left my Cour in Paris" T-shirts.

Voices rang out above the relative quiet of the street, and I spied a man and woman locked in a heated conversation next to one of the market stalls. Her back was towards me, while his face lay obscured in the shadow of a crisp white fedora. A rapid exchange of French passed between them, too fast for me to understand. My grasp of the language was marginal at best, but anyone could tell they were arguing. Her voice kept rising until she threw both hands up in the air and yelled in perfect English, "Well who then?" Feeling slightly self-conscious about eavesdropping on their conversation, I was starting to walk away as he lifted his head, revealing a square jaw and hawkish nose.

"*Le Garcon*" he said, looking directly at me.

I looked around me in confusion, as a man walking by gave a low, appreciative whistle. Without skipping a beat, she favored him with a bewitching smile, coquettishly batting her almond-shaped eyes. Her admirer slowed, but then redoubled his pace at the raised middle finger she held before her. She smirked at his hasty retreat, and I found myself grinning along with her. Despite a fierce demeanor, her fine boned features possessed a delicate quality. It contrasted nicely with the slight pout of her lips and shock of jet black hair, shot through with a single bolt of electric blue. Before I knew what had happened, she was standing right in front of me.

"*Vous Aimez?*" she asked, her eyes full of malice.

My mouth opened and then shut like a human nutcracker. I risked a glance over her head for the man in the fedora, but he was gone.

"See something you like?" she repeated, her tone sharp and challenging. I returned my attention to her face and blinked, disoriented. Her eyes were unnervingly opaque, like gazing into the depths of a deep well.

"*Bonjour,* I mean Hi! I was just..." I stammered and then gestured behind her, "Uh, admiring the cool souvenirs."

The corner of her mouth curved upwards.

I know what you were looking at and it certainly was not souvenirs, her expression said. She sniffed once in dismissal and spun on her heels to walk back to where she'd been standing, turning her back to me once more. Displayed on a table before her were an assortment of glass globes, each depicting some iconic French tourist destination.

She picked up one that held a miniature replica of Mont Saint-Michel, and turned it over in her hands, inspecting it before giving it a determined shake that called forth a white tempest upon the magnificent city-island. In spite of my present embarrassment, the swirling flakes awoke within me an intense longing for home. Six weeks had passed since I'd boarded a plane in Kansas City and stepped off in *La Ville-Lumière*, the City of Lights.

There's nothing left there for me now, I thought with the unflinching certainty of youth. As she held the globe aloft, it was speared by a ray of sunlight that refracted within, imbuing it with a brilliant golden glow. The sun was just topping the tiled roofs that lined our quaint promenade. Paris had the market cornered when it came to quaint promenades. I found myself wondering, not for the first time, if this place was real, and not merely a waking daydream. As if to add to the effect, someone started strumming a guitar nearby. She turned toward the sound, her profile framed in a perfect halo of summer sunlight and music.

I had just turned 18, and the image captured me completely. A wave of such overpowering desire crashed through me that I felt my knees tremble.

The flesh is weak

The cold voice within my head doused the flames of my passion like an ice water baptism. My father, half a world away, was still trying to have the last word.

A sudden outburst of rabid snarling and barking shattered my reverie. It startled me, and I took an involuntary step backwards, bumping into a man standing with his back to mine.

What happened next, I attributed afterwards to an overactive imagination fueled by espresso and teenage hormones. The sound of the dogs fighting intensified and then a piercing howl split the air. The man next to me craned his head in the direction of the melee, providing a partial view of his profile. The dogs seemed to agitate him, for his body stiffened and a frown darkened his face. To my alarm his lips drew back from black gums, revealing teeth that seemed much too long. I stood there transfixed as his brow furrowed and bunched outwards, nostrils flaring wide. He must have sensed me watching him. He whipped his head towards mine, and *his eyes, oh Jesus why were his eyes yellow?* I cried out as someone seized me by the shoulder. I spun around with my hands upraised as if to ward off a blow, and there she was again. When I looked back the man had vanished.

"Did you see--?" I broke off, unsure of what to say. The street was quiet once more, and the dogs had ceased their barking.

Without acknowledging my half-formed question, she asked "Are you hungry?"

"Am I what?" I asked stupidly.

"Hungry." She repeated. "You know, for food?"

Say something you fool!

She was so beautiful. I managed to nod once.

"What was that?" she said putting a hand to her ear, "Oh, yes, I'd love to have lunch with you!" The whole thing was so absurd that I burst out laughing.

"So it's decided then." She said with a smile, and took my hand.

As we walked, her fingers interlaced with mine; and with her other hand she dropped something heavy into the front pocket of my jacket. Behind us the vendors continued to hawk their wares to passersby, less one snow globe perhaps.

We were inseparable after that. Our time together was spent drifting from one café to the next, a bottle of wine (or several) always on the table before us. Up until that point in my life, I'd never had so much as a single drink of alcohol. My father hadn't been able to start the day without one. I learned quickly that wine often led to greedy fingers fumbling at buttons and zippers in the dark. Overnight, I came to love everything red or white that came in a bottle. We drank, we laughed, and we made love. Three weeks passed in the blink of an eye.

* * * *

"*Mon Coeur*" I moaned, rolling off Celeste's glorious sweat-beaded body and collapsing onto the mattress next to her. I took a ragged gulp of air, my heart knocking against my ribs.

"It's hot in here. Africa-hot," I gasped, trying to catch my breath. It seemed that I had being trying to do just that for the last three weeks, and what glorious weeks they'd been, filled with wine, sex, and little else. As the room came back into focus, I amended my previous assessment. Africa was a vast trackless land, and our own *dehabilement* was cozy even by

European standards. Touching three of the four walls, the very bed itself seemed disgruntled with its confinement.

Celeste made a small sound, and I raised myself up on one arm to look at her face. She lay still, her eyes closed, skin and bare breasts glowing with the flush of our exertions. She made love like the world might end, and then slept as if it had.

The heat continued to press down upon me, so I rolled off the bed and lurched to the window. I grasped the sill with both hands and squeezed my torso through the stingy frame, reveling in the feel of the cool night air on my fever-hot skin.

Three stories below, tables spilled out into the street, the smells and sounds of feasting wafting up to our window. Our frenetic love making had left me depleted, and the heady aromas brought a gush of saliva to my mouth. I took one last deep breath and pulled my head back under the window jam, careful not to crack it as I'd done an embarrassing number of times already.

The rise and fall of her breasts had taken on a slower, more natural rhythm. Her angelic repose contrasted starkly with the chaos of our accommodations. The bed was a shambles, the pillows and sheets tangled and bunched up into a miniature mountain range of fabric. Perched on the corner of the bed was a small wooden cutting board with the remains of our earlier *petite dejeuner:* bread crusts, a small wedge of Brie cheese, and a few grapes, all of which I gathered up in one hand and crammed into my mouth.

As I savored the salty, sweet morsel, my eyes returned to the young sylph before me, naked but for a silver necklace. It was unlike any I'd seen before, adorned with a thin cylindrically shaped tube that fell between her breasts. She'd told me that it carried the ashes of someone very dear to her, and never removed it, not during love making or even in the shower. To me, it merely added to her mystery and sex appeal.

As I stared at her, an unexpected and poignant sadness washed over me.

"You're just a stupid kid," my father's voice said with a sneer, *"Look at her."*

He was right. I knew such a wild beauty couldn't be possessed for long. She would grow bored and leave me eventually.

I didn't care. I would stay with her for as long as she'd have me.

"Hey." Her eyes were open, lucid once more, but they held a pensive expression I didn't recognize.

"Is something wrong?" I asked, placing a hand on her thigh, but she brushed it away.

"I need to go for a walk." She answered. "Alone."

"Is this another surprise?" I asked, trying to sound playful. She loved getting a laugh at my expense, from a random passionate embrace in a crowd to volunteering me as unwitting fodder for a street vendor's act. But she didn't rise to my attempt at levity.

"I'll be back in *cinq minutes*." she said and pulled a tight-fitting t-shirt over her head, not bothering with her bra. Desire stirred within me again. I was no match for this woman. I moved to kiss her, but she twisted away from me and was out the door before I could say another word. There was little to do but lay back down and wait for her to return.

I was awakened by her lips brushing my ear. "Get up lover, I do have a surprise for you after all." Half-asleep, I followed her out into the night and to my awaiting doom.

* * * *

After a three hour ferry across the English Channel, we embarked on an evening drive in a tiny two-seat Fiat across the rolling English countryside. Celeste, normally so full of laughter and mischief, drove in a determined silence, her face intent on the road ahead. When I ventured to ask where we were going her reply was curt, "I told you. It's a surprise. You'll see when we get there."

Knowing I would get nothing more out of her, I settled back in my seat and gazed out the window. In the darkness, the landscape was no more than a blur of indistinct shadows, their true form hidden and unknowable. I pondered how little I knew of my mercurial Parisian lover. Since the day we'd met, she'd told me her name and little else: not where she lived, whether she had any family, or if she even had a job. Somehow, she remained a complete mystery after almost a month of being my constant companion.

The miles rolled slowly by until she abruptly jerked hard on the steering wheel and pulled over to stop on the shoulder. I stepped out and stretched my stiff legs, puzzled as to why we had stopped there, without a building or driveway in sight. I yawned into the crisp night air, invigoratingly free of the city odors of sewer gas and car exhaust I'd become accustomed to.

Without a word, she took my arm and pulled me after her into the woods crowding close to the road. After only a few steps, the dense canopy quickly swallowed what little light the night sky had afforded. She did not slow, as surefooted in the darkness as if we were strolling down a street in Paris on a Sunday morning. We pushed further and further in, and still she offered no explanation. It occurred to me that I'd lost any sense of where the road lay. *Where in the name of Heaven was she taking me?* A nameless dread began to build in my chest. I felt an irrational urge to turn and run, but then my eyes discerned a gradual lessening of the oppressive darkness. After a few more steps, I could see a soft light filtering through the trees ahead, and exhaled a great sigh of relief, unaware that I'd been holding my breath. When we at last emerged from the suffocating confinement of the forest, I beheld a far stranger sight than I could have ever imagined.

Before us stood a glade hemmed in by the forest on all four sides. The trees were tightly wrapped in a thick woven mass of vines. It felt as though I had stepped inside an expansive green room, with walls that had grown up from the ground itself. At odds with the natural beauty and wonder of the space, stood an imposing wooden cross. It was a massive structure twice the height of a man, crudely fashioned out of rough-hewn timbers. It had been erected next to a fire pit ringed by a low wall of stone with kindling stacked high within. Four lengths of rope had been lashed to the cross in conspicuous locations, and I gave it a wide berth as I approached the source of light I'd seen though the trees. It emanated from hundreds of candles placed around the base and lower branches of a magnificent sycamore, standing like a sentinel at the center of the glade. Most strange of all, in front of the old giant sat a long table arrayed with a collection of marble busts.

Behind me I heard Celeste mumble something to herself.

"What did you say babe?"

"They're not here yet." She said.

I wasn't listening. My full attention was on the fantastic collection of sculptures before me. They all appeared to be quite old, their features smoothed by the effects of weather and time. As I walked down the length of the table looking into their faces and wondering who they might be, the chiseled bust of a young Adonis—his head framed by a mane of unruly, cascading curls caught my eye. His face tugged at my memory. I moved closer to inspect his strong jaw and full lips.

The hair rose on my scalp and an involuntary shudder ran through me. I felt like an archeologist uncovering Ra's Tomb—if Ra had been a hedonistic, drug addict with a death wish.

I was standing before Jim Morrison's headstone—stolen from his gravesite in Paris over two decades ago. To fans of The Doors, it still ranked as one of rock and roll's enduring mysteries. A thrill coursed through me as I reached out to touch the chiseled features, my fingertips playing across the graffiti and disfiguring pits and gashes where adoring fans had chipped away a small souvenir. "But why here?" I wondered out loud and was nearly knocked over as Celeste pushed past me, eyes darting from one bust to the next, her face a mask of concentration in the half-light. She raised a preemptive hand to silence me before I could speak, a look of irritation flashing across her features.

"But *which one?*" she moaned anxiously.

I watched her with a puzzled expression as she paced back and forth, occasionally stopping to touch a nose or put her hand on a bald palate.

"I didn't know you were so into sculptures," I said, "but there's one here that's gonna blow your mind."

"Please, I need to concentrate."

"Just look at this one right here."

"Thomas please, not now."

"Look at it!" I cried and pointed at the bust.

She sighed, glancing at it and then back at me. "So?"

"Don't you know who this is?" I said, unable to keep the excitement from my voice. "It's Jim fucking Morrison!"

"From the Doors?" I prompted when she didn't respond.

"But what on Earth is it doing here?" I said to myself, examining it once more to convince myself it was real. Even in its mutilated state, Mladen Mikulin's sculpture still projected a certain power and grace.

"There's a rumor that the sculptor hid something from Morrison inside it—a tooth or a lock of hair, maybe even a ring."

Celeste seized my shoulders and roughly pulled me around to face her.

"What did you say?" she hissed, her nails digging into my arms.

With an effort I managed to pry her hands away.

"Say it again." she commanded, her face a mask of intensity

"What's gotten into you?" I asked. Eyeing her warily, I rubbed my sore arms and continued, "There's a cult-belief that something's inside of--" I didn't get a chance to finish as her lips were suddenly pressed against mine. She pulled away, leaving me breathless, a wild light in her eyes.

"It has to be," she whispered, her voice shaking, "He said it would be hidden, somewhere no one would think to look, and he was right! Oh *mon amour*, you've found it!"

"Found what?" I said. "What the hell are you talking about?"

She looked at the statue once more, and then pushed me aside.

"Move back. Quickly!"

She dipped a hand between her breasts and lifted out the bullet-shaped pendant. With a jerk of her hand she snapped the chain.

Approaching the headstone, she twisted the cylinder, and a cap came off in her hand. I was burning with a hundred questions, but so intense was the look on her face that I held my tongue. She held the cylinder as if it were a viper that might strike at the slightest movement.

"Keep back, if you value your life."

She tipped the cylinder over the head of my favorite rock icon, and I watched horrified as a clear liquid splashed onto his marble hair and began to eat through it.

"What are you doing?" I cried.

"*Ne comprend pas*!" she snapped, such malice infusing her voice that I took an involuntary step back.

"You don't understand," she repeated more softly. "This is 37% pure muriatic acid, the strongest concentration you can distill before it becomes unstable. One drop on your arm and it would burn through it like a napkin."

She carefully replaced the cap as the hissing sound tapered off to a low sizzle. Using the cylinder again she lightly tapped the bust, and I watched dumbfounded as it split cleanly in two. She reached a trembling hand into one of the halves and withdrew a wrapped bundle of cloth.

"We must leave now," she said, "before they come."

As if on cue the clouds parted, bathing us in the preternatural light of a great amber moon riding high in the sky above us. It fell upon the giant cross and old tree, casting them in a queer and unsettling candescence. I stood transfixed until the moment passed and the sky veiled itself one more, sending us back into twilight.

Before who *comes?*

"I haven't been entirely truthful," she continued in a strained voice. "There's something I need to tell you but ..."

Her eyes grew wide with fright at something behind me. "Oh no," she said in a small voice. I swung around and watched as the candles began to go out, their light extinguished one by one as if by some invisible hand.

It's only the wind.

But not a breath of air moved among the leaves. The forest stood still and quiet as if waiting. Celeste grabbed ahold of my hand, pulling me towards the opening in the trees where we'd first entered, her head darting from one side of the clearing to the next.

"Wait a minute," I said, but she didn't respond, clasping my hand tightly.

"Just wait!" I yelled and wrenched my hand away. I grabbed her by the shoulders, the soft cotton of her silk foulard bunched in my fists as I pulled her towards me. When she met my eyes the first tendrils of fear uncoiled in my stomach. Her face had drained of all color and her body trembled in my grasp. The snapping of a branch discharged from the opposite side of the clearing and I released her.

"What was that?" I blurted.

Like a sudden shift in barometric pressure, the fear that had been building inside of me broke free of its moorings, unfurling into a mindless terror I hadn't felt since I was a child, cowering under a blanket in my room at night. It was immediate, irrational, and piss-yourself strong. It took every ounce of my self-control not to run. The only sound was my heart hammering in my chest as I looked into the impenetrable night of the woods surrounding us.

Snap!

My head whipped towards the sound. Had I seen something sliding from one tree to the next at the edge of the woods?

"Okay, you're right let's get the hell out of here."

No sooner had the words left my mouth, the woods exploded with a barrage of noise as if some unseen army were fanning out around us. For the first time I wanted very much to go home. Out of the corner of my eye I registered the last candle wink out.

The noises in the woods ceased as abruptly as they'd begun. I held my breath, sensing that others were watching us. A voice shattered the silence like a hammer.

"HALT."

I was assailed by an overpowering dread, rolling out in steady punishing waves from that voice. I felt naked before it.

"HALT IN THE NAME OF THE TWELVE."

Stone and glass ground together in my ears, boring into my head, guttural and relentless. If a mountain could speak it might carry such a voice. My spirit cowered before the awful implacable command in it. The sky cleared again, and my heartbeat surged with a new fear at what it revealed. At the opposite edge of the clearing stood a row of figures, shoulder to shoulder, unmoving. Their faces were hidden within the hoods of the long scarlet-colored robes each wore, the hems pooled on the ground at their feet. I had a brief, bright hope that perhaps they were actors putting on an impromptu play; a merry band of thespians performing a *Midsummer's Night Eve* in the woods at midnight. Folly.

Celeste grasped my arms again and pulled me to face her.

"Push me down and then run if you want to live!" she whispered in my ear.

The figures began to advance in a line towards us.

"Push me and run!" she hissed again. Her voice seemed to come to me from the bottom of a well. When I still made no effort to move she shoved me and staggered back, pretending to free herself. Off-balance, my feet became entangled and I fell to the ground, the impact jolting me from my stupor.

"Get Him!" she screamed pointing at me. I gaped at her in confusion and horror.

"Run Thomas, before it's too late!" she hissed.

A shout rang out from across the clearing and the formation splintered, the figures breaking into a sprint towards me. In disbelief I watched as one dropped to all fours. I scrambled to my feet and fled into the forest.

Time and space unraveled, my world reduced to putting one foot in front of the next. Stinging branches whipped my face and arms, conspiring to hinder my every move. I ran at a reckless pace, fearing with each step I would charge headlong into a tree and snap my neck. Hidden roots and tree limbs tripped me repeatedly, sending me crashing to the ground. Each time I regained my feet, expecting the clasp of hands that would drag me off to a dark and horrible end. The sounds of the chase resounded throughout the forest behind me, driving me on.

I stumbled, nearly falling as the terrain shifted, dropping sharply into a shallow ravine. Plunging forward with my arms pin-wheeling, I fought to regain my balance. A shape rose up before me and the next thing I knew, my back was on the forest floor, a searing pain swelling in my chest. I drew a single burning breath into my lungs before something dragged me to my feet. An overpowering musky odor invaded my senses. I gagged and tried to pull away, but was held fast in a crushing embrace.

Panic flooded through me, and I lashed out at my attacker in a desperate effort to free myself, punching and clawing with all my might. I tore a fistful of hair loose, and the next instant I was lifted into the air. I screamed as a horrible pressure crushed down upon my shoulder, puncturing my shirt, biting deep into skin and muscle. My cry was cut short as I was thrown against the trunk of a tree. I fell broken in a heap to the ground.

Unable to speak or breathe, I lay looking up at a patch of stars through a break in the canopy and thought of the first girl I'd kissed, Holly Simmons from 5th grade. Her lips had been soft and her mouth had tasted like bubble gum. All I could taste now was warm salty blood filling my mouth. The stars vanished as something loomed over me blocking out the sky. A familiar stench assailed me once more. I knew it for what it was, the smell of my own death.

As I waited for the end, I heard the snap of a branch. My attacker straightened and then whipped around as a citrine flash spanned the space between them, followed by a howl of agony that seemed to shake the very trees. A choking furnace-blast of burning hair and flesh singed the air, and the shape above me fled snarling and mewling into the dark. A moment later hands slipped under my shoulders and pulled me to my feet.

"Don't die," I heard Celeste whisper. Somehow she bore my weight as I lurched against her, my chest burning with a slow fire. I felt like I was dying. On the ground nearby lay the empty cylinder from around her neck, the last of its deadly contents spent. As we hobbled away, I looked up through a break in the trees to see the moon tracking our flight. Something crashed through the woods behind us, and then we pushed free into the open air, our blue Fiat waiting patiently before us. Celeste bundled me into the back, and leapt in to start the engine. Tires squealed, the car fishtailing as we sped off. In the rearview mirror a series of dark shapes burst from the woods onto the road. Celeste expertly shifted gears, and soon we were flying along, warm blood soaking through my jeans into the seat.

"Please don't die," I heard Celeste say again before I lost consciousness.

CHAPTER TWO

Five years later. Chicago. Fall.

The tip of my cigarette flashed like a beacon in the mid-day gloom. *A light shines in the darkness,* I thought sourly and exhaled, the smoke hungrily devoured by the whipping October wind. A bad joke made in poor taste—it brought the ghost of a smile to my chapped lips.

I was buffeted by a sudden gust of frigid air that swept up and under my thin army jacket, ballooning it out. Sharp, icy fingers did a quick tap dance across my stomach before I could yank it back down again. A shiver coursed through my body, though not from the wind. The cold didn't even touch me. I was burning up, a fever smoldering just beneath my skin. I wondered what the time was, but didn't feel like digging for my iPhone. I looked up trying to gauge the hour but with the sky the color of a dead fish, the clock had a way of drifting sideways. What I needed was a handful of aspirin washed down with whiskey and a bed to sleep off whatever had its hooks in me.

"To hell with this."

The whole trip out here had been a bust. I now had the joyless prospect of getting back to my apartment seven miles across town; an hour on the Brown Line into the City, and then a transfer to the Blue Line to head back out again. Getting from the northwest side to the southwest side was a losing equation on the CTA. The subway network had been built like the radial spokes on a bike – you had to go in to go out.

I ground the cigarette into the wet leafy mush with my heel, and crossed the street to a gangway that cut between two brick bungalows. The blocks were twice as long in this part of the city—another irritant. I'd be damned if I was going to walk two blocks out of my way to get to the townie bar I'd passed earlier with the flashing *Zymnie Pivo* sign. *Cold beer* were the only two Polish words I would ever need to know, as far as I was concerned. Providentially, the tavern also sat right across the street from the subway stop, and the shortest distance between me and that bar stool was a straight line. My present health aside, I always made time for a beer.

As I pushed open the low chain-link gate that led through the lot to the back alley, something shot between my legs. I turned my head to catch a glimpse of a long hairless tail as it slid around the front of the building. I shook my head in disgust. They were more brazen every year. It had been making good time—for a rat anyway. Even the way they moved repulsed me, humping along like bloated inchworms. Why couldn't they scurry like other rodents? The day I got used to rats would be the day I packed my bags for the countryside.

The homes were packed in tight here like most city blocks with about five feet between them. The narrow confines made an effective wind break, which I took advantage of to light another smoke. I looked down the short run that led to the yard in back, and then to another gate off the garage that opened onto the alley. I dragged the smoke into my lungs and headed for it—a vision of the beer sign flashing in my head.

As I stepped into the backyard I lost my footing on a patch of icy slush, coming from a surcharged storm drain by the back porch. It may have saved my life. As I slipped and fell forward, something clipped my shoulder and the side of my head, pitching me into the chain link fence. I hit it hard and it bent backward under the impact, bowing out into the adjoining yard before springing back to drop me on my knees on the frozen lawn. Blood roared in my ears as the world did a slow circle around me.

There was a sudden blur of movement towards my face and I brought an arm up. Something closed on it like a vice. A scream lodged in my throat as I stared into the eyes of a very large dog – one with my hand crushed in its jaws. I pulled my free hand back into a fist and punched it as hard as I could in the nose. A dog's nose contains thousands of more nerve endings than a human's does. It should have sent him howling across the yard, but instead he bore down even harder. Bad for me. I let loose the scream I'd been holding back as his teeth punctured my glove and then the soft fleshy meat of my palm and thumb. The week before, I'd shoplifted a sturdy pair of thick canvas gloves from Walmart. They were pretty good for softening a stray hammer blow or two, but were no match for inch and half long canines.

The taste of my blood must have excited him. The whites of his eyes grew bright as he dropped his haunches low to the ground and jerked backwards, pulling me off my feet. A more massive specimen of a dog, I don't think I'd ever encountered. He had to be north of 150 lbs. I fell to one knee and then quickly righted myself, forced to move forward with him. If he managed to move up more on my hand and get it between his back molars, he'd crush it like a beer can.

"Drop it!" I shouted, aware of how foolish it sounded - as if we were playing with a chew-toy and not one of my appendages. I tried to land another punch, but he shook his great head back and forth, ripping a fresh scream from me as he tried to gain the advantage.

The only self-defense training I could draw upon came from multiple viewings of *The Karate Kid: Part Two*. In a teaching moment with Daniel-san, Mr. Miyagi had stressed to use an opponent's superior size and strength as a weapon against them.

And so, in an act of profound bravery and stupidity, I stopped trying to free my hand and lunged forward, forcing my hand further into his throat. It felt like shaking hands with a wood chipper. My vision went momentarily black, but it worked. He recoiled and then gagged, releasing me. I tottered backwards, cradling my injured hand that throbbed like a second heart.

He shuddered and shook out a great hacking cough. I looked past him to the gate and to the alley beyond. It was so close, and yet it may as well have been a mile away. If I tried to run he would bring me down before I made it five feet. Once he had me on the ground things could quickly go from bad to worse. I looked at him again and it was my undoing. The white of his muzzle had been stained red by his coughing fit. My own personal shade of red.

The first stirrings quivered within me. Deep inside, storm clouds began to gather on the horizon of my inner landscape. The sight of blood and the agony of my injured hand called like twin sirens, compelling *IT* to awaken.

With a jolt, I realized I was just standing there letting it happen. In a panic, I raided my pockets, searching for my pills.

Where the hell were they?

Emboldened and unaware of the impending danger, he padded towards me, his lips curled back to reveal gums as black as night. Somewhere within the trackless and blasted terrain of my psyche it awoke. Deep inside the dank cave where it slumbered, a hideous shape arose and stepped from the entrance, its long tongue spilling out from its jaws in anticipation of the work ahead.

The throbbing in my hand flared up as if in response, and I gasped as it lanced up my arm into my chest, my very blood catching fire.

Jesus where are my pills?

It gathered speed, racing like a liquid fire through my veins, incinerating everything in its path. It reached my eyes and in a red flash the yard smoldered before me.

A low growl rolled out across the air between us and he stopped dead in his tracks, testing the air with his nose. We stood motionless, facing one another. With every beat of my heart, I could feel his fear grow, until with a quickness belying his size, he leapt, fangs bared to tear my throat. He moved with a speed admirable for his size, but I was ready. I turned my body in tandem with his. Seizing hold of his great head with both hands, I cast him to the ground. The impact broke like a wave upon the frozen soil knocking the breath from his lungs. I dropped down and lay hold of him once more. He gave a frenzied whine and whipped his head trying to shake me loose. I grasped his muzzle in both hands, slowly prying open the trap of his mighty jaws.

I hated killing dogs, but I was no longer myself. The air was split by the report of snapping bone, scattering the pigeons on the eaves above us into the sky.

I let the limp body fall to the ground once more. Swaying slightly, I peeled the shredded glove from my injured hand, and scratched at the dried blood there. My nails dislodged a shower of rusty flakes that drifted slowly down to the ground like ashes. Underneath it there were no punctures. No red, raw flesh. My wounds had healed in less time than it took to take a life.

Or smoke a cigarette.

What was a cigarette?

There were things I needed to remember. Important things.

The thought vanished: stolen away by the winds of the roaring tempest inside me.

My senses snapped to attention as my ears piqued to a new sound: a steady, rhythmic cadence. Snoring. It resonated inside my head as if I were standing over the sleeper, and not in the frigid air outside. I turned around to face the house.

Yes.

Inside.

Blood had been spilled, but not enough. I took a step towards the back door and a loud crunch issued from underfoot. I kicked at what lay there, my eyes following the object as it bounced across the brittle grass with a hollow rattling sound. Cylindrical and orange, it tugged at my memory.

Something to remember.

Someone slept inside.

A name. I have a name.

Crack their ribs

Remember!

Devour their beating heart

A name.

Lap up their blood.

The pill bottle you fool!

I dove forward and grasped it, tearing the lid off with my teeth. Tipping my head back I poured a stream of bright red capsules into my mouth and chewed. Choking on the bitter paste, I bit back against the rising bile in my throat and forced myself to swallow.

Work!

Work Goddammit!

Like opening a window onto a winter night, a coldness expanded inside me, and wrapped its fingers around my heart. I clawed at my chest, fighting for breath that wouldn't come. The vessel of my body filled with ice water, extinguishing the flames until the inferno hissed, sputtered and then died. At last my lungs filled with air and I collapsed to the ground, the muted winter colors returning to the frozen world around me.

* * * *

My eyes fluttered open and I slowly sat up. It appeared that I was lying in someone's yard surrounded by a gratuitous amount of dog shit. Judging by my own smell, the odds that I hadn't rolled in it were not in my favor. Oh well, shit washed out easier than blood.

But there's blood on your hands Thomas.

And by the way, is that a dead dog lying in the grass?

I looked at the body and it all came back to me in a rush. I managed to stand, and hobble over to it on watery knees. Silent and still on the frozen turf, its block-shaped head had been twisted around like a broken puppet. I recognized the breed, a Mastiff. No other dog grew that friggin' big. I'd bet a dollar his owner had named him Spike or maybe Killer. With numbed fingers I fumbled at his tags but they were scuffed and illegible. I studied his face. He didn't look like a Killer. In death he looked peaceful with a kind of dopey, sweet countenance, one that belonged more to a Charlie. My heart felt like a stone in my chest. Another mark against my soul. One more dark deed.

It dawned on me that someone might have seen the whole thing and could be on the phone to the cops at that moment. I looked over to the equally depressing yard next door – littered with crap the owner was too lazy to drag out to the alley: rusted bicycle frames, a capsized plastic kiddie pool with a gaping crack in the middle, an overgrown weed-choked garden plot sprouting an assortment of beer cans and soft drink bottles. A lone spindly-looking tree was festooned with plastic bags, trapped and fluttering in the bare branches.

This part of Chicago was alien to me. I was accustomed to the tightly packed two and three flats of my neighborhood with stoops that spilled right out onto the sidewalk. Out here the identical rows of brick bungalows with their tiny manicured lawns made me feel like I was in a different city altogether. I regretted accepting the job, and all I had to show for it were some aching ribs and a dead dog. The irony wasn't lost on me; I'd come to save a dog, not kill one. The jerk who called me about it had almost made me turn it down.

"Just bring him back or the kid'll be bawling til' next winter," he'd complained. "For five large he better not have a scratch on him, got it? And oh yeah, I almost forgot, his name is Duke."

Duke? Strange name for a diminutive Jack Russell. But the fee was five times what I normally got, so I'd taken it with no questions asked. In my experience missing pets didn't make it far from home anyway before being snatched by Animal Control or getting run over. I picked up his scent outside the courtyard of the apartment complex and tracked it right to the intersection of Brynn Mawr and Pulaski, both major streets. It didn't bode well for Duke's chances if he'd tried to cross there, but the Montrose and Bohemian cemeteries (a huge open expanse of grass for a dog to run free) were just on the other side. After spending an hour among the tombstones, I gave up and circled back to his neighborhood again. And here I was, back to square one.

"Hey!"

The voice belonged to the shriveled head of an old man, poking out of a window next door like a hairless gopher.

"Whatcha doing with that dog, mister?"

The geezer's voice was high pitched and wheezy but it still had some life left in it, maybe enough to pick up a phone and hit zero. Before I could make something up, the head disappeared back in its hole.

Time to go.

I squatted to retrieve a cigarette butt and my pill bottle, the less evidence the better. My spirits sunk when I saw the few lonely pills rattling inside. How many had I taken? What did it matter? I'd done what I'd had to. The drugs would hold it at bay, put a muzzle on it. But then why could I still feel its presence, like someone eyeballing me from the other side of a two-way mirror? Were they losing their potency already? As if on cue my heart rate jumped and then settled again, only not as slow as before.

I shuffled to the back gate and then froze.

Had I lost it?

I hurriedly patted myself down and then exhaled a sigh of relief, as I felt its hard outline through the fabric of my jacket. The flask that I kept for "emergencies" was still there. As I fished it out my pulse spiked again. I took a long pull. The whiskey helped, kneading its hot fingers into my muscles. But I still felt pinched, like I was stuck on an elevator between floors.

Keep cool Thomas. Everything's under control.

My finances would have preferred a two dollar bus fare, but being crammed on a bus full of people didn't seem too smart after what had just happened to Charlie. I'd learned the hard way not to tempt fate, I often lost more than I bargained for. I lurched down the alley to the street and hailed a cab as my stomach rumbled impressively.

I got in just as a police siren started to sound. We sped off, almost edging the business end of a garbage truck and zipped through the ghost of a yellow light. I nodded in silent approval. Give me a motoring sociopath over a Sunday driver any day. I wanted to get where I was going, and if I felt safe in the back of a cab then they weren't doing their job.

My face broke out in a sweat as an icy-hot flash coursed through me, a side effect from the mixture of barbiturates and beta blockers – Eric's latest concoction. I cracked a window and concentrated on my breathing to steady my pulse. The seatback in front of me had an advertisement of a man in a suit sitting at a table with a bowl full of lemons and a pitcher full of money. *When life hands you lemons,* read the caption, *trust First Bank to make the lemonade.* There was a vibrating buzz followed by Ozzy Osbourne singing "Hey yeah Bark at the Moon!" I fumbled my phone out.

"Ramsey's Retrieval Service. Ben speaking."

"You're an asshole," said a voice on the other end in a matter-of-fact tone.

"Grandma, what a naughty mouth you have," I replied.

"All the better to…oh fuck this, my head hurts too much." The voice said with a groan. It belonged to none other than Eric "the Red" Evans – friend, pharmacology wizard, and someone with a shared weakness for bourbon.

"Grab an aspirin and nut-up. There's been a minor incident," I replied. There was a momentary silence, broken immediately by loud cursing.

"Just tell me I won't have to get out a box of tranqs."

"Tranquilizers?" I said, raking my fingernails across my jaw, "That'll only make me angry." My face had started to itch like crazy.

"Not if I give you the batch I just cooked up. They pack enough carfentanil to take down a pissed off bush elephant. I also happen to be a damn good shot, and you know it."

A sour head could equal a sour mood, and his mood seemed a step above curdled milk. There was no arguing with him though. That much Zombie Dust would take me down for sure, and cheap whiskey was a gentle kiss compared to the hangover it would deliver.

"Look, everything's cool but your new pills are no good. I didn't even get a buzz."

There was a pause. "I seriously can't believe you forgot again."

And then it hit me.

Shit.

The cycle. With everything that had gone on the last few days I'd forgotten to check the calendar. It was inexcusable, pathetic really. I wish I could say it was the first time.

How can a werewolf forget about the full moon?

"Of course I didn't forget," I lied. "I'm on my way back now. No need to shoot me with anything yet." I said as I scratched my neck.

Eric was the first person I confided in all those years ago. He hadn't believed a word I'd told him, but after that night in the cellar he'd become a believer. He was extraordinarily lucky to still be alive.

I looked up, and in the rear view mirror the cabbie's eyes were as wide as dinner plates. How much had he heard? I tried to smile but his eyes snapped back to the road and he floored the gas again. It struck me as funny for some reason. A mild euphoria had taken hold of me, making me want to laugh.

Whiskey, pills, and a werewolf, oh my.

I slapped a hand over my mouth to stifle a giggle. "You better not be drunk goddammit!" Eric fumed.

"Hey, how's it coming with the latest tests?" I asked, trying to change the subject. "If the Professor keeps taking pieces off me there won't be much left to work with. Any promise with those protease inhibitors she's been tweaking?"

"Whatever she's got she's not sharing it yet. You know how tightlipped she can be." Eric replied sullenly.

I grinned at the thought of Penelope in her lab coat, frowning over the latest calculations, a lock of hair twisted tightly around her finger. She usually kept it up in a make-shift bun, a pen jammed through the center to hold it together. I preferred when she let it cascade freely down her back. I said as much once, and her reply was that she would either cure me or kill me trying to. Then she had smiled at me and put her hair back in a bun.

Considering how often she stuck me with something sharp, it appeared she'd been serious about the last part. Long ago she might have seen something different in me, but--M*mmpph!* My face smashed into the back of the front seat as the cabbie swerved violently to a tire-screeching halt.

"Out!" he screamed. Terror warred with disgust on his face. "You get out of my fucking cab, man!"

A car whipped past blasting its horn, and I caught my reflection in the window. An impressive amount of spittle hung like a string of Christmas tinsel from my budding beard.

That came in fast.

I also became aware of a cloying vomity smell of dog shit mingled with urine. I had apparently pissed myself, a sometimes side effect of the transformation.

I pulled out a small wad of crumpled bills, mostly ones, and held them up like an offering. I cringed to see a dark shit-like smear obscuring one of Washington's faces like a dirty caul. With an act of finality the cabbie jabbed his finger once in the direction of the door. I guess he'd had enough of this slobbering, hair-sprouting weirdo.

"I gotta go." I growled at Eric and hung up as he started to protest.

I stuffed the phone and the cash back in my pocket and stepped out the door.

When life hands you lemons!

"Have another drink," I finished, reaching again for my flask.

CHAPTER THREE

I tried not to live by too many rules, but over the years I'd settled on two. The first: Never follow a beautiful French girl into the woods at night. The second: Always stick with the first plan. Make a decision and execute it. No prisoners, no excuses.

It became clear my second rule needed re-examining, as I stepped out of the cab and onto a sidewalk that wasn't there. I felt a momentary sense of unreality wash over me as I realized where I was. I spun around to leap back into the cab but it was gone, the back door banging in the wind as it sped off.

In his desperation to be rid of me, the cabbie had kicked me out onto a bend on the east side of the southbound drive: a slender ribbon of parkway separating four lanes of traffic rushing past on either side. In all the time I'd lived in Chicago, I'd never seen anyone standing on these medians, not even a bum. The O-shaped mouths of a car full of kids zipped by, as they got an eyeful of the crazy guy standing in the median.

How long would it be before the cops showed up? In my condition that was the last thing I needed. I gathered myself to make a run for it, but each time I did a stream of cars would burst past right as I was about to go.

I closed my eyes and felt for the presence of the other within my blood. I had to keep it caged until I reached the mansion. There were too many people on the other side, strolling along the lake. If the wolf were freed now it would cut through them like a scythe through a field of winter wheat.

I waited. And just when it seemed the traffic would never clear, it did. I looked quickly in either direction and threw myself into the gap. I was across the first two lanes when my foot was swallowed whole, plunged into a hidden void of oily black water that sent me sprawling onto the pavement hard enough to rattle my teeth. The previous winter had made national headlines, the Polar Vortex spawning thousands of potholes-- notorious ruiners of rims and suspensions. I scrambled to my feet as the prodigious metallic bulk of a dump truck swung around the bend, a dangling chain from the back raising sparks as it scored the pavement. I stood there frozen in place as it bore down on me.

Tick.

In the limitless gulf that stretched between one second and the next, I beheld the unkempt profile of my executioner. A Chicago White Sox cap was cocked at a 45 degree angle on his head, the smoke trail from his cigarette escaping through a crack in the window. His bloodshot eyes widened in response to my own. Sitting on the seat next to him was the Grim Reaper. It waved.

Tick.

Breaking through the chains of my paralysis, I leapt for the sidewalk that lay an ocean of asphalt away. I hung suspended in the air as the ragged corner of the truck's bumper clipped the heel of my shoe, sending my body spinning through the air, to crash-land in a bruised heap at the edge of the bike path.

With tentative hands I did a quick inventory of my extremities. I was still in one piece.

Alive!

Shaking the dirt and leaves from my hair, I hobbled to a semi-standing position and looked around me, wondering if time had stopped again. I was surrounded by manikins, each staring unabashedly at the unkempt figure that had just fallen uninvited into their midst. Walking, running, pushing a stroller, or throwing a football, they were all as still as statues. An obese black woman even had a finger up her nose, frozen in mid-pick.

I swallowed and cleared my throat to speak. "It's alright. I'm ok…I…" I raised a hand and then let it slowly drop.

No one stepped forward to offer a hand or ask me if I was hurt. They just continued to stare at me in alarm, their wide eyes broadcasting, *hide the women and children*! Could I blame them? Hadn't I walked stone-faced past homeless women and children begging in the street? Life in the city could harden your heart. I was proof enough of that.

Still, I despised them. I met their eyes and something in my own made them turn their heads. *"What are you bastards looking at?"* I wanted to scream. My pulse drummed in my ears and for an instant I looked through a different set of eyes. Prey not people spread out before me, their hearts waiting to be ripped out. My hands bunched into fists as they hurried away, some on the verge of running. I glowered at them and then took off running, trying not to lope too much. The safe house lay a mere 10 miles to the south.

* * * *

My breath fogged out before me as the temperature dropped. Shrugging out of my army jacket, I tucked it under my arm and settled into a steady run. In minutes, sweat had soaked through my shirt and was pooling in my shoes. I longed to tear my clothes off and run naked.

Roller-bladers, bikers, and runners avoided me like I was on fire, some even veering off the path into the grass as they passed. I must have looked like a deranged hunchback, doubled over as if I'd been shot in the gut. I ignored them all, focusing with my full attention on the black asphalt path stretching away before me. It stank like a cesspit thanks to my heightened sense of smell.

As I passed the assiduously manicured greenery of the museum campus, the people began to thin out until I ran alone on the path at last. My body ached like I'd tumbled down a flight of stairs, but it was the discomfort of someone else's body, another person's pain.

Not much sand left in the hour glass.

The first whisper of doubt crept into my head. I grimaced and tried to coax more speed from my cramping legs. The transformation could be agonizingly slow.

In the movies the full moon always triggered the transformation from Joe Normal to a slathering beast, like flipping a switch labeled "werewolf." But in reality, one did not collapse to the ground and begin screaming in one instant, and then in the next chase some poor girl through the woods and devour her. My stomach rumbled again.

Instead, the transformation followed a gradual cycle with no true beginning or end. After that night in the woods outside London, I had ceased to be entirely human, but neither was I entirely inhuman. I was simply more of one or the other depending on the day of the month, with the exception of *one* night of course.

My metabolism swung back and forth on the pendulum of that ever approaching and receding night – a maddening business. For most of the month the changes taking place were internal: a gradual shortening of temper, trouble sleeping, and a general feeling of restlessness. It wasn't until the last hours on the final day of the cycle that I began to outwardly change, metamorphosing into something unfathomable to me and terrifying to everyone else.

However, six months ago things began to change, and I had no idea why. It troubled me but I knew it worried Penelope and Eric much more. For some reason, it no longer took a full moon to initiate the transformation. If I was injured, or allowed myself to become angry, things could spin out of control quickly. No one had said as much yet, but it was obvious to us all that the cycle was becoming more unpredictable and difficult to manage with each passing day.

I became aware of a warm wetness on my leg. I'd pissed myself again. But glancing down I observed a surgical-like tear in my pants along the outer thigh. Loping along with my arms swinging at my sides, my stiletto-like fingernails had sliced open my jeans like paper. Looking at my nails reminded me of a cashier at the grocery store last week. Her nails had been two inches long and painted with sparkling stars and squiggly lines. I'd quietly marveled that she managed to do her job at all, much less get dressed in the morning.

Something moved at the periphery of my vision. I turned my face toward the purplish bruise of the sky over Lake Michigan. It shimmered like a mirror and then rippled outward in expanding rings towards the horizon, as if a titan stone had been cast down from the heavens.

Fear and anticipation warred within me. As the transformation accelerated, a world that had been dead more than a millennia came to life once more. A foreign yet familiar landscape coalesced around me, draped like a second skin over the City. I ran along an asphalt path built by machines, but with each step my feet also fell on ground that my ancestors had ruled, back when humans still groomed each other for insects and hid in the forest. It was both beautiful and terrifying. But mostly terrifying.

I looked down at the path below me, superimposed upon a trackless grassland that stretched away in every direction to meet the sky. To the west, the shimmering city skyline rose towering into the sky, casting monolithic shadows out across the sea of waving grasses. My own shadow ran beside me, but not on two legs.

My body ached with hunger and a thirst for something not sold in six packs. In the failing light the outline of a man and his dog walking across the grass pulsed with a reddish glow. 31st Street beach lay just ahead. I'd covered over five miles in half an hour but still had a long way to go. I passed Burnham Park and then was up onto the footbridge at 35th that spanned Lake Shore Drive, the traffic a prismatic blur beneath me. I was going to make it.

I was not going to make it.

Two of Chicago's Finest were approaching from the opposite side. They were laughing, sharing some private joke until they looked across and saw me. Startled looks replaced their smiles as I hurtled towards them. I could smell their alarm, a spikey scent riding in the air between us. In unison they stopped, one dropping a hand to the holster of his firearm.

I lengthened my gait, took two bounding steps and then sprang into the air, the fortified muscles in my legs propelling my body forward like a massive hairy spring. I gave full voice to the howl that had been building in my breast, and they both fell backwards onto the path. "Jesus Christ!" one cried out as I shot between them, clearing twenty feet in a single leap. Without looking back I vaulted over the railing, and ran with everything I had towards Martin Luther King Drive three blocks to the west.

Back at the station they'd tell their buddies that they almost arrested *the friggin' big foot* and laugh a little too loud. But in the dead of night, lying awake next to their snoring wives, they'd wrestle with it alone: the knowledge that they'd seen something that should not exist. Sweet dreams coppers.

I raced between a pair of drab mid-rise apartments and straight into the side of a jet black Hummer speeding through the alley. The force of the impact rocked the vehicle as I ricocheted off the driver's side door and fell half-unconscious to the ground.

The square metal hulk squealed to a stop, a deep thumping bass rattling the windows from inside. I could hear muffled cursing as someone attempted to open the damaged door. It looked like it had taken a direct hit from a cannon ball. I rose unsteadily to my feet as I heard the passenger door open and then slam shut on the opposite side. From around the front of the car appeared the poster child for gang banger wannabes everywhere—a skinny white kid trying hard to be black. He angled toward me with one arm swinging lazily from side to side, imitating the ghetto swagger he'd probably picked up from watching actual gang members. The kid frowned, trying hard to convey a sense of menace while holding up his baggy pants with one hand. My hands itched to grab him and manhandle him into a belt.

"I'm gonna dust you punk!" He cried in a high pitched voice. "No one disrespects T-Rob's ride motherfucker!" He lifted up his XXL sized white tee, revealing the black handle of a Beretta tucked into the waistband. I just stared at him, bloody drool dripping from my chin. Then I showed him the pointed teeth crowding my mouth, my tongue making a lazy circuit across them. There was a moment's hesitation before he bolted back to the car, his pants tangling at his feet. In his desperation he managed to force the driver's side door open at last, and then double start the engine as he peeled off down the alley--a smart move on T-Rob's part. It prevented me from doing something both of us would have regretted later, although he would have regretted it a lot more.

I hunched over violently, a seizure tearing into me. Tendons creaked and bones popped as my body prepared to welcome its new host. There was little doubt I'd be leaving the tattered remains of my clothing on the street. Clawing my wallet, phone and keys out of my pockets, I threw them under a dumpster. With any luck I could retrieve them tomorrow.

A wail was wrenched from my lips as my tailbone straightened and then pushed out through the ass of my jeans. I dropped any pretense at being human, and bounded down the alley, my hands (pads) hitting the pavement in time with my feet. Hair flourished across my face. I crossed Rhodes Avenue, through an empty parking lot to Vernon. Claws capable of scoring metal tore grooves from the frozen asphalt. The brownstone lay less than a block away. Home.

RUN WITH ME.

The cellar door stood open, the unmistakable smell of blood wafting out into the cool night air.

SHE CALLS.

A name flashed across my mind. It used to be my name.

One hundred yards.

RUN.

FEED.

KILL.

Fifty yards.

My claws raked deep furrows in the grass as I skidded to a halt and tested the air.

Old blood.

And underneath it other smells, bad smells.

Metal and oil.

Words that men used, they hurt my head, alien and threatening. I lifted a leg and hot urine jetted onto the lawn, a warning to the pack. I backed away but stopped as a light shone forth from the cellar, illuminating the outline of a man. His pulse throbbed in time with my own. My nostrils flared, muscles bunched and ready to spring. He shouted something. He stood alone and vulnerable.

I leapt forward, and he disappeared back inside. I closed the distance between us in three great strides, and charged down the stairs.

Crack!

I skidded across the floor as a hot needle pierced my side. Two more retorts followed the first and my haunches burned. I struggled to reach the thorns in my skin, my jaws snapping futilely. My claws could find no purchase on the slick and cold surface beneath me. A door slammed shut, and I knew my prey had escaped. I gave voice to my rage, my roar echoing in the confined space. The scent of blood filled the room. I found its source: *a bucket* (the word formed by the dwindling and infinitesimal human aspect of my mind) filled with pieces of raw flesh - meat from one of the large stupid grass eaters. With a swipe of my claws I sent it spinning into the air, spraying its contents across the floor and wall. Something heavy clanged across the door to my prison. I threw myself at it and remembered no more.

CHAPTER FOUR

A breath of rain, no more than a mist (beneath mention by the standards of any true Londoner) drifted down onto the cobblestone pavers of Artillery Lane in the East End. At half past eight on a Friday the sidewalks teemed with revelers, freed from their cubicles for a few short hours in pursuit of inebriation. The sounds of merriment burst forth sporadically into the twilight like trumpet blasts, as patrons pushed their way into overcrowded pubs, or jostled their way back out to puff on a fag, the lapels of their overcoats held close against the chill.

The establishments lining the street swelled with the throngs of thirsty customers eager to be parted from their hard-earned pounds, except for one. It stood empty, or so it appeared. Less fashionable than its more exuberant neighbors, it lacked a brightly lit sign or freshly painted façade, in no hurry to welcome anyone inside anytime soon. Outside its entrance, a street light lay conspicuously dormant, and within a figure sat alone, turning a warm pint glass in a slow circuit on the table before him. The meagre light filtering in through the partially drawn blinds left most of the room cloaked in shadow. The only sound in the otherwise empty room was the soft scuffing of the glass as it turned round and round on the stained and pitted wooden table before him. Green eyes followed the brown swirling liquid, but the thoughts of their owner lay elsewhere.

The hands grasping the glass were thick and heavily callused, ridged with a network of scars. Some were as fine as a spider's web while others reflected older, crueler transgressions. They manifested a brutish, sullen violence, and stood at a marked contrast to the refined beauty of the twin rings adorning them.

Crafted from a thick and burnished gold, each cradled a massive blood-red ruby. The stones gathered within them the sparse light of the tavern, recasting it in the slow fire of an autumn sunset that played across the walls. The rings had a long iniquitous history, much like the man who wore them. Although pleasing to behold, they were unsettling to gaze upon for long, a sinister malevolence seeming to lurk within their ruddy depths.

The door opened, and the glass stopped its slow dance. Framed in the doorway was a piece of the night sky broken free. It hovered there for a moment before flowing out across the threshold to a seat opposite the man, where it coalesced into a rough human outline. A gash split its shadowy face in the approximation of a smile.

"Enjoying a pint are you, m'lord?" the shadow asked, a high pitched cockney accent heavy on its tongue. "I'm sure someone of your station prefers a fancier place, but this loo fits a skinflint like me just right, I'll admit ye that." The swirling smoke of its arms gestured at the worn and bleak interior.

The man with the ruby rings did not return the smile. He brought the glass to his lips and slowly drained it as he held the invisible eyes of the figure before him.

When at last he spoke, his voice betrayed a hint of irritation, and to the more nuanced ear, danger. "I haven't whiled away the evening in this dank hole to exchange idle chit-chat with a half-man, such as you and your accursed ilk."

With each word, the shadow lessened, diminishing further until at last there sat a man; middle aged and balding, with a stained and crumpled cravat tied loosely around his unshaven neck. An ill-fitting smoking jacket, one that was no stranger to the limited restorative powers of a needle and thread, hugged his portly frame in a less than flattering manner.

"N-No Offense, Master," the little man stammered. "Just having a bit of conversation is all. I'm your man sir, you can count on ol' Haggis you can."

The man with the ruby rings continued to hold his gaze, until cowed, the other dropped his eyes and looked away. "Tell your master I am most displeased that he has sent one of his minions in his place. I consider it an insult and will not tolerate it a second time. Now, what news? I have other matters to attend to this night, and have wasted far enough of my precious time in this...place." He spit the last word out like an offending piece of gristle.

Haggis brightened at the question, eager to please, "Marvelous news indeed sir!" he beamed. "Our lad is off and away. That cheeky yank bastard won't know what hit him, you can bet the Queen's crown on that," he said. While wiping his nose with the back of his hand, a pronounced ripping sound issued forth from somewhere on his person. "We've put our best on it," he continued. "He won't let you down, sir."

"He?" the man sneered. "It holds no claim to that distinction, and neither do you. *It* had better not fail me." His arms shot across the table, grasping the smaller man by the lapels of his jacket. "If it does, I will personally see to it that your filthy jacket won't be the only thing that needs mending when next we meet. You may be immune to the aggressions of mortal men, but I promise you an encounter with me will not be so easily born!"

And then, like a sudden break in a storm, the clenched muscles in his jaw slackened, his eyes tracking away from the figure before him. "How he's managed to elude me this long... but now, now he's shown himself! Quite an untidy mess he left for the police to pick over. So very careless." He looked up again, a kind of madness animating his features. He drew the thing known as Haggis closer still until their faces were nearly touching. "When news of this reaches them..."

"They'll send someone, sir?" Haggis finished, his voice betraying a slight quiver.

"Yes! And if they ever were to know of our *arrangement...*" he left off. "The Twelve are not to be trifled with." His lips drew back in a cruel smile. "And neither am I. It is worthless without the scepter, which I alone can deliver. Remind your master of that!"

With a shove of his hands he sent the squat figure tumbling from his chair onto the floor. "Now get out of my sight mongrel!" he roared, slamming his fist onto the table with such force that it collapsed under the assault. In a blur the little man fled the naked fury of that voice, a shadow slipping through the keyhole of the door.

The man with the ruby rings stood and walked behind the bar. He bent down and wiped his hands on the apron of the body lying there. "Filthy shadow spawn," he muttered. Once he had it in his grasp the Twelve would wish they had treated him better. To the wraiths he would fulfill his promise and bestow upon them their one true desire. Their first real breath as living beings would also be their last. He would sate his own appetites with their newborn flesh. The thought warmed him. He selected a dusty bottle from the glass shelf behind the bar. Pouring two fingers of bourbon into a glass, he drained it and gave a satisfying belch. "Thank you for the drink, good man," he said and reached into his vest.

"For your trouble."

He deftly flipped the heavy coin into the air to land heads-up on the chest of the corpse. It was a gold sovereign from a far older time, stamped with the worn, laconic visage of Henry VII. The man with the ruby rings smiled and exited the pub, flipping the "open" sign around to face the street once more.

CHAPTER FIVE

My head hurt. It hurt so much that I irrationally wanted to hurt it back. I lifted a shaking hand to inspect it and was surprised to find it whole.

Where was I? What had happened to me? Had I been drinking paint thinner? Perhaps I'd tripped and fallen into a bathtub full of gin with my mouth open. I needed an aspirin the size of New Jersey. I winced in pain at the creak of a door opening nearby. Like an avenging angel sent to punish me, a blinding white light blasted away the darkness of my cocoon. With my eyes held tightly shut, I heard a voice, and with it came an awareness of where I was.

"You're in deep shit hombre," Eric said. Not the words of comfort I might have hoped for. "She's hotter than a spark plug and talking about quitting for good this time."

I'm in the slammer again.

Terrific. Not only was I suffering a level of pain that would make Mr. T cry, a beautiful woman was angry with me. I dared to open my eyes the merest sliver, and through a blur of agony took stock of my surroundings.

The Ritz it was definitely not. The Bates Motel had more to offer. The room didn't have so much as a stick of furniture. There were no windows. Security cameras, protected within metal cages, had been bolted into the walls (also metal) in each corner of the room. Two gray metal doors stood opposite one another. One lead to the cellar doors and the backyard, while the other opened to the rest of the basement. The floor and walls looked like they'd been painted by Jackson Pollack--with a palette of red only.

With a queasy stomach I spied the remains of an empty plastic bucket, shredded like tissue paper. Dried gobbets of meat peppered one wall in a blast pattern. I swallowed and gagged at the bitter taste in mouth. My tongue felt swollen and sore, as if I'd been chewing on a burlap bag full of pennies.

You've got a bad case of bucket breath, my friend.

Gritting my teeth, I held a hand up in supplication. Eric hesitated, his eyes registering the rusty coloring of my skin and nails with little bits flaking off, but he shrugged and pulled me to my feet anyway. We both knew he'd seen worse. My head and body protested, but my self-esteem got a small boost from being off the floor. I leaned into him as my head spun and heard him breathing through his mouth. I must have reeked like something recently escaped from a rendering plant.

"Thanks," I managed. "I owe you one."

"Again" he finished for me, a grin lifting the outline of his goatee. Wearing a ZZ Top T-shirt and acid-washed jeans, he looked more like a roadie than a pharmacist. Without his help, I would have either been locked up or sleeping in a cardboard box under an overpass. Penelope may have been the brains behind the operation, but Eric understood what I needed to wake up and make it through another day: drugs, and lots of them.

Like a modern day Doctor Jekyll, he kept his experiments secret; mixing, grinding, and measuring ingredients out of an old broom closet under the stairs that he'd repurposed into a makeshift apothecary. He wouldn't let anyone else in, locking it when he was done. I'd caught a glimpse once of a crate on the ground filled with packets of Benadryl, Alka-Seltzer, and Ex-Lax. Better not to ask.

I offered up a silent thank you for my undeserved luck in having such a loyal brother-in-arms: the very first person I confided in about my condition. I still didn't know why I'd chosen him, but I think I'd known instinctively that if anyone could handle the shock, it was Eric. He'd taken the experience surprisingly well, considering he'd nearly been eaten. He'd kept the down jacket from that night as a souvenir, the stuffing falling out from the claw marks across the back.

"Sorry about the *eau de carcass,*" I offered.

"Yeah, you're no daisy," he said wrinkling his nose. "In your current pungent state, I'd say you remind me strongly of someone I met once."

"Never going to let me live that down are you?" I moaned.

At one o'clock in the morning the drug store should have been empty. I'd needed to restock my supply of Valium, Codeine, or whatever else I could get my hands on. Hard drugs were the only thing keeping me sane back then.

I was sweeping pill bottles from the shelves into my backpack when Eric stepped around the corner. He told me later that he'd fallen asleep trying to catch up on a backlog of prescriptions, and a noise must have woken him. Without hesitating, I clubbed him to the ground with my flashlight and continued my shopping spree. When I turned to leave he was blocking the exit with a gun in his hand, the front of his shirt soaked in blood from the head wound I'd given him. I begged him to shoot me. He was dialing the police when I broke down and the whole crazy story came pouring out of me in a confessional flood.

"This particular young man," Eric continued, ignoring me. "Had the nerve to break into my place of business and accost me."

"It was less than you deserved," I said in mock disapproval. "Sleeping on the job."

"Yeah, well you're about to get what *you* deserve." He laughed.

"Where is she?" I croaked.

"In the lab, where else?"

"I want my one phone call."

"We'd be the only ones stupid enough to answer it," he laughed again.

He was right. It seemed best just to get it over with and return to the less complicated agony of enduring a massive lycanthropic hangover.

Eric led me to the door and banged on it twice with his fist. After a series of clicks and whizzes the reinforced four-inch steel plate door swung slowly outward, and a robe was thrust in my face. Although muffled through the cloth, I detected the tell-tale sound of heels clicking away. The robe did not stink of blood or metal, and I allowed myself a moment to luxuriate in its terrycloth embrace, before gratefully putting it on and proceeding into the next room.

Well past its glory days, the old house still retained a shadow of its former opulence. It had "good bones", a term I'd heard realtors use when they were trying to unload a money-pit that should be condemned. The top three levels were gutted and all but unusable. All of the home's original architectural details were long gone, scavenged and sold off to scrappers and architectural resale shops years ago. Even the bathroom tiles and fireplace mantel had been stripped away. The grand staircase and 15-foot ceilings spoke to a bygone era, when the south side of Chicago had been the playground of aristocrats and robber barons. But for our needs, its present shabby condition was perfect.

Leasing a space in some warehouse would have cost money, which none of us had. The rent at the "mansion" was hard to beat, as there was none. From the outside it looked abandoned with all the windows boarded up, just like every other building on the block. We had ceded the top floors to the rats, and set our sights on retrofitting the basement from a former wine cellar into Frankenstein's laboratory, with Penelope as the Doctor and Eric as Igor. The role of the Monster fell naturally to me. Electricity was pirated from a pole in the alley, and run to a small army of space heaters that kept it from falling below 60 degrees most of the time.

Stepping free of the safe room felt like being released from solitary confinement. The room we entered, the so-called observation room, was almost as sparse. It contained only a saw horse workbench that served as a makeshift desk, a couple chairs, and two laptops hardwired into the video feed from the safe room. On the hard drives of those laptops were hundreds of hours of video that I would never see. I would sooner die than watch it, the irrefutable evidence of what I was. Penelope admitted that it hadn't yielded anything useful yet. Sometimes I fought the suspicion that it held nothing more than a sick fascination for them, like video footage of Big Foot or Area 51, but *this time* someone had actually recorded the real thing.

Outside the observation room, we stepped into the main living and working area of our unlikely hideout. Like most basements it had become an overflow area for our collective crap. Cardboard boxes with names like *Eric 2011* and *Penelope, Trials K-1 through K-17* lined the walls. But there were also far stranger curiosities--gleaming modern machines of medicine that rubbed shoulders with relics from decades past. A functioning heart monitor and dialysis machine sat next to a 1930's dentist's chair, complete with wrist and ankle straps. Next to an ancient-looking hospital bed stood my personal favorite, a moth-eaten stuffed black bear with an eyeless salmon in his mouth. I'd always been an avid dumpster diver, and coming upon "Smokey" one afternoon in a Southside alley had been a moment of near spiritual ecstasy. Over Penelope's strident objections, I had insisted we adopt it and make it our official mascot.

"Hey there Smokey." I said, affectionately patting his mangy hide as we passed by, my hand coming away covered in fine fur. Along the west wall lay a long metal table arrayed with various microscopes, Bunsen burners, test tubes, and other implements that tended to either confuse or strike fear into me. And at last, tucked into a corner of the room flanked by three cherry-red humming electric furnaces, we arrived at an immaculate jet-black desk. A stiff postured, slender back sat at the helm, nails clicking at a keyboard, the words flashing on the screen of the monitor in front of her. I prepared myself to navigate the fine line between apologizing and lying.

"Don't even try to sweet talk your way out of this one, Benjamin Ramsey," she snapped, the tone of her voice imperious. In spite of my grim circumstances I marveled at the throaty baritone of her voice, so at odds with her slight frame. She swiveled around and her eyes harpooned me, standing there like a fool with my mouth open.

"I....ahhh....listen, it's not what you think," I mumbled.

Not a good start.

"No, I don't think I will *listen*," she replied in a level tone, rising from her chair to approach me. "It is *you* who will *listen* to ME," she commanded. "It is *you* that agreed to adhere to one simple rule, the rule that underpins everything we do. You remember it don't you?"

"I..."

"Avoid any and all situations that may trigger an EVENT."

"Penelope, let me...."

"Your cavalier disregard for this one simple rule places all of us at risk," she said and stepped closer. I swallowed. The choking and shaking were certain to begin at any moment.

"*You* are the one that doesn't give a damn whether we wind up in jail, or mauled, or worse!" She snarled and moved closer still, her face inches from mine. Her breath smelled like cinnamon, my own must have been unspeakable by comparison. "What if you'd killed someone? Anyone! US!" she screamed.

God, but she was beautiful when enraged and hostile.

I shut my mouth and did the only sensible thing I could do. I turned and I ran. I did not get far. I'd forgotten that my muscles were more or less brand new on the morning following a transformation. Both my thighs and calves seized up and I tripped, doing a quick two-step with Smokey before collapsing on my back, trapped under the not inconsiderable weight of his molting carcass. For my encore I delivered a monstrous sneeze. There was a brief silence, shattered by hysterical laughing. Pinned and half-suffocated, I mustered a rueful smile. Penelope's snorting laughter was the loudest.

CHAPTER SIX

After an unceremonious rescue from Smokey's persistent embrace, I sat slouched in an old dog-eared office chair across from Penelope, her rage in check for the moment. My fingers picked at the spongy stuffing bleeding from a tear in the pleather relic, as I pondered the nature of the very large needle stuck in my arm. To my bloodshot eyes it looked about the thickness of a meat thermometer, but I was used to it. Submitting my body to pricks and prods on a weekly basis had become part of a routine.

When she'd gotten wind of my pill-popping spree following the dog attack, Penelope insisted on a full set of panels to check my blood for everything from glucose deficiency to diminished electrolytes and white blood cell counts - for my own good of course.

The human lab-rat part of my life came into existence as a negotiated settlement. In hindsight, I'd negotiated poorly. In return for allowing Penelope to run an endless series of often painful tests on me, she in turn agreed to direct her not inconsiderable intellect towards the task of curing me of my wolfness, and in doing so, saving my life. I used to fear needles before I met her. I laughed at hypodermics now.

If I had not been desperate enough for money to respond to an Ad soliciting *young healthy males between the ages of 20 and 30 years old* our paths might never have crossed. I was paid three hundred dollars for the study. Eight years later I was still earning it. What began as a trial to identify genetic markers for breast cancer in men, became the foundation for Penelope's *other* research. My role could not have been more pedestrian. I showed up once a week to have blood drawn, that was it. But one day she approached me and asked if we could speak privately. When I sat down in her office she looked me right in the face and asked, "How is it that you're alive?"

Trisomy, she'd gone on to explain, was a mutation that occurred when the body produced a third copy of one of its 23 chromosomes, rather than just the two copies that all healthy human babies are born with. The birth defects from such an occurrence were so extreme that the body almost always aborted the fetus before the pregnancy could reach full term. The only exception occurred with trisomy of the 21st chromosome, which resulted in a child born with Down syndrome. My DNA had trisomy of no less than seven chromosomes. In addition, three of those seven were fused together, which also happened to make me infertile. I was a genetic impossibility.

Penelope was convinced that a virus had integrated my DNA, creating mutagenic effects that essentially reprogramed my physical anatomy. Like a computer, my DNA been corrupted with biological malware. I needed an antivirus, and she made it her mission to find it, or invent it, if she had to.

* * * *

"Ben!" she yelled, her voice jolting me back to awareness.

I favored her with my most winning smile and said "We have to stop meeting like this."

She ignored me. "You mentioned that after the dog attacked, you consumed…" she cleared her throat, "…a shitload of R29's," she paused to tap at the keyboard in front of her. "Do you have a rough idea of just how many you may have ingested? Ten? Twenty?"

I closed my eyes and tried to remember something. The change acted similar to a seizure, incapacitating both body and spirit. In sleep, fragments of the actual transformation would sometimes claw their way to the surface. The people renting the apartment below me had called the police once, after they were woken by the ragged screams coming from unit 3F, certain that someone was being murdered inside.

I focused inwardly and saw the pit bull charge again. I stood over its shattered body and then… everything went dark. I shuddered, not wanting to relive it.

"It's okay," Penelope said, her tone softening. "Maybe later…"

We both knew she was just trying to make me feel better.

"Let's assume that you managed to swallow most of the bottle," she began again.

I nodded. I had a bad feeling about what she was going to say next.

"That would be the equivalent of *hmmmm*," her fingers flew over the keys again. "40,000 units."

A low whistle sounded from behind me.

"That's a lot of canine NyQuil." Eric said.

"What can I say, I'm a party animal," I quipped. I looked from one blank expression to another. "*Party* animal," I repeated. "C'mon guys. That worked on several levels."

"Frankly, it's a miracle that you survived such a concentrated dose of narcotics," Penelope continued, her eyes examining a series of graphs on the screen, "but what I'm most concerned with is repeating the mistakes of R27 and R28."

"Immunity" Eric huffed the word out with a heavy breath. "Ah, shit man".

Ah, shit was right. It should have hurt my feelings that losing a batch of pills worried her more than my near demise, but Eric's words struck me like a blow to the stomach. The pills meant more to me than either of them could ever imagine. Sure they kept me from causing trouble, but they also made it possible for a decidedly abnormal guy to lead a passably normal life. Like Prozac for werewolves, they muzzled my aggression, suppressing the more primal aspect of my dual nature. They made me feel more human.

Penelope arrived at the initial formula by the same process that underpins all successful invention--long and tedious work combined with a massive amount of luck. There had been hundreds of trials, with one failure following on the heels of the next.

She'd confided in me one night, as we sat tired and discouraged from another day without progress, that it was like "trying to cure cancer caused by voodoo." The endless tests exhausted me and I fell into a deep depression.

And then one day, it happened. Lighting struck. Somehow she'd done it, brewing a cocktail of drugs that might even get Keith Richards high. With Eric's help she mixed immuno-suppressants, sedatives, antipsychotics, blood thinners, and God knows what else. *But it worked.* It repressed every manifestation of my condition. My nightmare was finally over.

We embraced and shared tears, laughter, and shouts of triumph. *Cured!* I proceeded to get blind drunk. Penelope celebrated by getting more than a few hours of sleep for the first time in weeks.

That same night a fire in the lab destroyed everything. Eric discovered it first and burned his hands trying to put it out, but he arrived too late. In a stroke of incredible fortune, a single sample of the serum had survived, the test tube tucked forgotten inside the pocket of Penelope's lab coat. In her happy exhaustion she had forgotten to return it to the refrigeration unit in the lab that night. Her formula to make more of it was gone though, the hard drives that stored the data reduced to molten lumps of melted plastic.

Nine months later, precious little of that miracle drug remained. Every attempt to recreate it had failed. Eric took on the task of eking it out, extending its life by cutting it with Valium, Vicodin, and anything else he could snitch from the pharmacy.

The problem with the pills lay in their watered down potency. Sooner or later they lost their effectiveness altogether. The last batch, R-29, had shown some promise. Two or three pills a day and no one got hurt. I'd been a happy user for a full week.

By flooding my system, I may have accelerated the process, and so it was back to the lab to start on R30. If only I'd walked just a couple of lousy blocks out of my way.

The consequences of a life without those little red pills raced unfettered through my aching brain. I'd have to avoid all public transportation. No more going to the movies. No more concerts. No more sex – well that wasn't much of a problem anyway. Worst of all, even catching a beer buzz would be risky.

"Guys, let's not go nuclear." I pleaded.

"Ben, this is serious. You need to lay low. We can't have another-" she dropped her eyes and looked away. There was no need for her to finish. The periods between pills were the most dangerous.

Two weeks ago while walking across the UIC campus after a late night of studying, she'd been attacked. She had texted me earlier that night, excited by a new test the university was developing to isolate a gene linked to hair loss in rats. With her phone on mute, she'd missed my reply that I was coming to meet for a beer to hear more about it. Not that I'd really cared, it was just an excuse to see her.

They jumped her on her way out of the building and dragged her to a wooded area between the Behavioral Sciences building and an empty parking lot, where the trees blocked the view from Harrison Street.

Unfortunately for them I'd taken the 74 Bus to the Harrison stop. I was crossing the street when I smelled the blended sludge of violence and lust in the air. They were surprised at first when I burst through the trees, but then laughed at the skinny white boy armed with nothing more than a can of Diet Coke. There were four of them, young and stinking of malt liquor and weed. I saw one of them struggling on top of her with a hand over her mouth, and the other working at the zipper to her jeans below. I charged straight at him. A fat kid wearing a Miami Heat jersey stepped in front to intercept me. They stopped laughing when I snapped his neck. After that I can't remember anything but screaming.

The first homicide detective to arrive on the scene, a twenty year veteran of the force, said it was the worst thing he'd ever seen. They cordoned off the entire medical wing of the campus to get all the "evidence." Every news outlet and blog from Boston to Beijing ran with the story, until something more important like Kim Kardashian's breast size pushed it off the front page and into obscurity. It didn't go away for me though. I couldn't, *I wouldn't,* go back to that life again.

"I can't be sure until I've run a few more tests" Penelope said, examining a series of printouts. I hung my head and contemplated weeping, but then the makings of a plan began to take shape in my mind. In my experience, "a few" meant at least a dozen, and sitting in the lab and getting stabbed with a needle for the next week was the last thing I wanted to do. Besides, Duke was still out there, and I was going to need some help if I was going to catch him. It was time to pay a visit to my old pal Jonesy. He happened to be the best informant hard liquor could buy, in spite of the fact that he no longer ranked among the living.

After a quick change of clothes, I mumbled something about needing some fresh air and was out the back door before either one could protest. Stopping only long enough to fill my lungs with the brisk autumn air, I grabbed my skateboard leaning against the wall and took off.

CHAPTER SEVEN

The first stop was back to the dumpster where I'd ditched my stuff. I almost cried in relief when my outstretched fingers touched the outlines of my phone. The rest of it was still there too. My keys were sticky, and it looked like something had gnawed a hole in my wallet, but I was ecstatic. Maybe my luck was looking up after all.

I headed east and was soon bent over my long board into the bracing lakeshore air, crystalline tears forming at the corners of my eyes. My mood improved with each push of my foot against the pavement. I preferred my other board, called a "Pop", or Popsicle, for its resemblance to one, but it was made for cutting the ramps and bowls of Wilson Skate Park. By now it'd be overrun with kids. That's why for me and the rest of the old timers, early morning was the only time to go there.

I cut across 57th street, the copper-plated dome of the Museum of Science and Industry glittering in the morning sun like a colossal turtle's shell. Rumor was they had a giant Tesla coil inside, and I would have loved to see it in action, but my destination lay further west in Hyde Park. I needed to speak with someone there.

* * * *

He was the first of his kind I got up the nerve to talk to. I'd been too scared to approach the others. And believe me, there were others. I began to hear voices shortly upon returning home. The attack I suffered in the woods, and Celeste's murder afterwards had exacted a heavy toll on my psyche. Enemies lurked in every corner. Passing strangers seemed to leer at me with evil intent. I lived in constant fear of being discovered, of being caught.

Then one afternoon my fears were realized, although not in the way I'd envisioned. As I was exiting an alley after relieving myself of half a bottle of Irish Rose, a high reedy voice called out to me by my real name. I froze, my heart in my throat, but there was no one there. The seconds stretched to minutes and still no one appeared. I convinced myself that the voice had just been a figment of my booze-soaked brain, and resumed walking, which soon became staggering. I stopped to steady myself on the faux wrought iron fence of a stately Queen Anne. The front yard had been transformed into a tiny urban oasis, replete with gurgling fountains and a lush multitude of flowering trees and sculpted bushes. A handful of weathered, ivy-covered lawn ornaments and statuettes stood or kneeled before a pool of still water. As my eyes lingered on the moon-shaped face of a dryad, it raised a delicate porcelain hand and waved to me.

Winded after the first block but unable to stop running, I somehow covered the remaining ten blocks to my apartment and collapsed on the couch, the first werewolf to almost die of a coronary. I vowed never to take another drink. Two days later I was bellied up to the bar at Rothschild Liquor Mart. It remains my personal best for abstinence.

My next encounter didn't occur until a full three months later, during which time I made certain to steer clear of all gardens, lawns, or even suspicious looking shrubs. Being flush with cash from a busy week of pet rescuing, I had upgraded my beverage of choice from bum wine to a fifth of Jameson's. It was lucky for me that I did. Without the whiskey I never would have made the acquaintance of a certain wayward spirit, or *Doctor Lattimer Jones* as he preferred to be addressed. I preferred to call him Jonesy.

* * * *

I executed a decent Ollie up onto the curb and approached the entrance of a three-flat Greystone. My fingers drummed against the vest pocket of my jacket, and the small silver flask concealed there. Flasks were cheap at the Navy-Army Surplus, and it was a good thing for me that they were. Small personal effects weren't easy to keep track of when you kept literally bursting out of your clothes. My current bankroll nixed the purchase of anything better than Jim Beam, but knowing Jonesy it would do. I'd learned that you didn't have to be human to be a first class lush. I got to the door and took a measured breath to compose myself: conversing with a spirit, even one as harmless as old Jonesy, still made my skin crawl. Grasping the ring set in the mouth of the frowning old man on the door, I rapped twice and waited.

For a moment the face remained placid, until with a faint metallic click, twin sets of flinty eyes opened to glare balefully at me. I knew the drill. I took hold of the ring again, twisting it until it popped free with a squelch, like a boot from the mud.

I watched as the old man worked his mouth like a horse with its bit removed.

"It's been too long--" I began, but got no further, as he screwed up his mouth and hawked a glob of phlegm at my feet.

With a sigh I looked down at my shoe. How I wished I could hold down a normal job, one that didn't involve moonlighting as a way station for some door knocker's lung luggage. Jonesy had probably watched my approach with anticipation from blocks away, working one up the entire time.

I wanted badly to return the favor, but I needed him. Duke's face floated before me, dollar bills circling it like a halo. I had to find him, and if it meant getting spit on, so be it. If this job fell through I'd be back to the nickel and dime jobs that barely paid for the rent and some ramen.

The only upside to my so-called profession was that I never lacked clients. There were times when it seemed every light pole in the City was plastered with handwritten pleas that cried "Reward!" and "Answers to Skipper!" I even saw a flyer for a lost bird once. *A bird.* I had to stop and read it twice. Even my tracking skills had a limit.

As I pulled out a Kleenex and bent down to clean up the ectoplasmic loogie, Jonesy cleared his non-existent throat and began to address me like his long lost chambermaid.

"For what piddling affair have you so rudely disturbed my slumber?" he demanded with a sniff.

Not this again.

When a foul mood took hold, he acted as if we'd never met. He just wanted to hear me beg to puff up his ego.

I usually played along with it, but today I was in no mood. He wanted to play games? No problem. I knew how to deal with his type. "Disturb your sleep?" I replied. "One thousand apologies. I'll just take this," I said flourishing the flask before his face, "and be on my way."

Tipping it back I took a long drink and smacked my lips in pleasure. With an expansive grin, I turned around and strolled back down the steps. I didn't get far.

"Sir! Wait Sir! Beg Pardon Good Man!" Jonesy blurted out in a panicked frenzy.

I took another pull before reversing course, making sure not to hurry. The face on the door beamed with a benevolent smile. "Apology accepted," he said, as if I had been the one to insult him.

"Now, in what manner can I render the great value of my services? I can assure you with all confidence that there is no one with a more definitive knowledge of the goings on in this fair city than myself."

What a windbag.

I leaned in closer. "Your assistance in certain matters would be most helpful indeed, but I must warn you sir." I glanced quickly from side to side. "There is something foul afoot in the White City!" His comic look of horror was too much. I coughed into my hand and continued.

"Can I presume upon your complete fidelity in this matter?" I asked.

"But of course, sir!"

Jonesy was a sucker for theatrics. And whiskey.

His enthusiasm ebbed when he learned that I sought after a mere dog rather than some evil criminal mastermind, but my intuition had been right. He had seen Duke. He didn't care much for dogs though, *"ill-tempered mongrels!"* He told me that the *disagreeable beast* had crossed in front of his home the previous afternoon, even stopping to mark his territory on the bushes out front.

"And I say good riddance, sir!" he pronounced indignantly, eyes straying once more to the flask in my hand.

"And where did he go?" I pressed, slowly waving the flask before him like a snake charmer.

He screwed his eyes shut in concentration. "He was...he was....he was picked up!" he exclaimed.

"By who?"

"A blue motor vehicle, a *van* I believe your kind calls them. After gathering him into the back and shutting the doors, it turned onto Western and went northward until it passed out of my realm."

I'd learned that spirits were fiercely territorial, dividing up between themselves every inch of their little fiefdoms. The information was not quite the lead I'd hoped for, but it was better than nothing. I held the flask to his lips and watched it pour from his mouth to pool on the doorstep. Why did he even bother? Perhaps it reminded him what it felt to be human again, at least for a fleeting moment. I let him drain it, and then despite his comical efforts to avert his mouth, jammed the ring back between his lips. The vehicle that had taken Duke seemed to fit the description of a police paddy wagon, but it might also belong to some random dog napper as well. Whether it was kidnapping dogs or kids, vans seemed to be the preferred vehicle of social deviants.

I considered turning back and questioning Jonesy in greater detail about the van, but the empty flask in my pocket made me reconsider. I'd be lucky to get one word from him. Maybe I could try to talk to the others.

The others.

I shuddered at the thought. Unlike Jonesy *the others* couldn't be placated with a flask of cheap whiskey, and what they seemed to want I was in no position to grant. I must have presented the ideal host with one foothold in the spirit world, and the other firmly in the mortal one—a living bridge between the two. It would be a profound understatement to say that the last time I tried talking to one of them hadn't gone well. Getting chased down the street by a flying stone gargoyle (that you alone can see) can definitely ruin your week. Demonic possession was not on my bucket list.

I hadn't set out to make a living by bribing door knockers and recovering wayward pets, but the smallest thing can sometimes change your life, like stepping off a train in Grand Central Station and smelling your dead lover's perfume.

* * * *

The moment I'd entered the main concourse it hit me like a strong blow to the head. I staggered for a moment, before I could gather myself. I looked about wildly, searching for her face among the crush of commuters, even though I knew she was dead. I'd seen them drag her body from the Seine with my own eyes. But I couldn't help myself. I allowed her scent to lead me out of the station and down the street. Like an invisible sensory noose, it wrapped around my neck and pulled me along. Seven blocks later, the trail ended not with Celeste, but with a young redhead at Starbucks, checking in for her Barista shift. My heart ached with disappointment. At the bar later, it struck me that I might have something I could use to my advantage.

Within a week, I'd put down what remained of my earthly fortune on a shoebox sized office on the upper west side. There was just enough room for my desk, a folding chair, and a Ficus that doubled as my secretary. Even then it was more than I could afford, but once I'd gazed out of the small window looking out over Riverside Drive to the blue ribbon of the Hudson below, I knew I had to have it. I hung a sign on the door that read "Ben Ramsey, Professional Tracker," and I was in business.

My mind was filled with film noir fantasies, where lovelorn blondes with hourglass figures and cherry red nails wept prettily in my office. Those daydreams were dispelled in short order. My first commission involved a husband that had disappeared along with the couple's bank account. The cops had no leads, which meant of course that they could care less. It took me less than a day to find him, shacked up with an underage prostitute in an old motor lodge outside of East Newark.

One client at a time, my reputation grew. My services began when you walked in, and ended the minute I'd found your missing person. If you wanted them back – that was a job for a bounty hunter. They carried guns and charged a lot more than I did.

Things were going pretty well until the day my past finally caught up with me. I was locking the door one night, when I turned to behold a woman that would have given Rita Hayworth a run for her money. With curves that a runway model would get fired for, she took my breath away. When her story started to spill out, I found it hard to breathe for a totally different reason. Her breath was beyond foul. It smelled like she'd eaten a clove of raw garlic and chased it with anchovies. I was shocked that such a beautiful woman could be so unaware of her own dental hygiene. Much later I discovered that I could literally smell when someone was lying, just like a spoiled piece of meat waived under my nose.

Her husband of twenty years was messing around on her. Tears streamed down her face as she told me how ashamed she felt. She had been so stupid, so blind, and so on. She wanted proof. I didn't like peeping Tom jobs, but she was beautiful and had insisted on paying upfront in cash.

I waited for him on Broad Street in the Financial District. When he pushed through the revolving doors and onto the packed street, I followed him. He took a taxi up to Lower Manhattan, where he met a young brunette with big fake boobs. They got a table by the window, not even trying to hide. I got seated a few tables over, waited for them to kiss and then got the evidence while pretending to take a selfie. Easy Money.

The next day I felt agitated and restless, and hadn't slept at all the night before. The full moon was approaching but I had no idea. I still didn't know what I'd become. A part of me knew that I'd murdered my father, but I couldn't remember a thing. I'd woken up naked, scratched all over, and filthy in my bed twice in the last 2 months, with no recollection of how or why. I didn't trust doctors or risk drawing attention to myself either. The only explanation I could come up with was that I must be blacking out or sleepwalking or both. I started mixing Benadryl and whiskey at night, hoping to knock myself out.

I called her the next day and she wasted no time in getting to the office. The same sour odor struck me again when she walked in. It was strange because she hadn't said a word yet. Her face betrayed no emotion as she examined each picture. She set them down on the desk, and then she lost her mind. There was no way *NO WAY* that was *her* Frank. I should be arrested. I should be in jail. I should pay for what I'd accused him of. I can remember her eyes, wide and rolling, while the invective spilled from her lips. Perhaps what I'd mistaken for bad breath had instead been the stench of madness. I backed behind my desk and opened the drawer to return her money.

But that's when it struck me. What if there was no Frank? What if I'd tailed some random guy and his girlfriend enjoying a night out together? What if she'd fabricated the whole thing as part of some demented fantasy? My fears were confirmed as I looked up and she had a pistol in her hand. My hands were only half-raised when she pulled the trigger. I fell to the floor, blood spilling through the fingers clutching my gut. She stepped around the desk and lowered the gun to my head, a look of arousal flushing her face.

And then somehow my hand was around her ankle. She looked down, her smile faltering, and I snapped her fibula like a pencil. The wolf took care of things from there. Disposing of a body was a lot easier when there wasn't one.

It seemed like an opportune time to take a sabbatical. Her fee paid for the train fare to Chicago and the first month's rent. And so, the third act of my life began. In time I came to understand and even accept what I'd become, as impossible as that seemed. I switched to chasing dogs instead of people, but decided to keep the "P.T." on the end of my name. Pets didn't pay as well, but they didn't shoot you either.

CHAPTER EIGHT

"Another?"

I smiled at the bartender and nudged the empty pint glass forward. She whisked it away to return it a moment later, full and lightly perspiring. Life could be good if lived squarely in the moment.

Perhaps someday I would open my own bar, a secret club that catered exclusively to werewolves serving only rare, roast beef sandwiches and dark beer. The entrance would be hidden down a dead end alley, requiring a cryptic password to enter.

While drinking our way across Paris, Celeste and I had once stopped at *Le Galeux de Queue*, the Mangy Tail, in one of the poorer neighborhoods (yes, Paris has poor neighborhoods). It was rumored to have once catered to a small cadre of aristocratic degenerates and their forbidden cravings for human flesh. A friendly drunk at the bar (they're all friendly when you're buying) had divulged the supposed existence of catacombs beneath the cellar, where the blue bloods had indulged their less than Christian appetites back in the bad old days. Being drunk, his attempt at speaking softly failed, and we were all shown the door, and none too gently.

Macabre fantasies aside, I preferred my watering holes to adhere to a few simple criteria. No televisions. I went to a bar to relax, not watch some redneck haul another fish into their ridiculous Bass Boat. The juke box should be stocked with rock and roll and blues. I was there to drink not dance. Bright lights were *verboten.* If a Jackalope, or stuffed squirrel happened to be mounted on the wall next to a faded Polaroid of the owner's mother, all the better. The right mix of eccentricities gave the place a soul.

The best places made you feel like you were drinking in someone's home (if their home was a bar of course). And the golden seal of my approval was reserved for only those very rare gems, in which an old man showed up at the same time every day, had the same drink, and after enjoying it in silence, got up and left. Mic drop.

The bar I was sitting in, The Uptown Pub, was one of my favorites and met all of my time-honored criteria and then some. It sat on a street corner in the middle of the East Village neighborhood, refusing to adapt to the gentrification around it. Turn of the century greystones rubbed shoulders with gleaming new monolithic condos that tried too hard, or perhaps not nearly enough. They all looked the same to me: temporary yuppie rest stops for the future denizens of Suburb X.

The Uptown refused to oblige these painfully cheerful newcomers. It sat on the corner like an odiferous bum itching his crotch. Whenever the door opened a heady waft of stale beer and the ghost of a thousand cigarettes assailed passersby, clinging to the air around the building like the jowls on a fat man. Inside awaited a cave-like atmosphere: dark, dank, and with a bathroom so filthy, you were tempted to unzip and aim for the toilet from the threshold.

At three in the afternoon I had the place more or less to myself, which suited my mood. I brought the beer to my lips, and the front door swung open, a ghastly bright blanket of daylight enveloping me. I resisted the urge to yell "It burns, it burns!" and instead pivoted my stool to shield myself. Natural light only served to remind me and every other barfly inside that the real world waited for us like a parole agent outside. I spied a shadowy oasis at the far end of the bar and made for it like Noah for Mount Ararat. As I settled into my new hiding place, my pocket began to vibrate.

Could there be no peace for a troubled Lycanthrope? One whose sole desire was to drink between 7 and 10 beers? I took it out and looked at the screen. It was Eric. I couldn't send him to voicemail fast enough.

The floor boards creaked loudly, and I swore softly. I didn't need a wolf's ears to know that someone was standing behind me. How had he found me so fast? Had they put a tracking device on me? I envisioned myself walking around the city with a tag through one ear and a giant antenna strapped to my back.

"Eric, can't you give a guy a..."

I turned around to face a very large man in a snug fitting rugby shirt looking down at me with an unreadable expression on his face. He was built like a Panzer Tank with a square jaw and a crew cut. An uncomfortable moment passed as he seemed to be sizing me up. His eyes were nearly colorless – like the thin skin of early spring ice on a pond. The waitress returned with two pints and plunked them down in front of us. A generous smile suddenly transformed the man's face as he held up one of the pints and sat down on the stool next to mine. "Prost" he exclaimed in a thick Germanic accent.

I was nothing if not a creature of habit. To turn down a free beer and a toast would take a voluntary and unnatural act of will power. I answered him with a time honored response I reserved for such occasions, "Fuckin' A." I found myself grinning back at him and saluted his glass with a solid rap. As it flowed across my tongue I recognized it instantly, Dortmunder – my favorite Pilsner. God love those fanatical Krauts and their Reinheitsgebot.

CHAPTER NINE

I stood alone in the middle of Michigan Avenue in my dream. I knew I was dreaming because no one stood in the middle of Michigan Avenue, unless they wanted to get flattened by a double-decker bus full of tourists. Sidewalks normally choked with shoppers wrestling voluminous brightly colored bags, stood empty. My dream-self held no opinion of this irregularity. Emerald-green street trees rose towering up to a sky so blue it hurt my eyes, while the parkway flower beds burst with pinwheels of color. Everything was a little too perfect, like a movie set.

A dream thought occurred to my dream self. Where was the atmosphere? Leaves fluttered yet there was no wind. The sun shone bright and fiery above my head, and yet no warmth touched my skin. There was no discernible dream weather. I stood within a vacuum.

Before me the empty street stretched out straight as the line on a map to the curvature of the Earth. I could sense something was about to happen at the edge of the world, and strained my eyes, searching the horizon. There was a red flash, and then it began to rise like a sunset in reverse. No longer the beaten and battered survivor of the modern age, it rose in the sky an alabaster conqueror, equal to the Earth, a challenger to the sun itself.

I stood rooted to the spot, entranced by the Moon Goddess rising above me. The breeze quickly became a wind, and the wind a gale. Trees thrashed in ecstasy. Flowers tore free of the soil and flew upwards in a rip-current of air. It swallowed half the sky and rose still.

A network of varicose cracks and fissures sped across the streets and sidewalks. Manholes rattled angrily and then burst into the air like champagne corks. The pop and boom of windows hundreds of feet above me resounded in the air as they exploded outward. Nothing living could withstand the furor roaring around me, and yet I was unharmed, protected and cradled in the Moon's embrace. Buildings made of steel began to fold back from the street, bending like reeds.

The Moon continued its ascent, and then began to age rapidly before my eyes. I observed the devastation wrought from eons of cataclysmic bombardment. I longed to caress the scars on her face, ravaged but still glorious. The shattered ruins of the city trembled around me and then disintegrated at last into dust as they surrendered to the tempest. She had devoured the world. My body rose, floating towards her. Soon we would be reunited, and I would be welcomed home.

Time slowed and then stopped. I hung motionless, a single mote in the vacuum of space. I reached out a hand, the tips of my fingers straining, searching, grasping, and then at last, I touched the great belly of my mother. As my fingers trailed along her skin it started to change, the smooth skin becoming sticky and coarse. I pulled my hand back, the fingertips dripping with viscous ropey strings of congealed blood. My eyes widened in horror at the new landscape spread out before me.

Bodies, torn and mutilated beyond recognition, encompassed everything. Piled one upon another in an endless profusion they blanketed the surface of the planet. I screamed as I was pulled towards them. Their hands extended out to me, scores of swollen lips grinning in anticipation.

CHAPTER TEN

My eyelids fluttered open. Indistinct shapes and colors shifted and swirled like smoke before me. The world refused to come into focus. My stomach knotted into a fist and I shut my eyes tightly once more. The ground that I lay on was warm and moved rhythmically in a way that was simultaneously comforting and disorienting.

Was I dead? The last thing I remembered was plummeting toward the surface of the moon, but unlike other falling dreams, I hadn't woken up this time. The impact shattered my bones into a thousand pieces. Hadn't I read somewhere that dying in your dreams was supposed kill you in real life? With trembling hands I touched my head, chest and then my legs. I was definitely sore but nothing felt broken. *Still Alive!*

My momentary elation was cut short as something warm and wet slapped across my face, coating it with a foul-smelling slime. I gagged as it struck again, getting in my mouth on the next pass. "Stop!" I croaked, flailing my arms before me in an attempt to ward it off. I opened my eyes again and froze, lips pursed in mid-spit. Two bright golden orbs floated before me like jack o' lanterns. I stared, transfixed by their otherworldly glow. They blinked. I scrubbed hard at my eyes to dispel the last remnants of dream haze and found myself face to face with a wolf. Not just any wolf but the largest of its species – a timber wolf.

The wolf looked at me for a moment as if deciding whether I'd go better with a bottle of red or white, and then with a plaintive whine, rolled onto its back. With its paws in the air, it looked up at me with an expectant expression. I'd seen that expression before but never on the face of a wild animal, especially one capable of disemboweling me in the blink of an eye.

Aww will you look at that honey? The timber wolf wants a belly rub!

With great care, I lowered my hand to gently scratch his underside.

A hand that was coated in dried blood.

A familiar feeling of dread settled around my heart. The wolf whined in pleasure beneath me, as I inspected my other hand. The band of the watch on my wrist was frayed but unbroken. After scores of lost watches, I'd gotten smart and switched to elastic. Through the smeared dirt on the face, the hands pointed at ten minutes to six. AM? PM? With one last scratch and a belly pat, I put my palms on the ground and pushed myself up.

Away from the ground and my hairy, albeit smelly, companion, the air was freezing, and I shivered in my nakedness. *My nakedness.* How had I missed that? My hands involuntarily began searching for my wallet, keys and cell phone, as if they were somehow duct-taped to my bare thighs and ass. No money, ID, or credit cards. No way to call anyone or pay for a ride to my apartment. Thankfully I'd hid a spare key. I fervently hoped my longboard was still laying against the wall at the Uptown.

That's it! That's where I'd been! But where was I now?

Through the branches of the trees overhead, I discerned a handful of stars flickering weakly. Something about the sky bothered me. It wasn't really very dark at all, almost as if it were lit from below. *Of course!* What I beheld could only be the pseudo half-light that passed for night in the city. But that made no sense. How could I be in the city and yet also be sharing the den of some friendly Timber Wolf? As if aware of my ruminations, it stood up and stared at me. It wanted something, and somehow I understood what it was.

"Set me free." I said aloud to the night.

I paused and looked at the wolf again. It had a thick leather collar around its neck.

Oh shit.

Just when it seemed like your life had finally hit ground zero, you discovered a whole new subfloor. I stood naked and covered in dried blood in the cage of a Timber wolf *at the Lincoln Park Zoo.* I'd changed again, but how? There was a soft *click*, and a beam of light hit my bare chest. I froze and watched as it traveled slowly up to my face, the glare blinding me. I held up a hand to shield my eyes, and the light lowered a fraction. A young and startled looking security guard stood on the other side of a glass observation wall. "Prost," I said with a smile. The flashlight clattered to the ground and I took off running, the wolf at my side.

* * * *

As I raced through the enclosure I sensed other shapes, their movements fluid and graceful alongside me. More wolves, an entire pack. I was grateful they'd decided we were on the same team. I searched for an exit door as I ran, anything I might use to climb up and over the walls. Not surprisingly, the enclosure had been designed to prevent such an escape. No trees, artificial or otherwise, stood within ten feet of the large, interconnecting panes of thick glass. Ahead, I heard the gurgle and splash of running water. My eyes had adjusted to the dark and I saw a waterfall cascading down a series of rock outcroppings to a shallow pool. I had to give the zoo credit. The forest around me felt real, much more than just some stale space to pace back and forth in.

Things I hadn't noticed before jumped into focus; a bright green inchworm easing itself up a maple leaf, the sharp intermingled odor of wet fur and rotting leaves. It should have been impossible after such a recent transformation, but I could feel my blood starting to respond to the wolves all around me. I slowed to a brisk walk and focused on taking deep measured breaths. There were enough wolves around without adding another to the pack.

A shout issued from somewhere behind us and was immediately answered by another voice from up ahead. They had entered the enclosure, which could mean only one thing. They were armed. Were they afraid I might hurt the wolves? I looked over at the huge shadow at my side. No, I was the one they were here to protect. That guard had seen my naked and blood-streaked body.

I felt a dampness on my hair and skin and looked up at the sky. A light rain had begun to fall. The stars were nearly gone, which meant daybreak couldn't be more than half an hour away at most. Even if I managed to escape, how far would I get running naked through the middle of Lincoln Park? I needed some clothes, any clothes. A plan took shape in my semi-wolfish brain. For it to work I'd have to move fast. I squatted down and held a hand out to the wolf beside me. He sniffed it once and then licked it, looking at me expectantly. I thought about how I had been able to read his thoughts before, and closed my eyes, concentrating on what I wanted him to do. When I opened them he looked at me for a moment more, and then took off back the way we'd come, the pack following him. They started baying in earnest as if in pursuit of something. I waited, praying my scheme worked.

"Over here!" someone shouted from the direction the wolves had run. Just ahead of me, a man cursed. I waited, the sound of his shoes splashing through the mud growing louder as he drew nearer. I crouched low to the ground next to the trunk of a tree that wasn't quite wide enough to conceal me completely and waited. He came into view and passed directly in front of me, a rifle cradled in the crook of his arm.

I stepped out behind him, jerking the rifle from his grasp. He spun towards me as I swung the barrel into the side of his temple. He staggered and mumbled something unintelligible before crumpling to the ground. I dropped to my knees and felt his wrist for a pulse. It thrummed beneath my finger, the blood making its way back up the basilic vein to join with the cephalic on its journey to his pumping heart. I opened my eyes (odd how I didn't remember closing them) and his face was inches from my own. I jerked back and let go of his hand. He smelled...good. Shaking slightly, I rolled him over and started with the buttons on his shirt.

* * * *

The entrance to the enclosure was a cleverly concealed metal door set into a faux rock face, painted to blend in. It was locked but opened smoothly as I inserted the key card. The rain had picked up, falling in steady droves, and my clothes were soaked through by the time I exited the enclosure. I walked at a brisk pace, careful not to run, towards the west entrance. I was steps away when a shrill whistle split the air. Cursing my bad luck, I broke into a shuffling jog.

"Hey Jose!" I heard a man's voice shout. "I thought you were off today!"

I stopped and turned slowly, keeping my head bowed with the bill of the cap pulled down low over my face. An attendant waved to me from beneath the overhang of the entrance to another building, the likeness of a beaver carved into the stone gable above his head.

"Did they catch him?" he yelled through his cupped hands. Word traveled fast in this place. I shrugged my shoulders and spread my palms, as if to say "How would a poor schmuck like Jose know?" I waved and then continued on, waiting for him to yell again or run after me. I gave silent thanks for the cloak of heavy rainfall.

Once past the gates, I broke into a full-out run. I needed to put as much distance between myself and the zoo, and fast. I crossed the park and ducked into a bus shelter, glad to be out of the rain at last. A quick search of Jose's pockets had yielded a soggy five dollar bill, more than enough for bus fare. Shivering and soaked through, I stuffed my hands into my pockets, shifting from one foot to the other trying to keep warm. The clothes were a poor fit, the pants stopping two inches shy of my waterlogged shoes. I stared down at the rust-colored water dripping from my body, and wished that the rain could cleanse me of my sins too. I wished that I could start all over again, clean and un-cursed. *"You'll never be clean,"* my father whispered in my ear. In my mind's eye the water around my legs rose, swelling to a rushing river of red that pulled me under and swept me away.

CHAPTER ELEVEN

Someone had been in my apartment. Or more accurately stated, someone had been *wrecking* my apartment. I stood in the doorway, unwilling to step inside and make real what was surely a hallucination. The newspaper I'd retrieved from the front stoop fell to the floor as my hands went slack and then closed into fists. What desperate idiot would choose to rob and then sack such an obvious shithole? Even un-wrecked, it never would have graced the cover of *Celebrity Cribs.*

A classic Chicago "shotgun" apartment, it had been built to the geographic dictates of a city lot – long and narrow. Ancient rope and pulley sash windows opened onto a cavernous, breezeless gangway, insuring an indoor climate that was hot and stuffy in the summer and cold and breezy in the winter.

Scores of books lay commingled with an assortment of moderately soiled clothing that had once graced the backs of chairs and my old leather couch. In the hallway, a small landslide of disposable razors spilled out from the bathroom like a booby trap. Not surprisingly, being a werewolf had turned my life into an unwinnable battle with my own facial and body hair. To keep from going broke, I ordered disposables in bulk from a wholesale distributor in China. From the picture of the masked assassin on the box I had dubbed them "Ninja Blades."

The stuffing from my threadbare lazy boy festooned the room like dirty snow. Every drawer from every piece of furniture was pulled out and overturned. I realized what else was bothering me - the walls were bare.

"Not the dogs playing poker too!" I wailed.

Even my meager collection of paint-by-numbers masterpieces had been violated. Floating above the detritus I detected something else as well. A foreign scent permeated the air, something a human nose would never register. To me it was as if a bottle of cheap cologne had been splashed with abandon about the room. Something about it nagged at me. Had I smelled it before?

With a hiss the steam radiators kicked on, and within a matter of minutes I knew the air in the room would achieve a sauna-like quality. The three bay windows that looked out over the street were closed, and I hopped over the wreckage to reach them. It squealed in protest, but I managed to force the middle window open and let in some air. Across the street a dog looked up at the sound and our eyes met. The effect was instantaneous. Its face split into a snarl and it began barking furiously, racing around the yard in a frenzy. Wolves greeted me as one of their own, but dogs knew better.

In the days leading up to a full moon, I was forced to turn down any offers for new work, no matter how badly I needed the income. Dogs could smell me from blocks away, and it drove them crazy. They knew the scent of a killer. Lately it seemed like they were barking at me all the time. I gave it the finger as the front door of the house flew open and a middle-aged Puerto Rican man yelled at it to "shut the fuck up!" It was still barking as I turned away from the window and again surveyed the disaster around me.

I was pondering where and how to begin the immense task of cleaning it all up when I noticed something else out of place. In one corner of the room sat an old roll top desk, shuttered and forgotten since my days as a private dick. The tambour had been opened, while the drawers had been pulled out and their contents overturned in a pile on the floor.

My shoes squished loudly as I navigated my way over to it. I reached down and picked up a dusty black and white photo booth strip and blew on it, revealing the two young faces recorded there. My breath caught in my throat. Mock terror comically animated Celeste's features as I pretended to choke her, a sinister looking fake mustache reposing at a crooked angle on my face.

"You must pay the rent. I can't pay the rent," I murmured.

A smile tugged at the corner of my mouth, but was quashed by a familiar weight that settled around my heart. Better days to be sure. Much better. But I couldn't change the past, no matter how much I might wish otherwise.

I grabbed the handle to pull the roll-top shut but then stopped. I reached back into the far corner of the desk and retrieved a bound lump of cloth. The parchment-dry rubber band holding it together snapped and a woman's silk scarf spilled out onto my hands. I pressed it to my face, inhaling deeply. Was it my imagination, or could I detect a faint hint of jasmine and cloves lingering there still? She had been wearing it that night in the woods. The memories it carried held nothing but horror and grief, and I reluctantly set it back down. Next to where it had rested, lay a faded article cut from an old newspaper. I picked it up and read the ominous sounding title.

Miller Mountain Monster?

A Mr. David Jeffries of Manhattan, NY was stunned this past Saturday to come upon a large creature of supposed unknown origin while deer hunting on Miller Mountain. The incident has been transcribed here with the permission of the Wyoming County Police Department, which recorded Mr. Jeffries ordeal at his own request:

"The blood trail [of the buck I had grazed] meandered through a thick copse of red pine, which then opened onto a broad upland meadow of mountain laurel and dogwood. I lost it there briefly, but picked it up again further down the mountainside where the way became impassible: choked with Mutlifloral rose, or as I've heard the locals refer to it, Prickerbush. Disheartened, I resigned myself to end the pursuit rather than attempt a way through the wall of brambles. At that moment however, a sharp cry rose from the thicket ahead of me, wavering high into the air to cease abruptly in mid-wail.

Believing it to be hopelessly entangled, I forged ahead so as to grant it the mercy of my 300 Savage. After a dozen tortuous feet I heard the sounds of what I took to be the poor animal's struggles to free itself, and I doubled my efforts to reach it. As I fought my way forward, a singularly determined thorn pierced the back of my hand, and I cursed in pain. As I paused to extract it a deep growl rolled out from the woods somewhere ahead of me, turning the blood to ice water in my veins. I knew then my error, and that I had suffered the great misfortune of disturbing a mountain lion in the midst of feeding. I wrestled to swing about the barrel of my rifle and froze as the head of the beast rose up less than 10 yards in front of me. I nearly fainted dead away from fright, for this was no species of predator I had ever seen or heard of. [Editor's Note: Mr. Jeffries acknowledged that he has never seen an actual bear or mountain lion in the wild]

What I saw then I will never forget for as long as I live. It was certainly not a Felis Concolor, and in no way resembled the head of a bear either. Its pelt was jet-black with a single streak of ivory running from above the ridge of one eye back across the massive head, like a skunk but off-center. The eyes were eerily prescient, full of cunning and guile. They were a vibrant hue of gold and blazed with a malevolent radiance. I was captivated in my terror by the obvious intelligence I saw reflected within them.

I screamed as the monster lunged at me, but even its powerful body could not force a way through the grasping net of brambles that lay between us. Before it could attempt a second charge, the sound of gunfire from nearby on the mountain gave it pause. It bared its teeth at me, and then dropped its head, taking hold of the deer in its massive jaws. I watched trembling as it bounded off through the woods and out of sight.

Later that day, as I warmed myself before a fire in my cabin and sent up a silent prayer to God for creating the Prickerbush, I took out a pencil and pad of notebook paper and began to carefully sketch what I had seen that day."

Beneath the article was a simple yet effective sketch of what was undoubtedly a wolf's head. Next to the head was an arrow with the note "18-24 inches diam." Underneath the head it read "total wt. est. 7-800 lbs."

The article concluded with an excerpt from an interview with Scranton Paleontologist Dr. Jonas P. Oglesby. The doctor categorically denied that the existence of such a creature was possible. He stated that while a full grown Pennsylvania male black bear could reach a weight of 600 lbs and in some rare instances exceed it, the largest species of wolf known today, Canis lupus, or the gray wolf, could at best attain a maximum weight of 175 lbs. The gray wolf did not inhabit Pennsylvania, but rather certain parts of Alaska, Wisconsin, Michigan, and Minnesota. He went on to say that even dire wolves, who went extinct over 10,000 years ago, did not come near to approaching the weight claimed by Mr. Jeffries. To find such a specimen one would need to look to the fossil record of the Miocene Era, 5.5 million years ago. There, one would find the first ancestors of all canines and bears, the amphicyonids or bear-dogs, also referred to as *bone-crushers* for their powerful jaws. They were fearsome hunters, the apex predators of their time, unmatched in power and brute killing strength. *"Obviously, the notion of such a creature somehow surviving into the present day is quite impossible"* the doctor concluded, and there the article ended.

Impossible? It was obvious the man had no imagination. But no one was supposed to have seen me to begin with. I'd intended to disappear from the face of the Earth into the oldest woods in North America. What better place than the Appalachians were there to get lost in? For a kid from the sprawling rangelands of western Kansas, the thick green density of the mountains had seemed like another planet. I wanted isolation, and I found it in a turn of the century lumberjack's cabin built up high on the mountain with nothing but the trees all around for company.

Except for mice. When I'd gotten the key from the toothless caretaker and opened the creaky door, the wood floor had a carpet of stale mouse turds. He'd told me that the boy scouts still used it on occasion but that had surely been a lie. No one had been there in God only knew how long. A wood burning stove provided the only heat, and the water from the pipes smelled strongly of sulfur. But there was an old spring-fed cistern not too far up the hill that I could fill gallon milk jugs with, and it was ice-cold and clear. The cabin suited my purposes perfectly. Not a soul in the world would think to bother me up there. I wouldn't have to worry about eating the mailman, and he wouldn't have to die a horrible death beyond imagining. But like all of our best laid plans, things rarely ended up working out the way we intend.

After our chance encounter, Jeffries' story of the giant black wolf spread like a brush fire, taking on a mythical status among hunters. The tale became an irresistible lure for every jack-ass with a rifle within 100 miles. The next full moon would be my last on the mountain.

Unbeknownst to me, a particularly ambitious hillbilly had purchased an infrared scope, tied a goat to a tree, and then waited in a deer blind up in the trees hoping for his shot. He got it too, and in doing so he laid to rest one of the most enduring myths regarding my kind. The bullet worked its way out of my back in the shower the following day. I held it under the hot water as the blood washed away to reveal a slug of pure silver. They found him a week later, his Ruger 10/22 still grasped tightly in the hands of his headless corpse.

I crumpled up the yellowed paper in my hand and tossed it across the room. The past had nothing good to say to me anymore. I sighed and resolved myself to see what the rest of the place looked like. As I passed the front door on my way to the kitchen I tripped over the *Sun Times* I'd dropped on the way in. I bent down to pick it up and the headline jumped out at me.

WASHINGTON PARK MASSACRE!

My eyes flew to the date of the article, October 21st. I raised my watch. It was October 22. I frowned and skimmed the story. Words jumped off the page at me like accusations hurled in my face; *mauled, after midnight, crime scene, bodies mutilated.* They'd printed a list of all nine of the victims' names. The pages fell from my hands, fluttering to the floor.

I sat down, missing the chair that wasn't there, and fell hard to the floor. White and black television static danced before my eyes. I fought against a wave of nausea as my gorge rose. I tried to stand and failed. I crawled to the bathroom and pulled myself up using the sink for leverage. Turning the cold tap on full blast, I splashed my face with icy water, making my damp shirt sodden once more. I had regained a small measure of myself when a sharp rat-a-tat-tat! on the front door echoed through the apartment.

"Police, open the door!"

CHAPTER TWELVE

If the English language held four words more terrifying to hear, I couldn't have told you what they were at that moment.

"Open the door, police officer!" the voice commanded again, followed by a volley of pounding fists that shook the old door in its frame.

RUN. RUN. RUN.

But I knew I didn't have it in me. My body trembled with exhaustion. I doubted I'd be able to make it to the back stairwell without flopping to the floor like an escaped Jell-O mold.

"Just a second!" I answered as I hopped around, shrugging out of my borrowed zoo duds. I tossed the sodden mess into the bathroom as the front door shuddered under another hammering.

How many were out there?

"I'm coming!" I yelled again and grabbed a towel, wrapping it hurriedly around my waist.

I ran towards the door and slipped on the wet floor, landing heavily on my right hip. With a groan I crawled to my feet again, eased the dead bolt back and opened the door. I stood face-to-face with a linebacker moonlighting as a cop. What did they feed these guys, the smaller cops? He had to be every ounce of 250 with biceps as thick as my thighs.

I hobbled back, holding my towel with one hand, while I gestured for him to come inside. His polished brass name tag read, *Officer Stone.*

"Doing a little rehabbing," I offered as he took in the devastation of my apartment.

His eyes made a quick sweep of the room while his right hand rested against his utility belt, the holster of his gun an inch away. I fought the urge to swallow and started to speak again, but he cut me off,

"Benjamin Ramsey?"

"Call me Ben." I replied stupidly.

"Just a couple questions," he said and pulled out a pen and a little pad of paper. "Where were you at 11:30 pm last night?"

I nodded and smiled as if I knew exactly where I'd been. The last thing I remembered was walking into the Uptown. After that it was a big black hole.

"I went out for a few drinks." I said.

Thinking quickly I added, "It was big fun until someone at the bar lifted my wallet. What is this about officer?"

He ignored my question and scribbled in his pad. The pen looked like a child's crayon in his meaty paws.

"What time did you leave the bar?"

I looked down, trying to buy a few seconds and spotted the newspaper page lying on the floor between us like a giant red herring. WASHINGTON PARK MASSACRE!

I coughed loudly and let my towel drop.

"Shit!" I cursed as he averted his eyes.

I bent down to pick the towel up and grabbed the paper, stuffing it between my thighs. "Jesus, sorry about that!" I laughed. "Could you repeat the question?"

Before he could answer, a miracle happened---the phone rang.

I almost dropped my towel again in my eagerness to reach it.

"My mom probably!" I called over my shoulder as I picked it up.

"Ma?" I practically screamed into the receiver.

"Holy shit he picked up! Ramsey, where the hell have you been?"

Eric, you beautiful son of a bitch.

Maybe I'd get out of this jam after all.

"Oh it's you!" I laughed. "I hope you're calling to let me know you found it," I said with my back to the cop.

Eric started to speak, but I cut him off.

"No wallet? That stinks! That's the last time I let you buy the drinks," I scolded him.

"Ben are you in some kind of..."

"Yep, tequila shots are off my list for a while thanks to you," I said, forcing a laugh. "That was some crazy time at the Uptown Pub last night.

Anyway, I'll have to call you back buddy, a cop's here and I can't talk right now."

"Hey wait..."

I hung the phone up and turned around.

"What a jerk," I gestured with a thumb towards the phone.

He opened his mouth to speak and the walkie-talkie at his hip squawked to life

"We have a 966 in progress at 515 N. Grand. Officer on site requesting back-up. Repeat..."

"Thank you for your time," he said and lumbered out the door. I shut it behind him and slid the deadbolt home with a sigh of relief. With my ear to the door, I listened to his heavy tread receding down the stairwell. I didn't relax until I heard his car door slam and the sirens speed away down the street.

The phone rang again, and I jumped. I reached over and ripped the plug from the wall. The line could be bugged for all I knew. Did they even do that anymore? What if it was the cops that ransacked my place, looking for evidence? I prayed Eric had picked up enough to follow my lead and back the alibi up. It dawned on me that the cop had never even told me why he wanted to question me in the first place.

As the adrenaline wore off my headache returned, with heartburn in tow. I used to think the acid reflux was a side effect of eating something no human should ever ingest. But now I had a different theory--it had something to do with growing all that hair. I read somewhere once that if an expecting mother has heartburn, it's a sign the baby will have a full head of hair. I grew enough hair in a month to keep a wig factory in high cotton.

I swallowed against the fire simmering in my gut and pounded a fist against my chest. *Jesus, that burned.*

Burned.

The vision of a struck match flared up in the recesses of my sub-consciousness, a shadowy figure holding it out to light my smoke. I'd quit smoking years ago, but everyone cheats when they drink. And it just so happened that I drank every day. I tried to tease more of the memory forth, but my mind was frazzled and wouldn't cooperate.

I pulled the paper back out and reread it carefully this time from beginning to end. The group was attacked while taking a late night stroll through Washington Park. A single victim had survived the attack, but lay in critical condition in the ICU at Saint Jude's Hospital. The cops had no leads, but suspected that due to the scale and swiftness of the attack (the coroner determined they had all died within minutes of one another) at least two perpetrators were responsible. The article was penned by one Brent Shelby. I made a mental note to call him when things settled down.

I refolded the article and stuffed it into the front pocket of a pair of crumpled jeans I picked off the floor. I needed time to think. There were holes in my memory big enough for Andre the Giant to walk through.

Bodies mutilated.

I shook my head but the words continued to ricochet inside my aching skull.

Mauled.

I dropped my head down between my knees and took three huge gulps of air. My thoughts continued to betray me, dredging up the faces of my past victims: my father, the blonde in my old office, the men attacking Penelope...

I blinked and Celeste's bloated face swam before my eyes.

"NO!" I screamed and lurched towards the kitchen in search of a bottle of something, anything--cooking wine would do, but there was nothing, not even a bottle of aspirin. I knew all too well that deep within the darkest recess of my memories stood a door with the word MONSTER scrawled across it in large uneven letters. The booze and pills were the only thing keeping it locked away. If only Eric were here with some drugs, any drugs. I'd take a dart in the neck with no questions asked.

Wait! The Vicodin! I had at least half a bottle left, a shield against the night and the phantoms of dreams and memory. I scrambled to my feet and ran back to the bathroom, flinging the medicine cabinet open. Prying the lid off, I poured the pills into my hand and tossed them back. Within minutes, I felt the muscles in my neck and back loosen as a deep warmth spread slowly through my body. The door receded, fading back into the labyrinth of my subconscious to wait for another time.

I took an unsteady step from the bathroom. The hall stretched out before me, seeming to go on forever. My room lay miles away. I fought against a sluggish weight as it settled upon my shoulders, seeping down to my legs. Self-medicating soothed the beast but delivered a narcotic lobotomy in the process.

I dragged my feet forward, one impossible step after the next, until by some miracle I reached the entrance to my room. A slow bass drum in my head kept time with the beating of my heart. The pain was far away and receding further with every labored breath. As my legs gave out I angled the fall of my body towards the mattress. I almost made it.

CHAPTER THRTEEN

I jolted upright with a start, sweaty and dream-blind. The thumping of my heart in my ears sounded amplified in the dark confines of my small bedroom. I must have been having another nightmare.

CRASH!

Or someone was shattering a window in my apartment. Cursing, I rolled off the mattress and kicked over an impressive stack of dirty dishes leaning against the wall. I winced as they toppled to the floor and waited for the resounding crash that would alert the intruder to my presence. But it seemed that getting my place ransacked had a silver lining: the thick litter of clothes, books, and other crap on the floor muffled the plates in its filthy embrace.

My ears perked to a scraping sound, followed by the unmistakable tinkling of glass falling on a hardwood floor. A square of glass blocks were set into the back stairwell door about chest high. It would take a direct hit from a sledgehammer to smash through them. A thought erupted in my brain, burning through the lingering fog of sleep.

"They've found you, you fool!"

The realization held me fast, rooting me to the spot. Was I so far gone that I'd forgotten the ones who had done this to me? Who else would be so brazen as to return to the scene of the crime and announce their entry with such disregard? They'd come to claim their sacrifice after all. In a panic I moved to open my bedroom window, but then stopped. I lived on the 3rd floor - a lofty drop even for someone of my unique constitution. What good was it to escape if I broke both legs in the fall?

That left the front door. Unless they were trying to flush me out that way! With a sickening certainty I realized I was trapped.

We don't need to run. Let me out.

The sounds of more glass falling to the floor came from the kitchen again. They would be inside any minute. I envisioned a clawed hand reaching through the remains of the shattered glass, searching for the doorknob.

They'll kill you, just like they murdered Celeste.

I stood in the clearing of the midnight forest once again as I faced the robed strangers. I saw their robes fall away to reveal beasts that walked as men.

Turn and fight!

A sudden spike of adrenaline kicked aside the crumbling firewall erected by the Vicodin.

My fear vanished like a leaf on the wind. The time had come at last to make a stand. All the injuries and injustices of my abnormal life rose up and boiled over in a seething rage. They'd taken everything from me. But they wouldn't take me without a fight. They would pay for what they'd done.

Edging around the bedroom door, I glided along the darkened hallway towards the kitchen. I didn't need a light to see, my eyesight had already improved. I tiptoed to the threshold of the kitchen and stopped. There was a hand sticking through the broken window, grasping at the heavy glass door knob. It was an original piece of hardware and had to be close to 100 years old. Getting it to open could be like trying to jiggle the lock on a safe.

I entered the room and an involuntary shudder rippled through me. The air felt frigid and heavy like the inside of a meat locker. The furnace must have gone out again. It resided in the bowels of the building and looked like a medieval torture device with its black iron housing and massive hinged door. The building superintendent usually managed to coax it back to life with a mixture of hammering and foreign curses.

The moisture from my breath fogged out before me, as I crouched down and cautiously approached the gloved hand that twisted and tugged futilely at the knob trying to open the door. Lunging forward, I wrenched the door open, dragging the intruder into the room with his arm trapped in the hole he'd smashed. I looked into his green eyes through the holes of his ski mask, and then delivered two vicious punches – the first to his nose and the other to his solar plexus. The first shot snapped his head back, while the second doubled him over, his arm sliding free of the door as he dropped to his knees. The stairwell stood empty behind him. Where were the rest? Were they so confident that a single assassin had been dispatched to deal with me?

"What are you doing in my home, asshole?" I demanded. Apart from the B-movie cat burglar mask, he looked disappointingly ordinary. Instead of relief, I felt a vague sense of irritation at having gotten worked up for nothing. "The Hope Diamond is in the next apartment over," I said and prodded him with my foot like a dead animal.

An internal alarm went off in my head as I realized he wasn't gagging like someone sucker-punched in the gut should be. Before I could step back, his hands shot out and grasped both of my ankles. With a jerk, he pulled me off my feet. I fell backwards onto the kitchen table behind me. It was a thrift store special and the legs gave out, sending me crashing to the floor. I looked up and somehow he was standing over me. His heel stomped down, missing my face by inches as I barely managed to roll out of the way. I scissor-kicked at his legs and he danced back, buying me just enough time to clamber unsteadily to my feet. There was a loud ringing in my ears and my skull throbbed where it had smacked against the table.

"Fuck you. You're not taking me back."

He didn't respond and just kept staring at me, eerily silent. He held himself with a poised athletic grace that as an awkward skinny kid I'd always envied in others, especially athletes. Apart from his stoic indifference to pain, something else bothered me about him. He smelled wrong. Or more accurately he didn't smell at all.

He had no scent.

Every living thing had one, like a set of fingerprints. *Every living thing.* Who or what had broken into my home?

The kitchen was too small for us to circle one another, so we stood there with our eyes locked, waiting for the other to move. I hate waiting so I moved first, feinting with a jab, and then following it with an ugly but effective heel-kick to his chest, slamming him back into the refrigerator. Unfazed, he easily dodged my follow-up right hook which connected with the freezer door rather than his face. The two blows were too much for it and a hinge snapped. The door dropped, hanging at an angle before falling with a crash to the floor. I cursed and shook my hand.

An imprint of my foot was stamped on his shirt where I'd hillbilly kicked him. If it bothered him he didn't show it, his eyes fixed on me with a million mile stare as he rocked back and forth on the balls of his feet. Behind him I could see my distorted reflection in the window that opened up to the backyard, thirty feet down.

Time would decide this matter soon if I didn't. What had started as a vague itching sensation on the back of my hands had manifested into a tickling, burning sensation over my arms and legs. It made me want to drop to the floor and tear my clothes off, which in turn would lead to slobbering, screaming, and lots of hair and blood. I was beginning to regret my decision to go on the offensive. He might be some kind of bad-ass ninja, but it was obvious he was no werewolf. The brotherhood hadn't found me yet, which meant I could still finish this as a human, knock back some more Vicodin and call it a night.

I waited for an opening, for him to look away for an instant or rub his eyes but his eerie, unnatural calm showed no sign of abating. My only hope was to overpower him with brute force. It wasn't much of a plan, but I'd never been much of tactician.

I charged.

Reflected in the glass behind him, I caught a momentary glimpse of a savage face with wild eyes and bared teeth. Under different circumstances it might have bothered me. What did bother me a great deal were his eyes. Like a broken traffic light, I watched as they flipped from green to red, and then it was my body crashing through the window three stories to the rock-hard earth below.

NO! My body jerked to a halt, as claws sprung from my right hand and dug into the rotted wooden sill of the window frame. Blood dripped down my arms from the ruin of my fingertips, savaged by the three-inch nails that had saved my life. I pulled my other arm onto the ledge and a foot smashed down, snapping the femur with an audible *crack!* I screamed in agony and fell back again, held aloft by the claws of my other hand. A shadow leaned out, looming above me like an executioner. He ripped off his ski mask, and I stared speechless at the horror that lay underneath.

He had no face, only the smooth featureless visage of a manikin with smoldering coals for eyes. He raised an arm above his head, his fingers sprouting razor-thin black needles like custom stilettos. I thrashed like a madman to free myself but my claws held me fast. I braced for the killing blow when an eruption of noise and shouting burst from the room behind him. In a blur he was gone, shooting over me and out of the window.

Relief washed through me, carrying away my anger and fear.

"Thank Gaaa – ah fuck!" my relief morphed into a scream as my weight shifted and my body lurched downward. My claws were receding.

I couldn't help but marvel at the great and cruel irony of this latest development. I had somehow managed to put the Genie back in the bottle just when I needed him the most. I was helpless to do anything as my claws gradually relinquished their hold and I fell. My strangled cry was cut short as a hand clamped like a vice around my wrist and pulled me up and through the window to safety.

CHAPTER FOURTEEN

After allowing me all of sixty seconds to catch my breath, Officer Stone told he was taking me in. In spite of having just plucked me from a window and the overwhelming evidence all around us of an epic melee, he no more than raised an eyebrow when I declined to file a report.

I flinched as a bolt of pain arced up my injured arm. "Didn't I answer all of your questions before?"

"Detective Hannity said to bring you in," he offered unhelpfully. "Now."

"Now?" I protested, "Can't this wait until tomorrow?"

"Now." He repeated. I looked into his heavy face for a hint of compassion and found none.

"Fine," I sighed, and then remembering something I added. "But I have to use the john first."

"We have a lavatory at the station."

"Can't wait," I said with a grimace and hurried to the bathroom. Making sure to grunt loudly every few seconds I quietly eased open the door of the medicine cabinet and pocketed an extra bottle of reds. Next I grabbed the faux shaving cream can I kept there for emergencies. The top screwed off to reveal two crumpled fives and a single. Exactly what kind of "emergency" such a paltry sum of money would forestall was a mystery. I cursed and jammed the bills in my pocket anyway. It might be enough for a slice of pie and a ride home later. I flushed and opened the door.

A few minutes later I sat looking out the rain-streaked window of a squad car. The back seat was sticky and stank of B.O. from some unlucky scumbag who'd ridden there before me. As we drove away I stared out at the contingent of neighborhood gapers who'd come out in the cold and dark to see what the excitement was all about. I wondered, and not for the first time, if the decision to live in a city of 3 million people was the smartest choice for someone like me.

The ride was short. I was relieved when he pulled into the parking lot of the Wood Street Station, a 10 minute walk from my apartment. Depending on how busy the night was, I could have ended up at the regional headquarters 5 miles south. Officer Stone opened the door and offered a hand to help me up.

"No, it's cool I got it," I said and rocked myself up and off the seat with my good hand. The thought of his meat hook clamping onto my broken arm was enough to send phantom lances of pain shooting up my shoulder. I also didn't want to draw attention to the injury, which would just lead to more poking and prodding. I got enough of that already thanks to Penelope. It would be a pointless exercise anyway. It wouldn't be broken anymore by the time I woke up tomorrow.

He led me up the steps and into the fluorescent-bathed interior of the station. It was a drab and dreary place. Faux wood paneling must have been all the rage when it was built. Officer Stone walked me over to the front desk where I was frisked and relieved of my measly amount of cash and to my great dismay, my pill bottle.

"Hey, I need those!" I protested.

"All personal items will be returned upon dismissal," the cop said in a bored voice and waved us ahead.

We stepped through a door with CPD PERSONNEL ONLY emblazoned across it and passed into a large and drafty space, honeycombed with interlocking low walls of homogenous grey cubicles. The water-stained tiles of the drop ceiling gave the room an added touch of neglect. The furniture dated to mid-century, but not stylishly; the desks were massive and made of a beige colored metal, the chipped chairs a hodgepodge of the old wooden swivel office-type. It hurt my ass just to look at them.

A handful of haggard looking cops in street clothes were hunched before the glowing screens of their laptops, deep in concentration or exhaustion, or maybe both. I was led twisting and turning through the maze of cubes to stop before a single metal folding chair parked in the aisle. "Sit down Ramsey. Detective Hannity will be with you in a minute," he said and left.

* * * *

A hand on my bad arm shook me painfully awake. There was a sheen of drool on my chin, and a nasty crick in my neck. I thought longingly of my filthy mattress.

"Coffee?"

A blurry but steaming Styrofoam cup floated in front of me and I took it, sipping gratefully. It smelled and tasted like cardboard, but at least it was hot. Hannity didn't exactly fit my idea of what a Chicago Detective ought to look like. He had a youthful face framed by closely cropped hair, and his jaw appeared clean shaven even at such a late hour. He wore a pair of faded jeans, a striped polo shirt, and running shoes. If it weren't for the holster and bulletproof vest bulging from under his shirt, I would say he looked more like a high school math teacher than a cop.

"I'm sorry for the heavy hand, but this case just moved to the top of my pile, compliments of the Mayor's Office," he said in a voice laced with fatigue. "Officer Stone also felt that you might be..." he paused as if choosing his words carefully, "a flight risk."

A flight risk.

I had to force down a crazy urge to laugh. If Officer Stone hadn't shown up, I would have been flying alright. I'd never been so happy in my life to have a cop lay his hands on me.

He reached for a manila folder from a precariously stacked pile, while I took another sip of my coffee and kept quiet. He seemed like a decent enough guy, but just because he had a good bedside manner, it didn't mean I had to spill my life story to him.

I nearly dropped my coffee in my lap as someone cuffed the back of my head. I looked up angrily, but then sighed as I recognized the flabby face of Captain Joe Kowalski, asshole extraordinaire. "Solved any canine capers lately, Mr. Private Eye?" he chuckled, leering down at me. In spite of his textbook comb-over and crumb sprinkled mustache, he struck an imposing figure in sheer girth if nothing else. His bulging midsection threatened to burst free from his belt and knock me sprawling into the aisle.

"Always a pleasure, Captain Kowalski," I said, using my middle finger to prominently scratch a phantom itch on my cheek. He laughed again and shook his head in amusement. "Canine caper…" I heard him snickering as he walked away.

Hannity shook his head as he watched the receding bulk of the Captain, a look of annoyance mingled with disgust on his face. I felt myself warm towards him in spite of my circumstances.

"So what are the pills for that we found in your jacket? They're unlabeled."

"Headaches," I said, thinking quickly, "I get really bad ones."

"I see," he said in a voice that implied he clearly didn't. "And you're a… what's the right word?"

"Tracker," I said. "I mostly just find people's lost animals."

"A pet detective?" he asked.

I felt myself bristle at the question, and waited for the inevitable smirk to creep onto his face. Instead he just sat there patiently waiting for me to answer. I was really starting to like this cop.

"Yeah, it's not as glamorous as it sounds," I said. "I'm also a finder of lost items and things – keys, wallets, cars, you name it. You could say I have a nose for it."

I took another sip of coffee.

This was going a lot better than I'd hoped.

"Interesting," he replied and then opened the file in front of him on the desk and quickly flipped through it.

After a moment he closed it again and then leveled a hard stare at me. "You really need to get current with your outstanding parking tickets, Mr. Ramsey."

My throat hitched, spraying coffee onto his desk.

"That's what I'm here for?" I wheezed. "I haven't driven in years!"

I tried to remember the last time I'd been behind the wheel of a car, but couldn't. I'd left my 93' Honda Civic at the side of the road one day and just walked away. Road rage and werewolves don't mix, so I switched to a much more compact four-wheeler, my skateboard. You never had to worry about a hit and run, and the only maintenance involved tightening a screw every so often.

"Isn't there a statute of limitations on these things?" I asked. He just shook his head and a sobering thought occurred to me: How many parking tickets qualified for someone to be considered a *flight risk?* I mentally catalogued my meager list of e-bay worthy possessions. I'd already sold my beloved tube amp to cover the gas bill a few months back.

"Um, Okay then," I said exhaling forcefully. "How deep is the hole?"

"Enough to put a nice dent in your rainy day fund if you have one," he continued. "Technically speaking though, the tickets were nothing more than a convenient excuse to hold you," he said, and grabbed a crumpled piece of paper from his waste basket, using it to mop up the coffee.

Technically.

I didn't like the sound of that at all.

"What do you mean, *hold me*?" I said, "You haven't even charged me with anything yet."

"I don't have to," he deadpanned. "Once you were brought in, I made a call to my friends over at the Department of Revenue and a detainer was placed on you. I can hold you up to 48 hours for each unpaid ticket, of which you have six."

This was bad. This could not be happening.

"But that's not why you're here and I think you know that," he finished.

He took a small key from the chain at his belt, inserted it into a locked drawer and pulled out a clear plastic Ziploc bag. He held it up in front of me so I could see what lay inside and shook it once for effect. "Any idea how your wallet ended up in Washington Park, Ben?" he asked.

* * * *

The steel gate slid home with a jarring clang. I dropped down onto the thin mattress and listened to the heavy tread of Officer Stone retreating down the corridor. Who knew that six lousy parking tickets could deprive a person of their liberty for two full weeks? At $50 a pop and then doubled, they had me on the hook for six large. Even if I did manage to find Duke, I'd just be handing the reward money right over.

I'd repeated to Hannity what I'd said on the phone in front of Stone, but he wasn't buying it for a second. I couldn't blame him. I probably wouldn't have fallen for it either.

It had only been five minutes, and I already felt like jumping out of my skin. Wolves hated being confined. To distract myself, I closed my eyes and focussed on the moment in the bar before everything went dark. Penelope had tried to teach me some yoga breathing exercises to exert some self-control over my condition. I'd more or less laughed it off, but now I had nothing but time.

I slowly filled my lungs, breathing in through one nostril and then back out the other. I repeated it until, little by little, I felt the tension in my neck and back start to loosen.

Still your mind.

The memory of her voice soothed me as I took another breath. An image began to take shape in the shadowy recesses of my memory. *Chank!* The rims of two glasses knocked against each other, beer foam sloshing down the sides. The camera of my mind's eye panned out. A large, thuggish footballer type with hair so blonde it appeared white sat hunched over the bar next to me. The room lurched and he turned towards me and laughed. His face was like a barren rocky mountainside, all blunt angles with heavy jutting brows and a square jaw. The room began to spin around me in a slow roll and I fell off my stool.

Breathe in, breathe out.

We were outside. I leaned heavily against him as he supported my full weight. Lifting my head seemed like an impossible task. The sidewalk was an endless runway floating below me, while a light from above illuminated my dragging feet and shadows that slithered across the cracked concrete like snakes.

I wanted to ask where we were going, but my tongue felt like a sock stuffed in my mouth. If he released his grip, I felt certain my body would collapse in a boneless puddle of cartilage.

He shifted his grip to gain a better purchase and for an instant I saw a shape on his wrist, no larger than a quarter and perfectly symmetrical. Where had I seen it before?

I strained to see more as the scene began to shift, receding from me, pulling away as if I were tumbling down an endless hole. I must have fallen unconscious then. The blackness grew to encompass everything and my eyes snapped open.

Sitting up, I swung my legs over the side of the bed and tried to make sense of what I'd seen, but nothing added up. Had I really been that drunk (a distinct possibility), or had the stranger drugged me somehow? Who the fuck was the stranger anyway? In frustration I drove my fist down into the thin mattress and was rewarded with a jarring jolt of pain up my arm from the metal frame lying beneath it.

I punched it again, harder. The mattress squealed in protest and the lights above me flickered in response. I looked up and a sizzling crack split the air. *What the hell?* In the corridor one of the long fluorescent tubes on the ceiling blazed up suddenly, bathing my cell in a blinding white brilliance before exploding in a shower of shattered glass and white powder. My cell was plunged into darkness as deep as a well. A gust of wind rose up from nowhere, ruffling my hair and shirt. It carried with it the unmistakable scent of cold, damp night air. I rubbed vigorously at my eyes but the ghostly afterglow from the lights was burned onto my retinas. I froze at a scuffling sound from the corridor. I couldn't see my own hand in front of my face, but I could sense another presence. And it was right on the other side of the bars.

CHAPTER FIFTEEN

"Hello?" I called out, the hollow echo of my voice ringing through the empty space.

"Helloooo?" There was no answer. I'd been relieved to learn I was the only detainee, but found myself regretting it now. Either it had been a slow night in the neighborhood, or they had emptied the other cells intentionally. Perhaps they were trying to frighten me into confessing.

A shuffling sound came from the corridor. I waited, listening intently, but there was only the hush of my own breathing. My imagination perhaps. But I hadn't imagined that light popping like a Roman candle. A power surge most likely, but then why weren't the back-up lights coming on? That gave me an idea. The locks could be electronically controlled. I slowly eased myself off the bed and stood up.

I trailed a hand from the bed frame to the wall, with the other extended in front of me. I took a few more steps and my fingers brushed the bars. With a hiss, I jerked my hand back. They were ice-cold. I instinctively put the frozen tips of my fingers in my mouth, and was surprised to find they were wet as if I had touched actual ice. I reached out once more, and again pulled my hand back again as if it had been burned. It was crazy but I could swear that the bars were covered in a thin layer of frost.

Just like my apartment.

No sooner had the thought entered my mind, I was seized and hauled forward with terrific strength into the bars. With a muffled crunch I felt my nose break and a warm wetness splash my chin. A swarm of angry bees buzzed in my ears. I struggled to free myself, smashing down with my good arm at whatever held me, but it was like striking a tree branch.

BBZZTTTT!

An emergency light above the door to the holding area kicked on. I squinted through the blinding brightness to see framed before me a figure dressed all in black. He turned to look behind him, and his head, *its head*, continued turning, rotating fully around on its neck like an owl towards the direction of the light.

It had followed me.

Red eyes flashed again in my mind. I quickly raised a leg up. With my foot against the bars and a knee to my chest, I pushed off as hard as I could. His head whipped back around as I tore free with a loud *RIIIIIIP!* and fell to floor. With a shriek that sounded only in my head, it threw itself against the bars, both arms reaching out towards me.

"Sorry, this cell's taken," I coughed, splattering the floor with blood. It twisted obscenely back and forth against the bars, squirming and contorting its body. And then I watched, as quite impossibly, *its hands begin to extend through the bars towards me.* Like twin snakes floating on the air they came inexorably closer, inch by inch. I couldn't move; my mind and body were locked in a paralysis of terror. The black tip of a finger brushed the heel of my foot and I screamed, just as a jangle of keys sounded from the other side of the door. The arms snapped back, recoiling like springs. It stood facing me as if unsure of its next move. I stared into its red eyes, and then the door opened. Without a sound it disappeared, just another shadow.

Footsteps approached my cell, and Detective Hannity appeared on the other side of the bars. He looked down the corridor, his brows furrowing and then shook his head as if to clear it. Looking down at me with a puzzled expression, he asked. "You all right, Ramsey?" Bending down he picked up the piece of cloth from my torn shirt lying on the floor.

Words wouldn't come. All I could still see were the long arms, black as cancer, reaching towards me, and eyes that blazed in the dark. As if my own demons weren't enough, now I had a real one to contend with. When I realized he was still standing there, I looked up.

"Looks like Christmas came early for you this year Ramsey," he said, looking not at all happy about it, "A guardian angel just paid your tab."

I stared back at him until the significance of his words finally got through to me. *I was free.* I stood up slowly and brushed myself off.

"Remember those headaches I told you about, Detective? I'm going to need those pills back now."

* * * *

I stepped out of the police station chewing on a bitter mouthful of reds, hoping they were more than just sugar pills at this point. The second assault from the black thing had left me severely weakened. The slightest provocation could wake my alter ego, the one who liked to punch holes in chest cavities. I'd taken some small pleasure in watching Hannity's face as the tech had handed him the results of the lab analysis of the pills. He crumpled the sheet of paper up with one hand and reluctantly handed the bottle back to me. I felt a mix of relief, incredulity, and (if I had to be honest with myself) disappointment that they hadn't tested positive for some kind of narcotic. Was Eric losing his touch? My wallet was not returned. DNA tests could take anywhere from days to weeks, unless you had your own make-shift lab on the Southside of course.

I breathed deeply, enjoying the brace of icy air against my face and my newfound freedom. *But free to do what?* I wondered. *Get killed?*

"Don't go chasing any puppies outside the city limits." A voice warned from behind me. "We're not through with you yet, not by a longshot."

I turned around to see Kowalski's fleshy carcass filling the doorway. He wasn't laughing this time. Having to release the prime suspect wasn't going to make the Mayor somersault with joy. Sure they had my wallet, but a wallet wasn't a murder weapon. They wouldn't tell me who had made me whole on the tickets, but there was really only one person it *could* have been. I could see her handing over the money and then storming out in disgust. How was I ever going to make it up to her?

"Do you know what a person of interest is, Ramsey?" Kowalski asked.

"Sure I do," I replied with a grin, "it means you don't have jack shit." I turned to leave, but his hand grabbed my shoulder and pulled me around, the fingers digging painfully into my bad arm. If I'd had any doubt it was broken, Kowalski just put that mystery to rest. I winced in pain and put my hand over his, trying to pry it off.

"It means, we'll be watching you, you piece of dog shit."

He'd made a mistake. I held his gaze, looking deep into his eyes. I watched as his pinched-up face slackened and his eyes widened in alarm. He tried to back away, tugging at his hand, but I held it fast, no longer interested in freeing myself.

"Captain, the Commissioner wants to see you!" a voice called from the door.

I looked past him towards the voice that had probably just saved his life, and he managed to pull free. He staggered backward, almost losing his footing - his hand cradled protectively as if he'd grasped the handle of a boiling pot. The cop in the doorway looked from Kowalski to me, a question on his face, before ducking back inside.

"Good luck Captain, I hope you get your man." I called after him, "Whoever he is." My voice sounded thick and gravelly and there was a buzzing in my ears. A flash of heat chased through me. I reached out a hand on the railing to steady myself. When I looked up again the door was shut. I stood alone at the top of the stairs.

I dug in my pocket and dropped some more reds in my mouth. I chewed and swallowed until I could feel the building tide ebb and then gradually recede. *Stay in control.* The levy was starting to show some cracks, maybe even a few leaks. It wasn't long before the whole thing busted wide open, and not a pill in the world would hold back the floodwaters then. I prayed Penelope had some good news for me when I got back to the mansion.

I looked down the darkened street and not a single lamp post was lit. Every shadow and darkened doorway looked sinister to me. How hard was it to change a fucking light bulb? That thing was out there. I couldn't just stand around and wait for it to attack me again, which also meant I couldn't go back to the mansion. Not until I figured out what that thing was and how to kill it, or least stop it. I sure as hell wasn't going to put Eric or Penelope in any more danger than I had already. What I needed was a place to lie low while I sorted things out.

The wind picked up, carrying with it the sound of Tejano music from somewhere nearby. Chicago was home to what seemed like half of Mexico. I'd become so accustomed to the sounds of a tuba thumping out of passing cars that it barely registered with me anymore. It gave me an idea though.

After wracking my memory to recall the number, I made a call from the grimy payphone outside the station, amazed that it still worked. It went right to voicemail. I left a short message and sat down on the curb to wait. It was a long shot. After a few minutes my fingers and ears began to grow numb so I got up and started pacing. I was just about to start walking when I heard it - the unmistakable rumble of an approaching car that had parted ways from its muffler. It built in strength like a multi-layered drum roll, until I spotted the headlights turning onto the street at the end of the block. The noise kept climbing to a deafening crescendo as the tank-like hulk of a 1979 sky-blue Chevy Nova came to a stop in front of me. The driver leaned over in his seat to roll the passenger window down.

"Hey sailor, looking for a good time?" he screamed, his voice barely audible above the roar of the exhaust. I smiled and stretched a leg out, hiking my jeans up to display a knobby ankle and part of a hairy calf. He flashed me a thumbs up and a quarter came spinning through the air to me. I palmed it neatly as I opened the door and got in. The noise was profoundly deafening inside, the seats actually vibrating in response. I tried to say something, but he held up a finger and then blessedly turned the ignition off.

"Justin-" I began, but he gestured once more for me to wait as he reached into both ears and extracted a pair of foam ear plugs.

"Cheaper than a new Smitty!" He said, still yelling, and we both busted up laughing.

His hair looked like it always did - unwashed but fashionably greasy, while his outfit consisted of a pair of ripped and faded black jeans and a T-shirt that read, *My other shirt is your mom.*

Justin was one of those friends that made you realize just how un-cool you were in comparison. His unequaled collection of vinyl was legend among his fan base, who knew him only as "The Factor", his Deejay handle in the local club scene. Not as well-known were his guerilla home economics skills. He brewed his own beer and wine, and even grew some decent weed - a modern renaissance man by any definition.

I had come to rely on him for a very different sort of expertise—a darker passion that he took great pains to keep private. If word of it were to get out, it might frighten away the ladies, at least the attractive ones that liked to listen to DJ's and sip $20 martinis.

To put it simply, Justin was obsessed with the Occult. He had amassed a trove of arcane tomes on black magic that had grown to rival even his fabled record collection. I had come to refer to him as Mr. Crowley, and I think he felt truly flattered by the reference. If there was anyone that could help me with the immediate problem of a black demon-thing trying to kill me, it was my cabalistic record-spinning friend.

"I need your help." I said as we shared a fist bump.

"Of course you do, Rams" he replied with a wink. Without another word he popped his ear plugs back in and fired up Old Blue again. I jammed my fingers into my ears as he dropped the pedal and we tore off down the street like a howling heavy metal tempest.

CHAPTER SIXTEEN

The grounds and walkways surrounding All Hallows by the Tower Church were empty and still, without a soul in sight. A crescent moon rode high in a cloudless sky, the air cold enough to sting your lungs as you snatched a quick breath. If the occupants of the cars streaming past along the lower Thames had bothered to look up, they might have been surprised to see a lone figure perched atop the wind-lashed cupola of the ancient Saxon cathedral.

The position afforded him an unobstructed view of the landscape below. He had been coming to the exact spot for years beyond counting. It soothed him. Untouched by the frigid wind, he waited for the cold ground below to awake. In a few moments more it would be teeming with life, depending on one's definition of the word.

The hands of the old clock struck midnight, and as the massive bell began to toll the hour, he watched. Far below him, shadows began to coalesce into familiar shapes. The mist rising from a manhole became a young woman in a Victorian gown pushing a carriage, smiling and cooing at the empty space within. A paunchy businessman in a three-piece suit hurried by, important papers tucked between his transparent arms. On his way he passed through a group of small children playing hopscotch on the chalk scraped sidewalks. They were legion, thousands of souls, oblivious to one another and to the reality that they no longer walked among the living. He saw them, but they did not in turn perceive him. He envied their blissful oblivion. They were all cursed, but he alone was fully sentient. "Yet less than human" he said softly to himself, "far less."

Long deceased Londoners were not the only apparitions to haunt those streets, however. He could sense them long before he saw them:

shadows that were not shadows. He looked on as one detached itself from a building. The spirits flowed past it like water around a rock in a stream. He watched as its hand passed through a young man like a flame through a cobweb. The ghost gave a soundless scream and vanished.

He knew that he should not care, and yet he did. He had been made differently from the others. Perhaps it resided in his nature, and that of his creator, to feel this way. He had been the first, and so retained a glimmer of humanity within his inhuman shell, a distorted reflection of his maker's soul. It gave him a measure of power over the others, but if they ever conspired to challenge him with their combined strength he would surely fall. He did not fear this possibility. With the sole exception of Haggis, a regrettable name the shade had taken for himself, the rest were nearly mindless and therefore controllable. They could communicate in a way. He had shut himself off from their blind desires long ago. He knew what they wanted. It was the same thing the old fool who created them had desired. Power. Their maker had amassed an astounding degree of it in his own time, perhaps more than any before him or after. But to what end? It had not saved him.

They followed him because he had promised to deliver it to them. He had absolutely no intention of doing so. The old scarred wolf expected - no, *demanded* - the same thing of him. He didn't know the beast's intentions and didn't need to. The wolf manifested a demonical evil and cruelty within his twisted brain unlike anyone he had encountered. He and his kind were regarded as little more than servants, which was as he had intended. If the beast opined his true objective, he would stop at nothing to see them all destroyed. He felt certain he could prevail if forced to engage the old wolf, even without the talisman. But why take the chance when he was so close?

When he finally had it within his grasp, he would grant them all the power that their black hearts lusted after. For what greater power was there than oblivion?

Another shadow appeared below followed by more after it. They were restless, drawn to his presence. He should leave. Perhaps they would follow him and spare the innocent spirits he felt oddly compelled to protect.

He averted his gaze as another met its end. There had been no communication from the one he had sent after the boy. He would have gone himself, but his presence here had been necessary to prevent his brothers from turning their attentions to the living. Such a thing could not be allowed to happen again. Still, if he received no news soon he would be forced to act. It would not slip away again. If the young cub had to perish in order to retrieve it, then so be it. A rising chorus of silent screams reverberated in the air below him. He gathered himself and leapt up and into the churning grey skies above. The day of reckoning was coming, and the streets from Chicago to London would shake when it dawned.

CHAPTER SEVENTEEN

On the peeling dashboard of Justin's car, two bobblehead figures faced off against one another: a benignly smiling, young, strapping Jesus, and a scowling red-skinned, pointy-bearded Mephistopheles. They were locked in what could only be described as The Eternal Boxing Match. Don King himself could not have dreamt up such a promotion. With each pothole and bump in the road, the spring-mounted forms engaged, their oversized heads colliding with one another.

I watched the endless back and forth, my imagination supplying the ringside commentary. *Good lands a vicious jab to Evil's chin. But Evil strikes back with a punishing right fist to the chops! Good retaliates with another Sunday special! But Evil hammers back again with a body blow to the bread box!* It appeared to me that they were evenly matched, or at least perfectly counterbalanced.

I couldn't help but draw a comparison to my own dichotomous existence. There had been a time when I'd held fast to the conviction that my better nature would triumph in the end. That notion seemed laughable now. Everything had begun to tilt out of control, and once again I'd committed terrible acts that I'd sworn never to repeat.

Or had I?

Had I really been there that night in Washington Park? It was all so hazy, my memories fragmented and incoherent. I didn't want to believe it was true, but it didn't look good. Not good at all.

The current sorry state of my life brought to mind a mirror I'd seen once in the bathroom of a coffee shop. It had been hung low on the wall directly opposite the toilet. When you sat down you were faced with a portrait of yourself in a less than flattering pose. In small neat letters at the top of the mirror it read, *Karma is a bitch.* I found myself contemplating the message inherent in those words, and the futility of struggling against one's own nature. But as it often seemed to happen in my life, fate chose at that moment to intervene.

A gust of icy wind shot through the window Justin had cracked for the cigarette cradled in his left hand. My eyes went wide as the current of air slashed across my face, carrying with it a scent that made my nostrils flare.

The man from the bar.

Some people have a thing for faces, but for a wolf like me it's a person's smell that I lock onto. If I get a good whiff of you, you can be sure I won't forget it. His scent was like a hot frying pan doused in cold water. I reached over and grabbed Justin by the shoulder, causing him to swerve briefly into oncoming traffic. "What the fuck?" he mouthed angrily at me. I jerked my thumb in the air over my shoulder then drew my hand across my throat, the universal sign for pull over and cut the engine, or in certain circumstances, let's pick up a hitchhiker and kill him. In a rush of words I explained that we had to back up and then go...somewhere.

"I know it sounds crazy, but please, just trust me," I pleaded with him, my hands forming a steeple of supplication between us. Even to my own ears it sounded loopy. But instead of laughing in my face, which he would have been more than justified in doing, he grinned and said, "Alright Ramsey, what the hell."

I loved this guy.

But that was just like Justin. I think he saw in me a fellow weirdo and co-conspirator. He never skipped a beat when I came to him with one of my - *a friend of mine thinks he saw something in the alley the other night.* He would listen carefully, nodding his head, and then if he couldn't offer any information on the spot, he would reference one of his many books on black magic for the answer.

We swung back around to the intersection where I'd first caught the scent. I rolled down my own window a fraction and tilted my nose up to the crack. My pulse jumped as I picked it up again - faint, but still there. The wind was blowing from the south, so I gestured for him to take a left and we followed the trail into the night – a Black Magic DJ and a deranged werewolf. From the corner of my eye, I saw the Devil land another crushing blow to the perfect jaw of God's only son.

CHAPTER EIGHTEEN

As I motioned for Justin to swing around and turn down another boarded up strip of decaying urban streetscape, he pulled over and killed the engine. Anticipating the question I said, "We're getting close man. I swear it on my grandmother's – No. I swear it on the scaly ass of Cthulhu himself." The passing reference to H.P. Lovecraft brought a grin to his face.

"Look, Ramsey. We're amigos and everything, but this tour of the sad side of town is pushing past two hours," he paused to light a smoke. "And you still haven't explained why, what, where, or any–fucking thing." He crumpled the empty pack and tossed it behind him to rest with a couple dozen others. I smoked on occasion, but at current prices it competed with other essentials. A pack of cigarettes could put you back more than a six pack of beer, not to mention being treated like a leper every time you lit up. You couldn't even smoke in Ireland anymore, for Christ's sake.

He exhaled and wagged his hand at a street sign. "We're out over our ski's here bro. 169th street? Are we even in Chicago?"

Justin was a city kid, but the boundaries of that city had been carefully drawn around Wicker Park, Bucktown, and parts of Logan Square: places where white people rode bicycles at night, and the corner food and liquor had been pushed out for pour-over coffee shops and sushi joints. There were still some tough blocks in those hoods, but they made less than one square on a chess board that stretched for miles into darkness and decay. From Justin's vantage point, the rest of the city lurked unseen somewhere in the distance, its hostile concrete ceded to gangs and poverty. I hesitated to tell him where we were, because it would be less then comforting. It held a certain kind of celebrity when it came to urban blight. We were in the birthplace of Michael Jackson, and a city rivaled only by Camden, N.J. and Flint, Michigan in per capita homicides: Gary, Indiana.

We'd been tracking and backtracking, taking a route with more twists than a David Lynch film. I knew better than to expect Justin to do this for much longer.

"I tell you what Justin, if we don't find him in the next – WAIT!" I shouted. Justin jumped in his seat and his cigarette ejected from his lips, to fall burning into his lap. Only it didn't, because at the last second my hand flicked out in a blur and plucked it from the air. I took a deep drag and then handed it back to him.

"This is it," I said. "He's here."

"Who's here?" Justin asked looking around, "This place is abandoned dude."

He had a point – our destination would never grace the covers of a Frommer's Chicago Travel Guide. We had stopped along a singularly desolate stretch of crumbling asphalt. Boarded up buildings and chest-high weeds alternated with empty rubble-strewn lots in a cheerless block of abandoned industry. Across the street from our car squatted a massive turn of the century brick warehouse. Faded and chipped letters across the facade read *Smithewick's Fireproof Storage.*

"Detroit just got some competition," Justin declared as he stepped out and flicked the butt of his cigarette, sending it spinning across the deserted street to vanish into the gaping maw of an open manhole. Following my line of sight to the warehouse he said, "Don't tell me we're going in there." Hidden beneath the distaste in his voice lurked something else. Fear? Yes, I could smell it on him. He was hiding it pretty well, but this place had him spooked. And why not? It was past midnight and we were standing in the perfect setting for a post-apocalyptic zombie flick. "You wait here," I said and gave him a pat on the shoulder.

"You said *He's here*," he called after me." "Who is he and what is he doing in this place? More importantly, what the fuck am I doing here?" he finished, rummaging in his pockets for another cigarette.

"I promise I'll explain everything." I lied as I crossed the street. "Just be here when I get back, alright?" My nose quivered with a new scent and I nearly fell over in shock. *Duke!* Unless my nose was failing me, and my nose never did, he was here somewhere as well.

Duke wasn't alone either. There were other dogs. Lots of dogs. What the hell was going on?

As I approached the front of the warehouse the canine smells grew markedly stronger, but it seemed unlikely anyone had entered the building that way. The walkway and steps were littered with broken glass and garbage. A pair of rusty, formidable-looking metal doors barred the entrance. The absence of handles suggested they might open from the inside. I gave them a push, but they didn't budge.

The side of the building was even less promising than the front, without a single door or window, so I walked to the back. I was turning the corner when an internal switch in my brain flipped. I flattened my body against the wall and held my breath. My ears strained for the sound of approaching footsteps, but there was only the distant drone of cars from the freeway. I waited to the count of ten before tiptoeing quietly to the edge and peering around it.

Under a dimly-lit awning stood a man. Presumably he had his back to a door, although I couldn't be sure from my angle. I could see the mist of his breath billowing out in front of his face, but he stood as still as a statue. He wore a long overcoat and top hat with matching white gloves. It reminded me of a doorman for some ritzy residential high rise downtown.

He faced a parking lot filled with what must have been over 100 vehicles; black Escalades with enormous shining chrome rims, beefy Hummers and Navigators, sleek Land Rovers and a handful of the ever popular 1984 Chevrolet Caprice Classic. They were all pimped out in some way, except for one. It stood out like a wart on a supermodel's chin, with its faded turquoise exterior and blacked out windows. *A blue van.* Could it be the same one that Jonesy had described?

My nose twitched at the myriad blended scents of a dozen dog breeds. Their combined smell was stronger than before, and joining it were the muffled sounds of shouting coming from inside the building. If I could barely hear it, then it wouldn't register at all to the naked human ear. Whatever was going on in there, they wanted to keep it hidden. Unfortunately for them they'd failed to factor me into their equation.

I reviewed my options, the most obvious of which required getting a jump on the doorman. I'd have to cover 20 feet in the blink of an eye. The gravel, broken glass, and trash would make stealth all but impossible. He might have a piece hidden under that fancy coat. Whatever was going on, it didn't exactly have the trappings of a legal operation. It was too dicey. I needed help.

Back in front, Justin was nowhere to be seen. I scanned the surrounding street and buildings but there was no sign of him. The black thing rose up like the Grim Reaper in my imagination. I whipped my head towards a sound. *There!* A large plywood board covering the 1st floor window of a warehouse had been pried off, laying at an angle on the ground. Voices were coming from inside. I raced across the street past a half-smoked cigarette and up to the window. Crouching underneath it, I edged my head up to look inside.

"Please man, I told you. I took a wrong turn on the Dan Ryan. I'm just trying to get home."

Justin, his arms in the air, and eyes white with panic faced two men, their backs towards me. A heavy-set truck-stop type with a John Deere cap was patting him down and emptying his pockets. His partner, a slender Hispanic male with a shaved head, held a semi-automatic lazily at his side. I ducked down as John Deere stood up and then turned around to spit out the window.

"He don't have shit Emilio," the fat one said, his voice a surprisingly shrill falsetto.

"Gimme those cigs," the one called Emilio ordered, his tone low and measured. Even from outside, he smelled awful, like a stale Swisher Sweet dipped in piss. But underneath that was something worse: the acrid burn of bleach and fake orange. Meth. A Tweaker, dangerous and unpredictable. I'd have to act fast and without mercy. My fingers curled around a brick lying on the ground near my feet.

I could hear the snick of a lighter and the inhalation of smoke.

"Take em' off," Emilio ordered.

"What?" the fear in Justin's voice was palpable.

"Take off your fuckin' clothes," he commanded. There was a soft click as he disengaged the safety. John Deere began to giggle.

In one fluid motion I stood, stepped through the window and swung the brick with all my might. I would swear I didn't make a sound, but someone on speed is naturally paranoid I guess. Emilio whipped the gun around, but not before the brick smashed into the side of his head. They didn't fuck around back in the day when they made things, bricks included.

It hit his face like a sledgehammer, caving his cheekbone, the eye socket erupting in a fountain of blood.

I bent down, pried the gun from his hand and pointed it at John Deere, a wet stain darkening the crotch of his jeans.

I could feel Emilio's blood dripping down the side of my face, already cooling in the chill evening air. The wolf stirred, agitated by the violence and the smell of blood.

"Down!" I ordered, waving the gun. Both Justin and John Deere dropped to the ground.

"Not you, for Christ's sake."

Justin stood up warily, looking at me like he didn't know who I was. I decided right there that he would be the third person to know.

"Remember when I told you once that there was something about me?" I said, "Something different?"

I kept the gun pointed at John Deere.

"Yeah I remember," Justin answered in a voice that wavered. I think he was in shock. "We were both drunk and high, and you said…" his gaze wandered to that in-between place where people go when they're drawing forth a memory. "You said that it had something to do with why you were always coming to me for advice."

I nodded once.

"Is this where you tell me you're some kind of crazed murderer?" he said, and managed to get another smoke lit with his shaking hands.

"Maybe." I replied, looking at John Deere.

The volatile mix of fear, blood and piss in the air were starting to excite me.

"I'd wager 100 bucks that a bloodcurdling scream would draw about as much attention around here as a burst of gunshots, which is to say – none at all."

John Deere's eyes went wide and he shuffled back on his ass. "No!" he cried, as I took a step towards him and leveled the barrel straight at his head. "Please, please don't kill me, I'm sorry!" he pleaded, his voice breaking. I broke into a wide smile and threw my hands up in the air. "Just kidding!"

He looked from my face to Justin's, and then started to sob.

"I really should have been an actor." *A job where you pretend to be something you're not? Oh yeah, I would have been a natural at that one.*

"Rest easy you fat fuck, I'm no serial killer." I said and then turned to Justin. "I'm only a werewolf." To which he grinned, finally starting to relax a bit. "I'm not proud of it but I've killed people before." I plucked the cigarette from his mouth. "Just like this shit." I smiled and then ground the burning cherry into the palm of my hand.

"Jesus!" Justin hissed in alarm. "What the hell are you doing?"

I closed my eyes and concentrated on the bright searing pain in my hand. The blood, the piss and the fear weren't enough. I needed the final ingredient to draw out the wolf. "Pain helps to trigger it," I explained taking a deep breath, "A full moon will work in a pinch too."

"What are you talking about?"

"This." I said opening my eyes. His expression was a perfect window into what he saw: bright yellow pupils where blue ones had been just a moment ago. To his credit he didn't scream, and he didn't run. He just stared, his jaw hanging open. And then he stared some more. John Deere let out a strangled cry and fainted.

"That really does hurt like a bitch." I said, breaking the silence and shaking my hand in the air. I took the pill bottle out and shook two into my hand. There were less than a dozen left. I tried not to think about it. I chewed and swallowed, and waited for them to work. I would just have to hope they kept on working.

Justin's mouth moved soundlessly before he uttered "My God," followed by, "Holy fucking crap."

I turned my palm over and showed it to him. Where blackened skin had been a moment before, there was only a fading pink mark. "So," I smiled again. "How about helping an old friend out one more time?"

CHAPTER NINETEEN

There is no question that the future holds events which far exceed our current capacity to imagine them. Precisely such a thought occurred to me, as I explained my plan to break into a building housing some sort of criminal operation to a DJ in the middle of an urban wasteland in the dead of night.

After scouring the overflowing waste bins in the alley, Justin returned with a sizable, if somewhat frayed, length of nylon packing twine. Neither of us had been Boy Scouts growing up, so the integrity of our knots was a bit dubious, but we secured John Deere's legs and hands as best we could. Despite his pathetic pleas, I jammed a rag into his mouth and stuffed him into the trunk. When I explained what I needed done next, Justin nodded once.

"I've got some things in the trunk that might work," he said then looked at me. "Shit."

I shrugged and we opened the trunk again. John Deere must have thought we'd changed our minds about keeping him alive. As I reached for him he gave a muffled squeal, somehow managing to piss himself for a second time.

Grunting with the effort, I shoved his body to one side as Justin rummaged around until he pulled out a backpack. We split up, with Justin jogging around to the far side of the warehouse, while I took up my previous position and waited for his signal. In my head, a song began to play. It happened sometimes, my own brain randomly would select its own subconscious soundtrack. Lou Reed was singing about waiting for his man, when a voice tore through the silence.

"Lie down on the ground with your hands behind your head!" the voice thundered from close by. It was deep, loud as hell, and sounded like it belonged to a Marine Drill Sergeant.

"I repeat!" it said, and it did. The voice made it clear that it was in no way fucking around thank you very much.

"You have 10 seconds to comply!" it threatened. It seemed to be right on top of me. The urge to do as it ordered was undeniable.

The doorman reacted by basically shitting his pants in every way imaginable. His former composure evaporated in an instant, and he jerked his head from side to side, legs twitching with the impulse to run. He looked unsure of what to do and terrified not to do it.

The sound of gunshots split the air and the doorman jumped. "Those were warning shots! The next shots will not be, now GET ON THE GROUND!" the voice commanded. It was too much. He dropped down and prostrated himself, his ridiculous top hat rolling away to rest on the ground near him.

I burst from around the corner, sprinting towards the prone figure. "Don't fucking move!" I yelled in what I hoped was an approximation of the phantom cop's voice. He turned his head to look at me but stayed down. So far so good.

And then technology did what it always seemed to do when you needed it most. It failed. "Lay down on the ground!" the voice boomed again.

The sound startled me and I faltered, nearly tripping. The doorman hesitated for a fraction and then he was moving, his hands no longer on top of his head. I had to reach him in the next breath or I'd be dead. Leaping to his feet, he thrust a hand inside his jacket, withdrawing a handgun that Charles Bronson might have deemed excessive. I left the ground, propelling my body forward, leaping towards him as he pivoted. His arm slowed to a stop, the barrel trained directly on my forehead as my outstretched hand, the same hand that I'd used as an ashtray moments before, closed to a fist. His jaw gave way with a sound like the first bite from a fresh apple, red spray jetting from his nose into the air. He spun around once and dropped, his face pressed to the ground again.

I stood over his body. Unlike Emilio, he'd only been doing his job. I looked up to see Justin emerge from around the side of the building. He held an iPod and a pair of speakers, each the size of a paperback. His eyes went wide when he saw the crumpled figure on the ground.

"Is he?" he asked, looking down.

I shrugged, not knowing what to say and walked towards the door. I put my hand on the knob, and gave it a turn. It was unlocked.

"Wait here." I said, and then something made me look back.

"He was going to shoot me, Justin."

He was still looking down at the body of the doorman when I opened the door and stepped inside.

CHAPTER TWENTY

I once drove 22 hours straight from Kansas City to San Diego in a VW Bus so old, it must have come off the assembly line back when the Beach Boys still shared a collective head of surfer hair. My freshman year at college I let a Hawaiian girl stab out a tattoo on my ankle using a needle, thread and bottle of India ink from art class. At a distance, it could still be mistaken for a rudimentary cross or perhaps the letter Y. When I decided to drop acid for the first time, I wisely chose to do it in a cemetery. My point being, I've done my share of reckless, sometimes moronic acts, but most could be chalked up to youthful indiscretion, or as it's called nowadays, an undeveloped frontal lobe.

But violently forcing my way into an underground criminal enterprise wasn't merely reckless: it bordered on insanity. Maybe I was losing my mind, but who wouldn't in my situation?

Inside, a potent blend of human sweat and fresh blood hung suspended in the air, tantalizingly close. Down a dimly lit hallway of unfinished drywall stood another door. I put my ear against the wood and listened. I detected the muffled sounds of shouting, interspersed with the snarling and barking of dogs - a feverish pitch to their cries. The tide of shouting ceased for a moment before crashing back with a massive roar. It seemed to ebb and flow in time with whatever entertainment was taking place on the other side.

Was the mystery man from the bar really on the other side? I could still stop this madness, turn around and head back home; try to forget what I'd seen and done. But I knew myself too well. I hadn't risked my life and killed one (maybe two) men to give up now. Bracing myself, I grasped the doorknob, slowly turned the handle and then pulled as hard as

I could. If someone stood guard on the other side, I might get the jump on them. The door whipped inwards and a wall of sound rushed in after it, smashing into me. There were thick foam squares fit together in a tight mosaic like futuristic snake scales covering the inside of the door and the walls beyond.

Sound proofing panels. I'd seen them before at one of the swankier clubs Justin spun records at. They were pricey but highly effective at dampening background noise. Past the door a short landing opened onto a set of metal stairs and railings leading down. I crouched and crept over to edge of the landing, where a bizarre and macabre spectacle unfolded below me.

On the subfloor of the warehouse an arena the size of a hockey rink had been erected. Surrounding it on three sides were long rows of aluminum bleachers like the kind you'd see in a high school gymnasium. The esteemed clientele of the event, and the unmistakable owners of the Ghetto chariots in the parking lot, filled the seats. Cigars, drinks and fists of cash passed through the air as they urged on the gladiators forced to battle for their pleasure. Scantily clad waitresses weaved among the attendees, doling out Forties of beer and bottles of champagne.

A fresh outbreak of baying and snarling erupted from a holding area at the end of the ring, where a group of handlers waited with the next round of dogs. Although full body leashes crisscrossed their chests and necks, they strained to hold the dogs in check. They held the leash in one hand and a Taser in the other, a blue arc sparking occasionally from the business end. The dogs thrashed, lunging against their constraints, whipped to a killing frenzy by the explosive level of noise and violence. Most were large male Pit Bulls, but I also spied a few stocky Rottweilers and a lone colossal Mastiff.

I looked out over the killing floor and my breath hitched in my throat. His coat matted in dried blood and glistening with sweat, Duke stood alone in the ring, facing down a dog three times his size. He was nearly unrecognizable from the picture I'd been shown. They must have tossed him in the ring for a pre-match diversion and he'd surprised them by displaying more ferocity and tenacity than they'd expected. But bravado would only get you so far when you were trapped in the ring with a crazed Pit Bull. My mind raced, but I knew there was nothing I could do to stop it. I was helpless.

Fuck all that.

I decided right there that I'd rather die than live with another innocent death on my conscience.

I was preparing to jump the rail when the Mastiff broke free. It charged ahead into the ring, but rather than joining the fight, it kept running right between the two dogs. Picking up speed it bounded over the low wall straight into the stands. Shrieks of panic filled the air as the largest dog in the canine family tree began mauling the people seated in the first row. His handler rushed after it, Taser sparking in his hand. I watched him climb over the arena wall before a second dog leapt onto his back and dragged him down, jaws tearing at his back like a lion straddling a gazelle.

After that it was like a bomb went off. The handlers had lost all control. The dogs were everywhere, and the stands seethed with people trying to escape. Dark muscular shapes moved in and out of the stands, taking down their prey like silent assassins. People were there one second and gone the next, pulled down and under by an invisible current. The dogs were attacking anything that moved.

Among the heaving chaos of the stands, one man remained motionless like the last building left standing after a tornado. He looked comically large, as if Daredevil's nemesis the Kingpin had stepped off the page. I watched as a Rottweiler burst from the melee below, bounding up the stands towards him two rows at time. He didn't appear to see it. It reached him and leapt at his throat. It died. It happened too quickly to register, even though I was staring directly at him. He dropped the lifeless body of the dog and then he looked right at me. It was as if he'd been aware of my presence all along. His face looked...unfinished. A heavy brow jutted out over a wide square jaw and flattened nose, as if a sculptor had dropped his hammer and chisel after only a few crude strokes. Time skipped and I was back at the bar, three books of sheet music to the wind.

"What is your name my young friend?"

"T – I mean Ben, Ben Ramsey."

"A strong name. Have another drink my new American friend."

"Don't mind if I do Hans. Don't mind if I do."

It was him. The German. The stranger from the bar who'd bought me drinks all night and then drugged me. The one with the accent so heavy, his words punched into your eardrums like fists. Before I could react he turned and vaulted over the back of the bleachers, reappearing below as he sped away from the turmoil. He moved fast for a mountain.

Between us lay a war zone. Screams filled the air as the dogs drank the blood of their former masters. I jumped the railing, plunging headlong into the chaos. Every dog loves a chase.

CHAPTER TWENTY ONE

Entering the fray, I bobbed and weaved, cutting and spinning like a running back through the thick press of bodies and feral animals. I was desperate not to lose sight of my target. I focused my breathing and locked my eyes on his broad shoulders racing away ahead of me.

Inhale. I twisted from the grasp of a screaming young black woman, her hair dripping with blood from the ruin of her ear.

Exhale. I leapt over a pair of pit bulls, their muzzles worrying a limp figure on the ground.

Inhale. A slathering Rottweiler bounding towards me was rolled by the Mastiff, its massive jaws closing on the smaller dog's throat like a sprung bear trap.

Exhale. A man stepped in front of me, his left hand reduced to a bloody stump. Behind him I caught a glimpse of the German disappearing up another staircase. Without slowing I lowered my shoulder, hitting him hard right below the clavicle. He crumpled while I vaulted over his falling body like a springboard and kept running with everything I had.

I reached the bottom of the stairs in time to see a door click shut at the top. I bounded up the steps and placed my hand on the knob but then stopped. What if he was waiting to ambush me on the other side? The circumstances dictated at least a modicum of caution. But the beast that lurked within me would not be subdued. It was designed for this specific task: chasing down other living things and killing them. My eyes narrowed and I threw open the door to slam violently against the wall.

I stood inside a massive shuttered storage area, larger even than the fighting arena. Row upon row of wooden crates stacked 20 feet high, stretched away into the far dim recesses of the room. Above me a network of rusted iron joists crisscrossed the roof. An antiquated looking light fixture with a single lit bulb hung suspended in the void, its slow rotation moving in time with the massive blades of an industrial fan anchored at the roof's peak. The light it cast was worse than none at all. Shadows slid back and forth across the room like a ship on the waves of a turbulent sea.

Apart from the muffled screams filtering in from the other room, it was quiet inside. Perhaps he'd escaped through another exit. I opted to move along the perimeter of the room, reluctant to enter the corridors of boxes and the deep concealing shadows within. I'd taken no more than a dozen steps, when something moved at the edge of my vision. I whirled to see two blood red eyes glowing balefully in the dark. They came forward into the light. I grimaced as a large rat squeezed out of a ragged hole in one of the crates and dropped ungracefully to the ground. It skittered down an aisle before turning to appraise me, a stranger on its turf. Sniffing the air once, it dismissed me and disappeared from sight. I looked at the hole and thought of all the hundreds of crates, suppressing a shiver. There could be a veritable army of the vermin hiding in this place. As far as I knew they feared nothing, except perhaps the chemical arsenal of the Streets and Sanitation Department.

I continued forward, attuned to the slightest sound - my senses vibrating with super-charged sensitivity. From above, the light spawned an ever-changing landscape of shadows that rippled across the floor, making it appear to move beneath my feet.

As I passed another corridor, the swinging light above briefly lit its far depths, and I spied something lesser eyes might have missed. I stopped, a feeling of unease creeping over me at the thought of entering the long and narrow cramped space. I could be trapped with nowhere to run if the German came in behind me. But wasn't that what I wanted? A confrontation? A single man, even one as large and as strong as the German, couldn't hope to stand against the wolf.

Had I detected a flicker of fear when our eyes met? Perhaps he'd seen me change in the park, and knew what I was. Stepping inside the twin walls, I padded quietly to the end and picked up the small object lying discarded on the floor. I examined it in utter disbelief.

It couldn't be. Not here.

The light passed overhead again and I looked up to see the shadowy outline of a man speed across the wooden wall of crates before me.

Much too late I turned as a hand clamped onto the back of my neck and threw me into the air. I ricocheted off one and then another of the unyielding crates before the ground rose up and kicked me in the back. For a moment I was unable to move, but then an animal sound, something between a grunt and a snort passed my lips. I rose to my feet trailing a thin strand of bloody drool onto the floor and limped back down the passageway but it was empty. I'd misjudged things badly. No man, no matter how strong could have tossed me twenty feet through the air like a doll. The German was not the prey. I was.

In my clenched fist I could feel the hard contours of the silver pendant necklace Celeste had once worn. There could no longer be any doubt. The Brotherhood had found me at last.

A scraping noise sounded high above me. I lunged to the side as a heavy crate crashed down where I'd been standing a moment before.

Move!

I vaulted out of the way and barely escaped a second crate. It peppered the side of my face with splinters as it exploded next to me. I ceased to think and simply ran. Behind me a succession of crates crashed one after the other, the noise deafening. The gust of air generated by the last followed me as I flung myself clear. I backed up, bumping into a lone crate laying on its side, dropped from a forklift and forgotten perhaps.

I tensed, waiting for him to appear, and then hissed in pain as a jolt like a pinched nerve shot up my arm. The change was coming. Another burning twitch in my spine caused me to crane my neck back, and it was this simple act that saved me. Above me, I watched in disbelief as the German dropped from the rafters.

There was no time to think. Grasping the crate lying next to me, I heaved it with every ounce of my strength at the plummeting bulk of the German. I sure as hell didn't lift weights, or do much more than 12 ounce curls most of the time, but the wolf was strong and the wolf was pissed off. The crate slammed into the German and the German slammed into a wall of what else, more crates.

The sound of wood breaking has a subtle but distinctive difference when compared to bone. In fact, if one listens closely, a compound fracture has a truly musical quality to it. As he flew into the base of the column, his momentum smashed the supporting crates out from underneath those stacked above, and the entire tower came toppling down, crashing on top of him in a massive hammer of splintering wood.

It went on and on until the last crate settled in place with a final rasping woody creak. After a few moments passed without a sound from the German, I stepped forward to investigate but then danced backwards as a muffled voice issued forth from beneath the rubble

"Well played, *mein* friend," it croaked.

The pile convulsed and then surged outward in an eruption of broken boards. A battered and bloodied figure crawled out to collapse face down on the floor, his left leg bent at an impossible angle.

"You are like a little child lost in the dark. You know nothing! NOTHING!" he raged and then was overcome with a wracking cough, a bloody froth bubbling from his lips as he turned his head to one side. "I don't blame you though. It must seem like one big mystery, all questions and no answers, yes?"

If anger is a simmering fire, than true rage is a river of ice – crystalline and clean. I felt as if I had been set on fire and then submersed in a glacial lake. I hadn't felt such fury since witnessing Penelope's attacker laughing as he ripped her blouse open. I'd compensated by ripping his head from his shoulders. The brazen hubris of the German was almost worse. First, he roofied me in my favorite bar. Then he tried to flatten me with a crate. After that he'd done his best to crush me like a grape. And now he was mocking me? The fight with the doorman, the bloody carnage of the arena, it had all been building up inside of me. I took two steps towards him and drove my foot down hard onto his shattered leg.

His eyes bulged and bloody spittle sprayed from his lips as a hoarse scream stretched his jaws wide. My tongue felt heavy and my teeth had begun to ache. I wanted to know what his blood tasted like. I doubled over suddenly, stifling a cry as red hot needles pierced my fingers, a precursor to the claws that would soon sprout from the tips of my fingers.

Tear his throat open.

It was gaining momentum, but I still had the pills. I would make him talk first. I dropped onto his back with my knees, straddling him while wrapping my throbbing hands around his neck. I needed both hands just to encompass it. He gave another yell and twisted beneath me trying to throw me off.

I tightened my grip on his neck, his jugular throbbing with a drumbeat-like urgency.

"Wait! Just wait!" he cried, going slack beneath me. "I can help you. I know things. Secret things!"

I grunted as the vertebrae in my spine popped, lengthening to accommodate my altering physiology. Gritting my teeth, I pushed on through the pain. I had to hurry. "OK Hans, you can start with why you drugged me at the bar and what the fuck you're doing with this!" I snarled, shoving the necklace in his face.

"You know that you are responsible for all the death back there? You know that, yes?" he said ignoring my questions.

"Listen Hans, or whatever the fuck your name is, I want-"

"Call me Klaus," he said, "The dogs, always they are barking, yes?"

I lifted a clawed hand to slice his throat open and stopped. How could I have overlooked it? It was so obvious. How could I have forgotten?

"They are mindless but know a real killer when they smell one."

It had been me.

"It is a weakness of mine. I enjoy watching them tear each other to pieces. It reminds me of how far we have…evolved."

The dogs must have sensed me as soon as I'd come into the arena. My scent had driven them insane with fear. They'd only done what they'd been trained to do, kill. Now there was more blood on my hands.

"Shut up." I commanded.

"You are lost, but I can help you, I can -"

"Shut up!" I howled, my hands shaking as another seizure ripped through me. It was no use. The transformation had progressed beyond my control and had to be stopped. I released a hand from his throat and reached for my pills - *which were not there.*

"We don't need to be enemies," he said calmly, and then his body rippled like an eel and I was thrown off his back onto the floor. I scrambled to my feet as he stood to face me.

Stand? With that leg? Impossible.

I watched the tattered bloody rags of the pants on his left leg flutter, as if moved by a gentle breeze. And then the shattered leg began to repair itself, the lacerations on his arms and face vanishing before my eyes as if they'd never been there. I stared transfixed, as bone bent and snapped back into place, realigning itself. It was like watching the injuries happen in reverse.

He shook his head in a bemused kind of way. "How have you managed such a feat – staying alive all these years?" He said, his voice incredulous. "All this time hiding in plain sight when we have been searching, always searching. It was wise not to go home," he paused and a cruel grin curled his lips upwards, "But wait. You did go home, didn't you *Thomas?*"

I fell to my knees with a strangled cry as the transformation accelerated. My hips strained against my jeans, my thighs bunching with muscle.

"Looking for these?" he said, and I looked up through a haze of agony to see him holding my pill bottle, a smile stretching his face. "A pity, it must have fallen out when I tossed you like a plaything across the room."

"Give them to me!" a monster's voice roared from my mouth.

"Would she want you now, I wonder?" he continued, clearly enjoying himself.

"I would imagine she had higher hopes for you after snatching you from death's doorstep?"

I could still see Celeste's face the day she'd left the cottage. We'd been holed up for days. She promised to return the next morning. It was the last time I saw her alive. In a locker she'd left a backpack containing a change of clothes, three hundred Quid, and two passports. Thomas Spell died that day, and Ben Ramsey rose in his place. My father once told me that Spellman had been shortened to Spell when my great grandfather came over from Austria. The surname derived from the German word *spillen* which meant *to jest*. Of course the irony was lost on him, a man who was about as jolly as a headsman.

"And what did you do when you returned, my young cub?" the German continued. "Imagine my surprise when I located your family home only to find it in ashes."

It had been a mistake to go back to my father when I'd returned to the States, but there had been no one else to turn to. He'd welcomed me with tears and then flew into a rage when I told him I wouldn't be staying. One of my last coherent memories was putting down my backpack and turning around to see him sliding his belt free from his pants. As if I were still a frightened little boy that could be cowed into submission with a beating! I locked him in the basement that night before the moon rose, and in the morning I set fire to the house and never looked back.

"It's curious that the bones I discovered in the ashes were gnawed by an animal." the German went on laughing, "The prodigal young wolf returns home, and has his own father for dinner! Ah well, we are all guilty of transgressions against our fellow man, aren't we my friend?"

I fell forward onto my stomach, my tail bone popping as it extended.

"You have something that does not belong to you Thomas," he said, "If you tell me where it is, I will let you live."

"Don't know…what you're talking about," I panted.

"You've hidden it well. If it was in your filthy hovel I would have found it."

He bent over my shivering form and pulled Celeste's bracelet from my convulsing hand.

A smirk squirmed across his mouth like a slug. "Give it to me and I may even tell you the truth about her. After all, the dead whore was the one who stole it to begin with."

I could no longer speak

"Oh come now," he simpered, shaking his head in disappointment. "You've forgotten your little Parisian lover so quickly?"

I could see them pulling her from the river again. Her body grey and limp, the wounds awful to behold. I rolled onto my back, spasms wracking my body. He glared down at me through yellow eyes that burned with hunger and violence.

"You asked me about the necklace. Well here's a little secret for you wolf cub. I always keep something to remember the pretty ones by," he said with a sneer, "before I tear their throats out."

He winked, and in that fraction of second morphed into something that was neither wolf nor man. A wolf-man, just like all the Hollywood clichés. It happened faster than I could process, like a time-lapsed nature film sped up to a thousand frames per second.

"I'm afraid I can't allow the transformation to run its full course." He said, looking down upon me. "We are most powerful in our true form," he reached towards me, and with one hand wrapped around my neck and the other grasping my leg, he lifted me off the floor and then slammed me back down, holding me fast in spite of my thrashing limbs. Hot stinking breath stung my eyes. I could feel the heat radiate out from him in waves.

"You are nothing, Thomas. Less than a slave," he snarled. "And I am your master."

I wish I could say that I broke free of his grasp and savaged him, but no such thing happened. He lifted me up again by my throat. I struggled feebly like a small fish on the end of large hook. My feet, or claws, scraped for purchase on the ground as he shook me and screamed something in my face, but I could no longer hear him. The room began to dim and I knew that I was going to die.

While I had been waging an all-out war against myself, trying to stifle my *abilities* at every turn, the German had fully embraced them. Yes, I was a monster, but I also remained the same dope I'd been before. I still slept through my alarm, drank too much coffee and beer and forgot to buy toilet paper. I still cut myself shaving, paid my bills late, and the food in my refrigerator could only be consumed under threat of certain food poisoning. Was it any wonder I found myself in some random warehouse getting my windpipe crushed by a walking nightmare? I should never have gotten on that plane to Paris.

I'd left home to find myself and returned as a murdering mystery of epic proportions. There wasn't enough irony in the world to touch that one. What had begun in the twilit woods of the unspoiled English countryside would now end in the decaying heart of a dying city. My eyes closed.

I awoke with a start in my old room. I stretched, yawned and threw my legs over the side of the bed, kicking a soccer ball resting there. It rolled lazily across the floor to stop against the wall, where I saw that it had gray eyes and a face that I knew. I screamed and staggered away from the decapitated head of my father. My feet slipped on something slick and I fell to the floor. Blood covered my hands, chest, the headboard, and (Dear Jesus how?) the ceiling. I staggered out of the door and followed the trail to the basement where the door has been torn from its hinges. One cannot appreciate how much blood the human body holds until it has been spilled like a smashed vat of cheap Bordeaux.

I didn't want to remember this.

PARIS IS FOR LOVERS THOMAS.

No.

Please no. Not this.

HOME IS FOR BLOOD SOAKED SHEETS AND SEVERED HEADS.

My eyes fluttered opened. I was still being strangled. The pressure in my lungs built to a crescendo of unbearable agony and then...stopped. The terror and pain retracted their claws from my chest. I didn't care anymore. Let it come. I wasn't afraid anymore.

The vision of the grinning jackal before me faded away, replaced by a beautiful woman's face. We were walking through the market, our arms entwined, looking at trinkets. I laughed at something, or nothing. She turned to me with a smile, and a light shone from her face that grew to encompass the world.

CHAPTER TWENTY TWO

She smelled like sex and her mouth tasted of cigarettes and red wine. She pushed me onto the bed. I let my body fall backwards, anticipating the feel of her bare skin pressed to mine.

I fell but encountered no resistance, passing through the mattress as if it wasn't there. I tried to call her name but frigid water closed over my face, swallowing my screams. My body plunged sightless through the void until a flash of light split the darkness. I clawed my way towards it, bursting to the surface and into a tempest of howling winds and whipping waves. Lightning cleaved the obsidian sky, revealing my surroundings, and I despaired. All around me raged a mad sea without a spar of wood to me to cling to. Rising and falling with its enormous swells, I realized something was clasped tightly in my hand.

Another volley of lightning revealed a great wall in the distance, stretching from one end of the horizon to the other. And then in horror I comprehended its true form - a massive wave, a wall, yes, but of water - hurtling towards me. Nothing living could hope to withstand such a thing. A desperate thought entered my mind. I forced the air from my lungs, plunging beneath the surface once more. I would burrow underneath the mountain of water and emerge unscathed on the other side. Free of air I sunk like a stone, deeper and deeper into the limitless ocean. Suddenly my descent stopped and an unseen force began to drag me up to the surface once more.

I was sightless in the black water, but for a soft glow emanating from my hand. I opened it and pulsing within was a ball of light, beating with a life force of its own. Uncomprehending, I beheld a globe, such as a child might shake to bring forth a swirl of glitter and light. I brought it closer to my face and it moved, wriggling with a life of its own out of my grasp. I struggled in vain to halt my ascent, and could only watch as it plummeted into the depths like a dying star. The invisible force relentlessly pulled me up to the sky above, and as I broke the surface again I looked up to see the titan wave crashing down from miles above.

"Ben!"

"Ben! Wake up!!"

I opened my eyes. The ocean had vanished, and I lay on a cold hard floor. Someone shook me hard enough to snap my chin against my chest.

I tried to say something in protest, but a hissing sound was all that came out of my mouth. The agony of attempting to speak nearly caused me to faint. My head felt ready to split open and my throat ached as though it been scoured by sand and hot desert winds. The shaking resumed, doubling in intensity. I looked up at the figure holding me but he was concentrating intently on something else in the room. "Stop!" I finally squawked. Whipping his face towards mine, a look of terrified relief washed across Justin's features.

"Jesus-fucking-shit-thank-you-God" he blurted out. But instead of offering me a hand up he began to drag me along the floor like a sack of flour. I could see that he was caught in the throes of some hysteria, and didn't even notice when the side of a crate clipped my head.

"I can walk, I can walk!" I pleaded, unsure if I was telling the truth. He stopped and reluctantly released me. I failed at first but then gradually managed to rise to a semi-sitting position, causing a burst of firework-bright pain to go off in my head.

"What's going on?" I asked, "Where's the German?"

Justin leaned in until our faces nearly touched. "We have to get out of here," he whispered in a wavering voice, "NOW."

I tried to speak, but Justin covered my mouth with his hand.

"We leave now or we die!" He hissed.

I nodded and he dropped his hand. "Okay, let's just retrace our steps and go back the way we came in."

Justin shook his head violently from side to side. "It's a slaughterhouse back there. We can't… I can't go through that again. It's suicide."

"I think there might be another way out," I said and held up a hand. He pulled me to my feet and flinched as screams and what sounded like a whole showroom of furniture being smashed erupted from somewhere close by. I threw an arm around his shoulder and pointed the way. He braced himself and then hobbled forward, half supporting and half carrying me towards the doors I'd seen from the outside. When we reached them they were blocked by (what else?) another stack of crates. No wonder I hadn't been able to budge the doors earlier. I was beginning to fucking hate crates.

We inched along as the sounds of destruction intensified behind us. A voice cursed loudly in German. Whatever had his attention, it had my sincere thanks. When we finally reached the doors I insisted on helping Justin push, but they soundly rebuffed our efforts, unimpressed by our breathless heaving against them. The exertion caused black snow to dance before my eyes. I couldn't be certain if I was helping or merely using the crates to keep from falling over.

"Let's try rocking these motherfuckers," Justin huffed, his breathing labored. It took a few tries to get the timing just right, but then it actually began to work and the column began to sway. "Give it everything you have!" Justin grunted, and with one final heave the column toppled over with a resounding crash.

"Here goes everything," I said and tried to spit on the palms of my hands, but my mouth was dry as dust. I looked at Justin and we both grasped the handles and pulled in unison. A burst of cold night air ushered into the room as the doors glided smoothly open. We both stepped across the threshold as a voice issued from behind us.

"Where do you think you are going *mein* friend?"

Justin spun around, slowly craning his neck upwards to take in the hideous monster that I knew stood towering there. He made a small sound in his throat and then crumpled to the ground like an engineered demolition. I turned and looked into the grinning evil of that face. It had been an interesting life.

"Get stuffed you filthy Kraut bastard," I said, and flashed a grin of my own.

The leering canine sneer vanished and his eyes narrowed, smoldering with malice. I waited for his claws to open my throat.

He pulled his arm back to strike me, and then his muzzle split wide with a scream that sounded all too human. I stumbled back as something black whipped out from behind him and wrapped around his broad chest, squeezing tightly like a serpent. It moved like mist before my eyes, insubstantial and shifting. A dozen smaller tendrils branched off, racing up his face and *into his ears and mouth* like the probing feelers of some giant centipede.

"Verflucht Teufel!" he howled and grasped the choking coils between his claws, shredding them like the strands of a frayed rope. The indentations impressed on his face and heavily muscled torso attested to the thing's strength, as he turned back to engage it once again. From behind his broad outline I perceived something massive, writhing and flailing like a hundred tentacled octopus. I didn't wait to see what happened next. I knew what manner of nightmare he faced. I quickly grabbed hold of Justin's arm. I dragged him unceremoniously across the empty lot towards the street just as Justin's car, tires squealing, raced away. I bent down and picked up the John Deere cap lying in the street.

CHAPTER TWENTY THREE

I may be cursed for all eternity, afflicted with a disease that is gradually winning the battle for control of my body and perhaps even my soul. I may be piss-broke with an occupation a well-trained monkey could excel at. I may even be wanted as the prime suspect in a gruesome and foul murder that I can't be certain I didn't commit. I may be totally and completely fucked.

But when a small, furry shape darted past me and fled down the alley, I felt a tiny spark of hope stir inside me.

"Duke!"

"Uhhhhh-," Justin moaned beside me.

"We have to check the other cars," I said to myself and dragged him after me. "Maybe someone left a set of keys inside."

Most of the lot had emptied out already. The doorman was still lying where he'd fallen. As I walked past him, the light above the door reflected off something metal on the ground next to him. I set Justin down and picked them up. *Keys.* I pointed the key fob at the lot full of cars, pushed the unlock button and the lights of the blue van winked at me.

It seems our doorman wore more than one funny hat.

I bundled Justin into the Van just as the warehouse door flew open and a crowd of bloodied and traumatized people came streaming out.

With his still unconscious form slumped in the seat next to me, I laid hard on the accelerator and we tore out of the lot. I turned too hard at the alley, and for a terrifying moment the top heavy van was on two wheels before gravity reasserted itself and dropped us back to the earth with a spine jarring impact. It shook Justin from his terror-induced coma and he started shouting something about yellow eyes. I was about to slap him when something shot out from behind a pile of debris and ran up the alley in front of us.

"Duke!" I shouted, sticking my head out of the window. "Here boy! Good boy Duke!"

I don't know what made him stop, maybe it was just the sound of his name. I doubted his abductors had greeted him with anything more affectionate than "little shit" over the past few days. When I pulled up alongside him and put my hand out, he bounded over and jumped up to lick it. At that moment, I couldn't help feeling an affinity for the dirty little mutt. And then it struck me like a ball peen hammer between the eyes. *Why isn't he afraid of me? Where are the fangs and the terrified barking?* Every dog I'd encountered since changing had gone ape whenever I was within spitting distance. Had something about me changed or was Duke just too traumatized to care? I'd have to come back to it later when I had time.

Justin had stopped yelling and sat looking at his hands like they were alien to him, mumbling something unintelligible over and over to himself. I got out and opened the door, ushering a wounded half-crazed animal covered in blood and filth into the seat with him. In his excitement, Duke leapt up into his lap and then just as quickly leapt off and into mine. Justin cried out, rocking forward in the seat, both hands wrapped around himself in a protective embrace.

"You alright?" I asked. "The little guy's just excited and...hey wait a minute, are you hurt?" His eyes were clenched tight, his face a mask of agony.

I gently pried one of his hands away revealing a dark, wet stain that had already soaked through his shirt.

"One of those crazy-ass dogs," he grimaced. "It's not as bad as it looks. All I need is a few stitches and some aspirin. He's the one that needs a doctor," he added with a nod towards Duke.

I hesitated, but he waved me off. "I'll be okay, really."

I did a quick visual inspection of Duke's many wounds. His body was a patchwork of matted blood and angry welts where the fur had been ripped away. He'd lost most of one ear too and the stump looked angry and infected.

"Don't worry. We're going to get you fixed up," I promised. He licked my hand again, as if to say, "OK, I trust you." Dogs are pretty incredible animals.

The simple act of petting a dog was such a satisfying and natural feeling. I realized just how much I'd missed it. I found the spot behind his good ear that every dog has. As I scratched it his little foot thumped against the seat in pleasure. I patted him gently on the head and then popped the stick shift back into Drive. A few blocks later I slowed down to ask a bum on the corner for the location of the nearest quick shop.

"Ain't no foo and likka down hah, boy," he answered through a handful of teeth. He smelled worse than Duke, which was saying something. I continued breathing through my mouth and nodded encouragingly.

"But thah a Marathon two block weth," he offered, pointing down the street. "Thwich hand a few year back. It'th not ath good ath Mobile yoothed to have," he continued somewhat wistfully.

Waxing nostalgic for the liquor selection of one gas station over another – at least I hadn't hit that milestone yet. I groped around for the change slot, and scooped what little was there into his waiting hand. He blessed us as we drove off. I didn't care what kind of beer the Marathon had, as long as it was cold and had alcohol in it. I might even share one with my new buddy Duke. All dogs love beer.

Right then I made up my mind. I wasn't giving him back.

* * * *

Half a can of Old Style and two Red Hots later, Duke had rolled onto his back and was snoring loudly on the seat next to me. He grunted and pawed the air once, his hind legs hanging languidly off the edge of the seat. It reminded me of a kid dangling his feet off the end of the dock in the summer. I felt a stab of love for the little shit and scratched his belly in affection. He reciprocated by letting loose with a trumpeting fart entirely out of scale with his stature. The food and beer must have done a twisted tango in his gut, so we fled for the safety of the curb and the marginally cleaner air there. As we sat there, fatigue settled in and I slumped in silence, feeling numbed and lost in my own thoughts.

I could sense Justin's eyes on me but when I turned my head he looked away. The color had returned to his face, which I took as an improvement. I'd found some fast food napkins in the glove box and had pressed them against his wound to try and staunch the flow of blood. It seemed to have worked. Thank God it had been a dog bite and not something else.

Where do you think you are going mein friend?

I shuddered and rubbed my hands together at the chill in the night air.

"What the hell happened back there Ben?" Justin asked. I sighed, "I'd love to lay everything out for you buddy, but I'm a little short on answers myself at the moment." "Well can you at least tell me what, I mean *who*, you are?"

The silence grew between us again as I contemplated what I should say. To buy a little more time I stood up and jogged back to the van. Before sticking my head in I took a deep breath and held it. Even taking such precautions, the toxins in the air were nearly visible to the human eye. Duke could have given a carrion flower a run for its money. I snatched what was left of the 12-pack from the floor and gratefully pulled my head back out.

I tossed Justin a beer and cracked one for myself, draining half in one long pull. The carbonation burned pleasantly at the back of my throat. Letting loose with an expansive malty belch, I wiped my mouth with the back of my hand and began the tale. I kept my true identity to myself of course, but somewhat to my surprise I told him about Celeste. If only I could have saved her. If only she'd confided in me. If, If, If.

The story was long in the telling and when at last I said, "So there it is," the beer had been depleted along with half a pack of Camel Lights. Examining the cigarette in my hand I smiled at an old memory. When smoking was still fun back in high school, we used to prod each other to burn the cigarette all the way down to the filter. "Smoke it to the camel's balls," my friend Adam would say.

I flicked the butt away, watching its trajectory as it disappeared behind an overflowing trash can next to the men's room. Unburdening myself hadn't made me feel any less burdened. If anything, it had only served to reinforce how hopeless my life had become, with scant promise at improving anytime soon. What Justin said next did little to disabuse me of that notion.

"Wow," he said, absently twirling the beer can on his palm. "That's brutal."

"Brutal," he repeated with a shake of his head.

"Thanks a lot, Captain Fucking Obvious," I wanted to say, but I held my tongue.

"So you don't know anything about those guys who attacked you?" he asked.

"Celeste referred to them as *The Brotherhood*," I said, "They must have found her once she left the house." *And then tortured and killed her when she wouldn't reveal where she'd hidden me.*

"We should go to the police," he said. "It's too much of a coincidence, I mean what happened in the park and that German guy showing up," he paused to swallow. "He must have been the one to murder those people." *Or maybe it was you.* I could hear it in his tone, and I couldn't very well blame him. Still, he wasn't thinking straight.

"Are you nuts?" I spat. "Maybe it was the German, maybe it wasn't. Who fucking knows? And what am I going to tell the cops? *I know this sounds crazy, but I'm being set-up by a German Werewolf, and oh yeah there's also some black ninja thing trying to kill me.*"

"Well what about the German, what does he want from you anyway? I can't believe I'm saying this," he said pausing to look around, "but he's a fucking *werewolf*!" he whisper-yelled.

Who did he think he was talking to? I realized he'd only seen my eyes change color, but wasn't that enough? If it was more proof he needed I could always rip out his liver and show it to him.

"I know!" I whispered back, my eyes round, "And I think there were mummies in those crates too!"

He stiffened in anger. "I didn't ask to be dragged into this, you know."

He was right about that part, and I owed him my life.

"That wasn't fair. I'm sorry. I'm just bone-tired. You're right about the German. He's the key to this whole mess." *But whether he was still alive was another matter.* "He said I had something that belonged to him, but I have no idea what he was talking about. I just know he wanted it bad enough to kill me for it. And I'm certain he would have too, if you hadn't come along. How did you find me anyway?"

"When I saw a woman come running out of the door screaming with blood on her face, I figured something had gone pretty wrong," he replied, his eyes growing distant as he relived the memory. "I was shitting my pants, but after no one else had come out for a few minutes I got up the courage to make my way inside. It was fucking awful in there, blood and bodies and rabid dogs everywhere. I don't think I'll ever get that out of my head. I was damn close to run screaming from there myself. I got turned around and went back up the wrong stairwell. When I opened the door, there you were." He stopped and looked at me. "I thought you were dead, Ben."

I coaxed the last few drops of beer out of my can and crushed it. "You and me both," I replied. "If you can help me figure out what the hell that black thing is, maybe we can find a way to fight it. It's tried to kill me twice, and I'd like to avoid the charm if you know what I mean. Look, it's late, you're hurt, and we're both exhausted. We can circle back to it tomorrow, but for now let's get out of here."

Rising somewhat unsteadily to my feet, I offered him a hand up. We started back towards the car and then I remembered that the jalopy had only half of a tank of gas. The last thing I wanted to do was to get stranded down *here.* As I walked towards the pumps under the rusting canopy, I drew my hand back to aim the crushed beer can at the trash can two stalls over and stopped. Something about it seemed off, like a picture that'd been photo-shopped too many times. Why was it in shadow when the florescent lights above it were working just fine? It was as if the light couldn't quite make it all the way to the pavement. "That's weird," I started to say, but the words caught in my throat. I whirled around and grabbed Justin by the arm, half dragging him behind me as I ran to the car. I looked back over my shoulder in time to see the shadow do something very un-shadowlike. It pulled free from the trash can and started to move towards us. Fast.

I wrenched the driver side door open, shoved Justin in and then leapt in after him. His mouth started to form a question.

"Keys!" I screamed in his face.

We both began fumbling through our pockets. I risked a look in the side mirror to see it billowing towards us like a fog bank rolling in off the ocean at night. Justin jerked around in his seat, seeing it for the first time

"Go, Go, Go!" He screamed, his eyes white with terror.

Panic incapacitated me, and then my eyes caught the glint of something shiny on the floor. Thrusting my arms down between my legs, my hands closed on the keys. I jammed them in the ignition and the engine rumbled to life. I slammed the lock down with my fist and a second later the door disappeared with a wrenching metallic shriek, ripped clean from its hinges.

Black smoke poured in through the opening. I stomped hard on the accelerator as the smoke engulfed my foot and shot up my leg. It was like stepping through the ice on a frozen lake, and everything went instantly numb up to my knee. The tires squealed, spinning on the crumbling asphalt before finally gaining purchase. As we lurched forward the vapor hardened into tendrils that coiled around my leg and began to pull me out of the car. Justin lunged across the seat and wrapped his arms around me. With one hand on the steering wheel, I beat at the black tentacles around my leg to no effect. Inexorably they pulled us both across the seat until I teetered on the edge, the pavement roaring by mere inches away. Justin yelled something into my ear but it was torn away by the wind. He screamed again and made a gesture with his hand as he pointed straight ahead. I looked through the windshield in confusion. And then I understood.

As we came even with a parked minivan, I pulled hard on the steering wheel, sideswiping it in a screeching crescendo of metal and sparks. For an agonizing split-second the tendrils constricted even tighter before recoiling in a rush, releasing their hold on my leg. I didn't dare look back, pressing down hard on the gas pedal once more, eager to be away from the nightmare behind us.

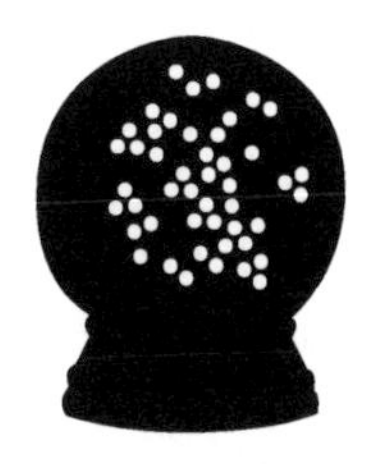

CHAPTER TWENTY FOUR

A half hour later the first snowflakes of the season started to drift down as we turned onto my street. Watching them fall reminded me of something. I just couldn't put my finger on it. Justin suddenly slammed on the brakes, violently throwing me forward to crack my head against the dashboard.

"What do you know, my headache's back," I said, cradling my throbbing skull in both hands and glaring at him. At least most of the feeling in my leg had returned. After 20 minutes I'd begun to fear it might stay that way forever.

He pulled over and killed the engine, his arm pointing down the street. I lifted my aching head to see flashing lights. Two squad cars were parked right in front of my building. I moaned and closed my eyes again.

When will the world stop shitting on me?

All I'd wanted was a change of underwear and my toothbrush, but I knew that returning home had never been a terrific idea in the first place. That *thing* knew where I lived, after all.

We had to figure out how to stop it or we'd both be dead inside of a week. How did you stop something that could turn into smoke? Maybe the snow would slow it down.

Snow.

My brain twitched at the word again. There was definitely something about the snow. Snow balls, snow cones, snow man...I wracked my brain, knowing it held the answer if I could just find the right question.

Falling snow. Gently falling snow. Whirling around-

"Oh my God!" I cried out.

"What? Are the cops coming this way?" Justin frantically scanned the street.

It couldn't be. What the German sought - had it been right in front of me the whole time?

"No. no. Look, I know this sounds nuts, but my favorite board is on the back deck and I don't want the pigs snatching it."

"A skate board? Are you fucking serious?"

"I have to. Keep an eye on the little dude." Duke looked at me the way all dogs do when they know you're leaving.

"He's a tough little—whoah!" Justin had been about to give Duke's head a pat but quickly snatched his hand away. The hackles were standing up along his spine and his teeth were bared, a low growl warning Justin to keep his distance.

"Must be loopy from the loss of blood," he said shaking his head. In spite of the chill, sweat stood out in beads on Justin's forehead. The thought that Duke might have contracted rabies from one of the other dogs flashed across my mind, but I didn't have time to worry about it. I reached out to scratch Duke under the chin and it seemed to calm him down.

I exited the car and started walking towards my building, but stopped in front of an old Greystone two doors away. The old wrought iron gate opened with a squeal. I scampered silently along the narrow walkway to the back yard and alley beyond. Darting from one trash bin to the next, I edged closer to my building. Peering above the top of a can overflowing with garbage, I felt a wave of relief wash over me. They hadn't put a look out on the back fire escape.

I took one last look and then dashed for the rusting metal hulk of the rear stairwell. It was unlit and seldom used by the other tenants after dark.

Rounding the second story, my foot kicked an empty clay flower pot over the edge. I froze and held my breath, ready to run. When no one appeared I breathed a shaky sigh of relief and continued to the 3rd floor landing and the rear door to my place. Wind and snow whistled through the gaping hole where the window had been smashed in by the black thing. I really needed to come up with a better name for it than *black thing*.

Positioning myself below the broken window, I popped my head up for a quick look. The lights were off in the kitchen, and at the far end of the hall there was a cop talking and gesturing with something in his hand.

My nose wrinkled at the sour stink of pastrami on rye with hot giardiniera. I loathed pastrami. There happened to be one prick I knew who loved the stuff. Of course, out of all the cops in the precinct it would have to be him. He turned and his barrel-shaped profile was briefly illuminated before he moved out of sight. It was none other than Captain *(I'll gladly pay you Tuesday for a burger today)* Kowalski. I'd bet my last nickel he was telling everyone how he always knew *that weirdo* was no good. Another cop emerged from the living room with a clear plastic baggie in his hand. They were cataloguing evidence, clearly not expecting me to show my face again.

I had to get in there before they found what I'd really come back for, not that they'd suspect it as anything other than...*a worthless trinket.* And maybe they'd be right. I reached a hand through the hole, my fingers locating the smooth glass of the doorknob. Giving it the expert twist I alone possessed, I slid the door open, whipped inside and gently eased it shut. Out of the rushing wind, I could hear what they were saying.

"Hey, did you hear that Golden Dog got shut down by HD?" Kowalski said.

"No shit?" replied his partner, his voice a little too loud and eager sounding – must have been a rookie.

"Fucking rat turds everywhere, even found some in the fryer!"

"Jesus! Good thing I'm a beef guy, you know?"

I grimaced in disgust. Golden Dog stood at the top tier of my list for red hots. "*You've eaten worse things,*" my father's voice reminded me. They both resumed their pillaging. I stood there wondering if this was maybe the worst idea I'd had yet. They were bound to come into the kitchen eventually and then what? At that moment a frenzied tirade of barking erupted from across the street. I risked a glance down the hallway and their backs were towards me, looking out the window.

"Someone needs to shut that damn mutt up!" Kowalski growled. I gave silent thanks for my neighbor's timing and tiptoed as fast as I could to my bedroom, ducking inside and flattening myself against the wall. I had just begun to relax when the wooden floors in the hallway creaked loudly.

"What about the slob's room?" I heard the rookie say. My heart flew into my throat as I saw his hand reach around the door frame and grope for the light switch.

"Nah, leave it for forensics!" I heard Kowalski yell from the other room. "It smells like the little piss-ant crapped his shorts in there."

The hand retreated, and I heard the rookie snickering as he walked away, "Good one, Cap'n." Well, the fat prick had almost been right about something for the first time in his life. I had just almost shit myself.

I looked in dismay at the undulating terrain of my bedroom floor. It spread out before me in a jumbled mass of clothes, bed sheets, dishes, books, and God only knew what else. I had no choice but to blindly sift through it. My hands passed over object after object, gently discarding them in a pile after a quick assessment of their shape and weight. *What if they'd already bagged it? What if I'd thrown it away? What if it lay somewhere in another room in the apartment?* And then my hand closed upon something. It had a semi-oval shape and while not exactly heavy, it carried a solid heft like a small paperweight.

My heart began to pound as I brought it up to my face. It glimmered in the wan light of the room, the city on the island, Mont Saint Michelle. It looked just like I remembered it all those years ago when I'd first seen her hold it in her hands.

Keep it safe, Thomas.

I jumped at the voice. Her voice.

Remember me.

I looked about the room in alarm.

"Celeste?" I called softly, slapping a hand over my mouth too late.

From the living room a voice said, "You hear something?"

Oh fuck. Footsteps approached from the living room. I was trapped.

Keep it safe.

I would.

I stuffed the globe into my coat pocket, and quickly scanned the floor for anything I could use. A garishly painted Chinese mask lay discarded atop a pile, the lower half of the face broken off. For years it had hung lopsided above my bed, where any self-respecting person would have put an actual headboard. I forced it over my head, raking my cheek on the jagged edges where it had snapped in two. It might just cover enough of my face to keep them guessing.

Grabbing the heavy brass reading lamp next to my bed, I waited on the edge of the doorway for the telltale floor creak. It was mandatory for all cops to wear a standard issue Kevlar vest, but it was heavy and hot as hell. I'd never actually seen Kowalski wearing one. Maybe he was too fat for it to fit properly. I prayed that he'd left it outside in the squad car. I clutched the lamp tightly and braced myself.

Click. Light flooded the room. I swung that lamp with everything I had - right into the expansive and exposed midriff of the unprepared Captain K. His breath exploded with a "Whufff!" and he toppled backwards into the kitchen.

"Bonsaiiiii!" I screamed like a maniac, throwing the heavy lamp at the rookie behind him, who was fumbling for his firearm. He pulled it free just as the base of the lamp slammed squarely into his crotch and sent the gun clattering across the floor.

Without looking back, I ran for the back door, whipping it open as the wood frame above my head exploded in a shower of splinters. Outside I glanced at the metal stairs and knew they'd pick me off before I reached the 2nd landing. I hopped up onto the railing.

"Stop! Police!"

I leapt into the white sky.

As light as the falling snow.

The first snow always made the city look clean and pure, hiding the grime beneath a concealing cloak of white. My brief flight ended almost before it began as I slammed down onto the tops of a row of garbage cans lined up along the side of the alley. They took the brunt of the impact before toppling over, dropping me bruised but unbroken to the pavement below.

I gained my feet and took off down the alley as two more shots ripped into the pavement behind me. I could hear the sounds of someone stomping (and hopefully falling) down the metal staircase.

I tore through the gangway, leapt over the gate and raced for the van. "Drive!" I screamed, wrenching the door open and leaping into the passenger seat. Justin jumped straight up, hitting his head hard on the ceiling, but somehow holding onto his cigarette. The tires spun in the snow as he backed up and then jammed the stick forward, lurching down the street. Duke bounded over the seat and into my lap, happy to be in a vehicle racing towards somewhere again. My heart was thumping in my chest but I felt in control. I had to move very carefully from here on out. My chemical arsenal was gone, confiscated by the German. Only frail human willpower remained. I hoped it would be enough.

* * * *

Sticking solely to the side streets, we switch-backed our way half a mile west into Humboldt Park. I signaled for him to pull around and park in a narrow alley behind a shuttered taqueria. "Sorry about that," I said as Duke yawned and then dropped his head into my lap, asleep almost instantly. "I think we're safe for now."

He blew out his breath and then looked over at me. "What happened?" he asked.

"They spotted me and I barely got away. You were right, it was a stupid idea. I don't know what I was thinking."

"It's okay. I have a few prized possessions of my own I wouldn't let go of without a fight." He said. "So what now?"

What now. We couldn't just sit there all night in the car. I couldn't be sure they hadn't gotten a look at the van. Either way they'd be searching for me. Penelope and Eric might not like it, but my options were somewhere between few and none. We had agreed on certain ground rules some time ago. One of those entailed not involving anyone else in our little "club" before consulting with the rest of the group first. Well, they would just have to roll with it. It wasn't the first rule I'd broken.

I turned to Justin. "Look, this is about to get a lot weirder and a hell of a lot more dangerous, so if you want out, we can part ways now with no hard feelings. I can go back to getting chased by a black demon, and you can go back to your records and pentagrams and shit. I'll more than understand." I looked him in the eye and smiled, "But if you're in I have some people you need to meet. There's a place in Bronzeville. It's old, creepy, and probably haunted. You'd love it."

He sat there is silence, and so after a few minutes I nodded once and turned the door handle.

"Wait."

Reaching for his smokes he shook one out for me and lit one for himself. He filled his lungs and exhaled, his words wreathed in smoke.

"There's a book in my library." he said. "It's one of the oldest things I own. There's a chance it could help us with whatever did…that." His eyes darted to the space where the car door used to be.

I took the cigarette and tucked it behind my ear. The way things were going it very well might be my last, and I wanted to savor it.

"I may regret this," he said, a grin tugging at the edge of his mouth. "But I've been playing around the margins of this sort of thing my entire life: Black Magic, the occult, voodoo – you name it. I always hoped that it was real. It may sound a little crazy, but in a way this is like a dream come true for me."

"No, it doesn't sound a little crazy at all, but completely bat-shit insane? Most definitely."

"Maybe," he replied. "But I'd be lying to myself if I said otherwise."

I realized I couldn't argue with that. My entire life felt like a lie.

"So you're sure about this?"

He nodded. "I'm in."

I shivered and looked at the snow blowing freely into the car, collecting in a small drift near Justin's feet. "We may freeze to death before the black thing can finish us off." I said.

As he turned the key in the ignition a terrifying thought entered my mind. If that thing could find me in my apartment, and then a jail cell, and even track me all the way to an abandoned warehouse in Indiana, what would prevent it from going to--

"Floor it!" I yelled. "Let's see how fast this piece of shit can go!"

CHAPTER TWENTY FIVE

As it turned out, pieces of shit travelled exactly as fast as you'd expect. Dropping the accelerator merely produced a greater degree of shaking and a heightened sense of impending doom upon its occupants.

Every fiber of my being screamed with the urgency to reach Penelope and Eric, but Justin insisted on first retrieving the *Necronomicon*, or whatever tome of ancient evil shit he needed to help us defend ourselves.

He left the engine running and ran up to his apartment while I waited in the van with Duke. His flat was above a nondescript townie bar in the East Village called Czacki's, catering mostly to Polish day-laborers. I'd been there for a beer once, but the dour faces hovering over glasses of warm vodka had made it a short visit.

He came out five minutes later carrying a grocery bag with a massive book clasped under his arm. I looked in the bag and saw duct tape and trash bags. The book looked exactly as I'd imagined: black, old, bound in leather, and spooky as hell.

"Is that human skin?" I asked with an upraised eyebrow.

"You've watched too many Vincent Price movies," he said while lovingly stroking the cover. "Scored this baby in a backroom deal in Prague. Cost me a pretty penny too, or a pretty Koruna. Anyway, the old priest knew it was valuable, but if he'd known what he had, he wouldn't have sold it to me at all. He would have destroyed it. Good thing he was illiterate."

"A priest?" I cried, "What the hell was a man of the cloth doing with a book on black magic?"

Justin flashed a wicked grin. "Cash is King, especially in the Church."

"Why do you have to keep making sense," I asked. "So what is it worth anyway?"

"Let's just say, I could have bought the guy a brand new church and a bitchin' rectory to boot and still had enough left over for a decent retirement," he said. I gave a low whistle. "Let's hope it lives up to its evil potential then."

After erecting a makeshift wind block from the tape and bags, we were off again. I took the wheel so he could examine the book as I drove. We didn't have time for side roads, so I took a risk and headed for the freeway. As we merged onto the Dan Ryan, I sighed with relief – no traffic. It was only in the hours before dawn that expressways delivered on the promise inherent in their name. We zipped south in less time than it took to get a bad haircut. As we rolled to a stop before the mansion I surveyed the outside for any signs of trouble. It looked like it always did, dark and thoroughly uninviting. It was a necessary illusion orchestrated by design, not happenstance. Abandoned buildings were ignored by everyone except rats. We'd surrendered the top floors to them a long time ago.

Justin had been productive during the short ride and bright orange stickie notes sprouted from the pages of the old book like fake flowers on a grave. Leaving Duke, we stepped out of the van and into the night air. The wind cut into us like a scythe, and we hurried around the back. Winter was merely God's way of punishing every Chicago man, woman, and child, for our collective summer hubris.

With Justin shivering behind me I tried the cellar door and wasn't surprised to find it locked. In spite of all the precautions and protocols, we'd somehow never planned for this exact contingency; me being drugged, getting arrested, and then losing both my keys and phone. The fact that I also couldn't use the landline in my home, on account of my home being occupied by the Chicago police, further complicated things.

I realized that I would need to fall back on my considerable talents as a lock pick. It took another tortuous five minutes to pry a paving stone free from the frozen ground, but it served as an effective battering ram – bashing in the plywood board that covered one of the first floor windows. As I squeezed through the opening and stepped into the pitch black room, the business end of something cold and metallic pressed against my temple.

"I wouldn't take another step if I were you," warned a voice from the abyss.

I raised my hands behind my head, my fingers brushing the cigarette I'd placed there earlier.

"Got a light?"

I could almost feel him shaking his head in the dark.

"Don't let her see you smoking it," he warned as he lowered the shotgun. Eric didn't smoke, but you'd rarely catch him unprepared. A soft *click* sounded in the stillness of the empty room, and a small flame illuminated his face before he extended it to me. I filled my lungs with smoke, glad that I'd waited. This time around at least, he was the one that looked like hell.

"You look like hell," I said, and it set him off.

"Yeah, well you have a *hell* of a way of making an entrance." He griped. "Why didn't you call, man? I could have blown your head off just now. You know how this neighborhood is. And where--"

"It's a long story," I said, cutting him off before he started in on one of his notorious tirades. "Believe me. I would have called if I could." I remembered that Justin was still waiting outside. He must have been frozen half-solid by now.

"There's another thing," I said. "I'm not alone."

I stuck my arm out the window and motioned to Justin. And then remembering, I said "And get Duke" He frowned, clearly not happy, but ran back to the Van and opened the door. Like a pistol, Duke sped across the sidewalk and leapt through the window with ease. Justin followed him a moment later. I could actually hear his teeth chattering.

"This is a good friend of mine," I said. "He saved my life the other… uh, what day is it anyway?"

Eric flicked the lighter back on and fixed me with a hard stare. "How bad is it?" he demanded. He knew I wouldn't take this kind of risk unless I had no choice.

"Let's go where there's some heat and I'll explain everything," I offered. The memory of black smoke enveloping my leg, made me reach out and grab him by the shoulder. "Have you seen anything strange around here lately?"

He was quiet for a moment and then erupted with laughter. It dawned on me how ridiculous that question was, especially coming from me. I began to laugh too, and it kept building until we were slapping our legs and crying, each using a hand to hold onto the other to keep from falling over.

"But seriously, there's this black thing…" I continued, still giggling.

"Come on, tell me about it downstairs," he said. When I told him about Duke, he just shrugged his shoulders. "Penelope has a thing for stray animals." He turned to look at me. "She'll be glad to see you," he said, "but after that she may kill you." Flicking the lighter back on, he led us through the gutted kitchen to the head of the basement stairs, our breath puffing out in great gusts above our heads.

"Speaking of chilled to the bone," I said. "Is that bottle of Beam still stashed in the fail safe?"

With a last snort of laughter, he replied, "It's good to have you back *Wolfman*."

* * * *

I had barely set foot inside the lab when I was physically accosted, although not in the way I'd feared. With a breathless cry Penelope flung herself at me, wrapping me in a fierce embrace. Her body crushed against mine, the soft mounds of her breasts pushing up into my chest, her lips pressed hard to my own. My senses reeled with her heady scent, taste, touch and--*SLAP*. My neck popped as her palm caught me flat-handed across the jaw.

Eric's prognostication had been dead to rights, but I couldn't have cared less. I managed to catch hold of her hand as it swung again. Undeterred, she switched to her other hand, but I hooked that too and after a brief struggle she gave up. I released her and she stomped away without a word. Men and women may not be from different planets, but if they were, the one inhabited by men would have been annihilated long ago.

What Penelope lacked in stature she more than made up for in tenacity, and great aim. As I rubbed some feeling back into my cheek, I looked at Eric and said, "It's time we lessened Smokey's burden."

"Damn right it is," he agreed, and crossed the room to the old stuffed Black Bear. Without fanfare he proceed to jam most of his arm up old Smokey's backside. Having been deceased for decades, Smokey didn't protest. With a grunt, Eric withdrew a dusty bottle of brown liquor and held it aloft like a trophy. Toughing it out for three years with a bottle of whiskey up your ass - the old bear had earned his stripes, no doubt about it.

"And now," Eric pronounced, placing three chipped rock glasses on a tray. "Why don't you tell me what the hell you've been up to for the last 48 hours."

"None for me thanks," Justin said while looking around the room. "This place is awesome," he added, barely getting the last word out before he was seized by a coughing fit that he muffled in the crook of his elbow.

Eric either hadn't heard him or, more likely, had pretended not to, and filled all three. "Skal!" he proclaimed, and handed out the glasses. It's what he called an *Irish pour*; I had to sip a little off the top just to keep it from spilling over. Justin reluctantly accepted it, holding the glass like it might bite him. Eric slowly sipped his drink, waiting for me to begin. I tipped mine back, drained it and held it back out for more.

"Glad you haven't changed on me," he said, and refilled it. I took a more moderate sip and began. When I got to the part about the dog-fighting ring, Justin nervously took a sip of his drink and was wracked by another bout of coughing, nearly spilling it all over the book he'd brought. I made a mental note to have Penelope check his wounds after she was finished with Duke. The little rascal had taken to her right away, jumping up into her arms and nuzzling her neck. Although not an RN, she still knew a lot more about basic medicine than the rest of us. Once Justin's hacking subsided, I picked up the story again "...and then the black thing..."

"Wait, is this the same thing that attacked you before?" Eric interrupted.

"I'm not positive, but I think so," I replied, "and somehow the German was able to hurt it, or at least destroy the shape it had taken."

"That's closer to the truth than you know," Justin interjected, flipping around the book he'd brought, holding it up for us to see. "I think I may know what this black thing actually is."

"I never doubted you for a second," I said, leaning forward eagerly. My speech sounded slow to my own ears - the whiskey was going down a little too easy.

My eyes danced over dense rows of illegible and spidery script that covered one of the massive yellowed pages. The opposite page held the queer etching of an old man in a flowing robe, a walking stick thrust out before him towards a dark-skinned mirror image of himself.

"Very interesting, an old timer and his twin brother from another mother. Now how do we kill it?" I asked.

"He's not just any old man," Justin replied. "And what's worse," he said, his voice turning serious. "I'm not sure it *can* be killed."

"What?" I said, nearly dropping my glass. "Why not?"

"It's hard to kill something--.

"That's already dead?" Eric finished.

"Something like that."

"Lovely," I said, and the room went black.

CHAPTER TWENTY SIX

"Nobody move," I whispered. "Eric, where's the 12 gauge?"

"Shit. I left it by the door," he cursed. "It wasn't loaded anyway."

"Where are the shells?" I whispered louder, straining not to shout.

"In the boiler room," he replied.

"What does it even matter?" Justin interjected. "You can't shoot smoke."

"Well you can fucking try!" I nearly yelled.

Justin had a valid point, but a loaded Remington 870 seemed a lot better than an unloaded nothing. That thing had torn the door right off the van for Christ's sake. I stood up and then froze at the sound of a door opening from across the room. For one desperate moment I contemplated trying to force the transformation. *You'll kill everyone in the room, idiot!* Besides, I didn't have any way to do it. If there had been a knife handy I guess I could have plunged it into my leg, but what was the point? I was the one the black thing wanted. If I could delay it for even a few minutes, it might give the others enough time to escape. I strained to detect its location in the room, readying myself, tensing for its icy embrace. The darkness was suddenly split by a blinding white light. I shielded my eyes to see Penelope standing before me, holding a flashlight, her face a blur from the afterimage burned onto my retinas.

"Sorry if I scared you," she said, sounding not at all sorry. "The centrifuge must have blown one of the fuses again." Behind me Justin was seized by another fit of coughing that quickly progressed into ragged and phlegmy hacking.

"You alright buddy?" I asked. Maybe we should get him to a hospital after all.

"Peachy" he croaked, shivering as he held the massive book in in his lap.

Penelope cleared her throat. "I need some help with finding the right thingy to replace the broken thingy with," she said, looking pointedly at me. Why was she talking like a ditz? The wiring in the mansion was ancient and the power cut out all the time. She never had a problem dealing with it before.

"Yeah, sure," I said, and moved my lips mouthing the word *-what.* She fixed me with a look that said *not now.* She produced another small flashlight from her back pocket and tossed it to Eric.

"Can I borrow that?" asked Justin. Eric handed it to him, and he resumed his feverish note taking.

"Hang tight, fellas," I said and followed Penelope across the room. Something was definitely wrong. She walked like she was trying not to run. The electrical box was upstairs in a pantry that had once served as the cozy drug den of a former tenant, replete with used needles and the requisite stained mattress thrown in the corner. We walked in silence up the stairs. In light of our previous encounter, I opted to play it safe and keep my mouth shut.

When we reached the pantry I could see the panel door to the box already hanging open. I scanned the row of fuses. One was missing. I turned to Penelope, and she had it in the palm of her hand.

"I'm sorry," she said. "But I couldn't think of another way to get you alone so we could talk. Something's very wrong with your friend, Ben."

"I know there's something wrong with him," I said. "A dog mauled him earlier, and he's hurt – pretty badly I think. Not to mention our encounter with the German and the black thing. By the way, he knows I'm a werewolf."

I could see her eyes widen and her jaw set, so I took a step back.

"I had to tell him. He saved my life. Anyway, it's a miracle he's still sane. I've been meaning to ask you to check him out. Why didn't you just ask me to come into the lab? You scared the shit out of everyone just now," I finished.

"I didn't want to take any chances," She said and stepped in closer. Putting her mouth to my ear, she said softly "His hearing might be as good as yours, the lab wasn't safe, and I didn't want to scare Eric."

My confusion mounted.

His hearing? Scare Eric?

"What the hell are you talking about?" I said, my tone gruffer than I intended.

"Justin didn't get bit by a dog, Ben. I knew it the minute he walked in."

"Yes he did, he told me himself after I woke up…"

My hand flew to my mouth as his words suddenly came back to me

"I've been playing around the margins of this thing my whole life. This is like a dream come true for me

…a dream…

…my whole life."

"Oh shit, we've got to--" A series of loud crashes sounded from downstairs, followed by yelling. We fled back through the kitchen to the stairs. I prayed we weren't too late.

Halfway down it struck me, "The lights!" I cursed.

"Just go! I'll take care of it," Penelope said tossing me the flashlight.

Another thundering crash came from the basement and then my hand was on the handle to the door, throwing it open. The light from my flashlight bounced around, illuminating a room unrecognizable from just a few moments ago. It looked like the inside of a ship caught in a storm at sea. Everything was knocked over and pushed to one side, as if the room had tilted at some crazy angle.

"Eric!" I yelled as I entered the room, unsure of what to do.

"In the tank!" I heard a muffled voice cry. It was our name for the room I'd woken up in a few days ago. It could keep anyone in, or anything out. "I'm alright! Watch out for--" something flashed at the edge of my vision, "Justin!" he finished as I spun. Something struck my hand, sending the flashlight skipping across the floor to roll behind an overturned love seat.

"*I feel better now,*" a thick voice said from close by. "*Much better, Ben.*"

"Justin, listen to me," I said, trying to keep my voice level and calm. "You don't understand--*HUFFF!"* a blow to my stomach drove me to the bare concrete floor – even the rugs had been uprooted in the upheaval.

"*You're wrong,*" I heard the Justin-thing say with an eerie calm. "*I understand everything now. I can…I can feel…Oh…* Oh God!"

The first time was bad. Really bad. It began with your body flooding itself with endorphins to brace against the oncoming assault. At first they made you feel invincible, but then the pain rushed in, and no amount of drugs could prepare you for it; your body being broken and reshaped into something else, something inhuman. He screamed again, and I could feel my own blood beginning to pound in my ears, my heart ramping up. His wolf was calling to mine. I had to stop this madness before we tore each other to pieces.

"Justin!" I yelled, spitting blood onto the floor. "I can help you. I know you don't want to hurt anyone." I gained my feet and felt a spike of adrenaline. My pupils expanded and a shiver ran down my spine like an electrical charge. Justin moaned loudly from nearby. I turned towards the sound and everything went white. Penelope had gotten the lights back on.

Half-blinded, I peered through squinted eyes at something convulsing on the ground next to me.

"Hang on Justin," I said, and realized my mistake. At the sound of my voice his head whipped towards me. His face had been erased, replaced with a hairy mass of quivering flesh and teeth. Howling, he scrabbled across the floor and launched himself at my legs, knocking me to the floor.

He clawed his way on top of me even as he shook, wracked by the seizures remaking him. We rolled across the floor as I struggled to free myself, my body beginning to wage its own war with humanity.

"Ramsey, move!" a voice yelled from above me. Justin's grip lessened for an instant. I wrenched free and rolled away to see Eric, eyes wide with fear and revulsion, the stock of the Remington held tight against this shoulder, the barrel leveled squarely at Justin's head.

Justin snarled and lunged for Eric. "Wait! Don't!" I screamed as he pulled the trigger. The concussion from the blast punched into my eardrums as the top of Justin's head flew apart like a bloody piñata, spraying the side of my face with gore. I tried to raise myself off the floor but someone held me down. Looking up, I saw Penelope's face floating above mine. Her lips were moving, but the ringing swallowed everything. I tried to ask her something as she put her palm gently on my forehead and plunged a needle into my neck.

CHAPTER TWENTY SEVEN

"Drink this," Penelope said gently but firmly.

"What?" I said, my own voice sounding muffled to my ears. The ringing had abated a little but showed no signs of leaving yet.

She pantomimed a drinking motion and thrust it into my hands. I peered inside the proffered cup, sniffing at its contents.

"I'm not thirsty," I said, pushing it away.

"It's only water Ben," she insisted, leaning forward and giving me her doctor-knows-best look. "You need the fluids. It will help with your headache."

"On one condition," I replied, accepting the cup. "Don't ever give me that…that…what did you call it again?" I asked, and tipped the water back. To my parched mouth it tasted better than any beer ever had. Almost.

"Propofol. It's a perfectly safe and effective sedative, approved by the FDA and recommended by the …"

"Tell that to Michael Jackson," I cut in. "Oh that's right, you can't because he's dead." It had knocked me out cold in record time. And the ensuing hallucinations and nightmares had come straight from the darkest pit of my subconscious. Try as I might, I couldn't dispel the vision of Penelope and Eric – their lifeless bodies shredded like so much cabbage. As if my normal nightmares weren't bad enough.

"They probably administer that shit to the inmates, right before they stick the final needle in their arm. Speaking of which, thanks for ponying up the juju to get me out of the clink. I wouldn't hold my breath for a speedy repayment, though." I said.

Her eyes narrowed, "Were you in jail?"

Oh shit. "What? Of course not, where's Eric?" I asked trying to change the subject. I decided I should get ready in case I had to run again, and swung my feet off the couch. Sitting up, a fresh wave of nausea hit me and I dropped my head down between my knees.

"Easy," she said, putting a hand firmly on my shoulder to keep me from trying to get up again. "Eric's fine. He's a little shaken but he's okay."

"I've been better." Eric said, stepping into the room, his eyes looked bleary and were circled in black. As he walked past a broken pile of furniture it settled with a groan and he danced aside, uttering a curse.

I decided to speak first, "I never would have brought him here if I'd known."

"Right," he replied.

He picked up a folding chair from the floor but then set it back down, wrinkling his nose. The room stank of bleach, but not in a clean way. Most everything had been splattered with gore and would have to be thrown out. Shooting someone in the head at point blank range with a shotgun tended to make a bit of a mess. Eric's clothes didn't look any better off.

His eyes caught mine and then looked away. "Everything happened so fast." He muttered.

Too fast. I thought, not wanting to feel anger but unable to suppress it. Justin's death weighed heavily on me. I never should have brought him into this. And why did it have to be the head? A blow to the arm or leg could have shocked his system and bought enough time to get him into the safe room.

"Lucky for me you weren't packing anything stronger than Big League Chew that first night in the cellar," I said, regretting it the second the words left my mouth.

"Don't fucking remind me," Eric said, his face flushing red. "And now you owe me *another* jacket."

"Have some respect," I said, standing up. "You just killed a good friend of mine, not to mention the one person with the knowledge to protect us from whatever's been trying to ace me!"

"I saved your lousy life!" he shouted. "All our lives!" he said rounding on Penelope. "That thing would have killed us all and you damn well know it!"

"Stop it, both of you!" Penelope shouted before either of us could say another word. "Attacking each other isn't going to solve anything. Just stop it!" Looking at me and then Eric, she said. "You two have been through too much together to do this to each other." She pulled her hands raggedly through her hair and stood wringing them before her. "What happened was traumatic for everyone. But we have to move on. We have to just..." she paused as she searched for the words, "...look at what we can *learn* from this."

Learn from this?

"Hold on just a minute," I said, my temper flaring. "He's in the lab, isn't he?"

She wouldn't look at me.

"Jesus Christ, Penelope!" I exploded. "He was my friend! Everything is not a fucking science experiment for you to play God with!"

"I didn't touch..." she began, "I wouldn't, not without asking you first." Her voice hitched and I could see tears beginning to well in her eyes. My fury vanished in an instant.

"I'm such an asshole," I said pulling her close and embracing her.

She pulled away, looking at me searchingly.

"I won't do anything if that's what you want," she said. "But Ben, it might be the only opportunity we have to try to learn something more about your condition. It might not reveal anything, but--" she broke off and looked away.

"It's okay." I said. "In a strange way I don't think he'd mind. He was into some pretty morbid and disturbing shit on his own." Penelope started to speak but I held my hand up. "I want to see him first," I said, "Alone."

I stood before the draped figure and fought against the desire to turn and run back out the door.

This is your fault. Don't be a coward.

Laid over Justin's body, the sheet looked like some frozen alien landscape, the cold bones of a giant lying hidden beneath a blanket of snow. Although I knew it was only a trick of the light, the scarlet crater at one end seemed to advance as I watched, fanning outward like a swarm of red ants. I tore my eyes away. *Did I really want to do this?* I knew what I was, but I'd been spared the horror of bearing direct witness to it. Would anyone willingly choose to gaze upon the darkest, most vile aspects of their nature if given the choice? I watched as my hand extended, reaching for the sheet. It felt like it belonged to someone else. "You owe it to Justin," I said, and tore the sheet away.

He had been in the throes of what modern medicine surely would have diagnosed as a severe seizure. His arms and legs showed deep purplish bruises where he had thrashed and flailed, beating helplessly against the unyielding concrete. My eyes filled with the horror at what had been done, unfinished as it was, to my former friend. Physiologically, nothing made much sense. The proportions were either too long or too short, the angles hard where they should have been soft. Unrecognizable as the person I had known, he had become a veritable embodiment of one of Doctor Moreau's failed experiments, neither man nor beast but an unfinished union of both. I saw myself reflected in his shattered form and it nearly broke my mind.

Unable to look anymore, I made to replace the sheet and as I did so my hand brushed against his. It jerked once with an involuntary twitch and I recoiled backward, tripping over the wheel of the metal gurney to send it spinning across the room, the corner of the bloody sheet still gripped in my hand. I forced myself to release it and scrambled to my feet. Throwing the door open, I pushed roughly past Penelope and Eric in my haste to escape the unspeakable abomination in that room.

"Ben, wait!" she called after me.

"Do what you have to." I rasped, my breathing labored. "But swear that when you're finished, you'll destroy it."

"Ben, I…"

"Swear it!" I cried and dashed for the stairs.

Outside, the whipping wind numbed my skin and scoured my mind, cleansing me of my fear and anguish. My nostrils flared wide as I filled my lungs with the frigid air, savoring the cold trail it burned down my sinuses. People from temperate climates would never understand the rehabilitating properties of truly cold weather. Chicago challenged a person in a way Southern California never could. Feeling as healed as I could hope to be, I decided to go back inside when a child's voice rang out from the dark,

"The golem approaches!"

I whipped back around and scanned the blackness of the yard around me.

"Who said that? Show yourself!" I shouted.

There was only the wind to answer, until an indistinct shape broke off from the shadows and began to slowly approach. My body tensed as I prepared to run, until the sight of a small garden gnome materialized before me.

It measured no more than a foot from the tip of its conical hat to its pointed boots, and was made from a cheap painted plastic that had started to peel. As if it were a stray kitten, I bent down and gently picked it up. The body was hollow and I could clearly see the ridge running along the outside where the two molds had been pressed together.

"It approaches. The golem approaches," It repeated and fell silent again.

"I see." I had no idea what it was talking about.

"The shadow is…" it began to say but fell silent as the door opened behind me. I held the gnome tightly against my chest.

"Ben, are you okay?" came Penelope's worried voice from the doorway. "Please come back inside, it's *freezing* out here."

"I'll be right in Nells, just need a minute more," I answered without turning around. I heard the door close again, just as the gnome squirmed out of my hands and raced away across the lawn.

"Stop! Come back!" I called, but it was a fast little bugger and already too far ahead to chase after. Before it turned the corner it stopped and called back, "It comes! Mister Jones said to tell you!" Then it was gone.

So old Jonesy had sent a warning. What the hell was a golem?

CHAPTER TWENTY EIGHT

"I've been looking through this thing." Eric announced through the blast of wintery air that ushered me back into the room. He held Justin's leather bound tome in the air before him with both hands, brandishing it like a preacher with a Bible.

"All I can say is that I don't understand a friggin' word," he finished, dropping the book into his lap. He didn't look at me, his fingers tracing the edges of the raised letters on the cover.

Penelope rose from her chair, concern etched on her face, but I motioned for her to stay seated and mouthed the words *I'm Okay.*

"It's written in some foreign language or something." Eric spoke again. "Could be in Portuguese for all I know."

He shifted the book from his lap, dropping it with a loud thud onto the coffee table. He picked up the blue spiral notebook lying next to it. "Your friend could read it though, and he took notes. Lots of notes. See for yourself."

I flipped through it, recognizing Justin's handwriting. He'd burned me enough DVDs of pirated music over the years, labeling them in his precise measured penmanship. The entries seemed to follow some sort of protocol, but the writing was comprised almost entirely of what looked like dashes, curlicues, exclamation points and other unrecognizable symbols.

"Most of it looks like gibberish, but there does seem to be a word that's repeated over and over," I said running my finger down the sheet. "M-Y-R-D-D-I-N"

"Yeah, I noticed that too, so I Googled it thinking maybe it was something important," Eric interjected. "Ready for this? It's another name for Merlin."

"As in *the wizard* Merlin? As in Knights of the Round Table, King Arthur and all that crap kind of Merlin?" I said, puzzled. "Why would he grab a book about Arthurian Legend?" I snapped my fingers, "Wait, before the lights went out didn't he say something about an old man?"

Penelope reached over and picked the book up, flipped quickly through it. "Here!" she exclaimed, her finger on the picture Justin had held up earlier. "He wanted us to look at this."

I carefully scanned the picture of the old man and his twin again. What if he wasn't holding a walking stick at all? The head was carved in the shape of serpent. What did every wizard have? *A staff.*

"He said it couldn't be killed," Eric said.

"Because it was never alive," I said, finishing his sentence. "But he said *maybe*. He wasn't sure." I looked at the picture again. There was something unsettling about his dark twin. "Ok, let me get this straight. Are we saying that Merlin has something to do with that thing that's been trying to kill me?"

Eric looked at me and burst out laughing, "Ramsey, listen to what you're saying. You're talking about Camelot! It's a made-up story for Christ's sake. Get your head out of your ass. God I need a drink," he finished, and turned and left the room.

"Don't you think I fucking know that?" I yelled after him, my voice rising. "But there's obviously something to it, otherwise he wouldn't have wasted his time on it."

"Let him go, he's worn out like the rest of us, "Penelope said. "By the way, I can read it."

"Justin may have been eccentric, but he wasn't stupid, he – what did you say?" I stopped, realizing my hands had become fists. I forced myself to unclench them.

"It's shorthand," she said, running her slender fingers across the symbols on the page. "I had a part-time job as an admin for a law firm once. Sometimes I had to take dictation." She held the book before her and began to translate, haltingly at first, but eventually falling into an easy rhythm.

1221 A.D. An account recorded by an unknown author states that in the Spring of said year, the magistrate of Hatherleigh (a small hamlet in Devonshire) declared Myrddin persona non grata, and then posted a list of the alleged grievances in the town square. Myrddin was accused of having invested the water of the town's well with a foul rotting odor, of cursing the cows and goats with a malady which caused their udders to run dry, and for afflicting the favourite pony of the magistrate's eldest daughter with blindness in one eye, making it unfit to ride. Upon learning of these charges, Myrddin vowed to take vengeance on the magistrate. He crafted a demon, a shadow invested with the form, bearing, and likeness of the wizard, and sent it to the hamlet in his stead. An attempt was made to apprehend this false Myrddin, at which point it became violent and injured three men, one grievously, before it was put to the torch and destroyed. Undeterred, Myrddin created a second, and then a third, and so on, sending each one on the heels of the last. The magistrate and his family disappeared soon after. The rest of the inhabitants, fearing their town had been cursed, abandoned their homes and fled. Soon after this incident, Myrddin's behavior became strange and his actions erratic, rendering him an increasing liability to the lords and gentry to whom he had been a benefactor and invaluable aid. He would appear at various locales near and far, unannounced and muttering to himself in a disheveled state. It was concluded that his mind had been damaged by the nature of his unearthly activities. When it became apparent that he could no longer be trusted to dispense the sage advice and wisdom so sought after by those in power, the king himself passed a decree declaring Myrddin unwelcome on the very soil of England, banishing him from his ancestral home. He was never seen again. It is widely accepted that he died penniless and destitute, buried in an unmarked grave in…

I followed the line as it ran down and across the page in an erratic slug trail of ink. I could see Justin wracked by the first tremor, his hand skittering across the page as it coursed through him. He must have known what was coming. *Why didn't he ask me for help?*

"Too bad he didn't finish," Penelope announced, stretching. "But I don't really see how this helps us." How could such a simple, mundane gesture be so attractive? She could probably pick her nose and I'd swoon.

"What is it?" she said, catching me looking at her.

"Nothing," I said and changed the subject. "Nells, do you know what a golem is?" I asked, feeling a little foolish.

"Golem?" She asked. "Do you mean like in *The Lord of the Rings*? Wasn't the little green goblinish guy named something like that?

Now I was really confused, "Forget it. It was nothing." I stood up and faked a yawn that quickly became real. "Getting late, think I'll grab a wink or two before the sun comes up." I looked at my watch and groaned. "In three hours? Hey, how's the little dude doing?"

"Out cold," she answered, "The wound to his ear was infected, and he was running a pretty good fever. I'm going to keep him sedated for a couple days so his body can heal itself." I must have looked worried because she gave me a reassuring look and said, "He'll be fine. Don't worry." Another yawn seized me, and I contemplated just laying down on the floor.

"There's a cot against the wall. You may want to sleep with the pillow *over* your head." She said as Eric's snores rumbled through the walls from the room over.

"No kidding," I said with a laugh. "What about you?"

"Oh, I don't sleep," she answered. "You know, aspiring doctor and all that."

"Right," I said, wanting nothing more than to wrap her in my arms. Instead I got up and retired to the cot, lying down in my clothes and gratefully shutting my eyes. As I drifted off, I felt a blanket gently draped over my body.

CHAPTER TWENTY NINE

A piercing shriek jolted me from my sleep.

Penelope!

I yelled her name as I struggled, my legs and arms entangled in my sheets. The door flew open with a crash and light flooded the room.

"Ben, what is it? Are you alright? Are you hurt?" Penelope said, squinting and looking around the room.

From underneath a sheet I said, "I heard someone cry out. At least I think I did. I guess it was just a nightmare."

"Oh," she said looking relieved, and then, "Who's Celeste?"

I froze. *Oh Shit.*

"Who?" I feigned, unwrapping myself at last.

"You were calling her name over and over. You sounded terrified, and…sad." A single line of worry creased her forehead. I very much wanted to hold her face in my hands and smooth it away.

Instead I shrugged my shoulders and lied. "Hmm. I don't think I know anyone by that name. I'm really sorry I woke you up for nothing." I sat back heavily on the bed, and then jumped back up. "Ow! What the ..." reaching under the blanket I pulled out a crumpled paper bag.

Keep it safe.

I quickly twisted the bag closed and set it back on the bed. I'd forgotten all about it in the chaos of the last hours.

"What's that?" she asked.

"Nothing," I replied and stretched.

"What are you hiding, Ben Ramsey?"

I recognized the tone and knew I had to come up with something quick. *Why didn't I just show it to her?* I wasn't even sure what it was, but something stopped me.

I flashed a guilty grin at her. "Just a little something to keep the chill away," I said and held the bag out towards her. "Night cap?"

Relief and sadness warred within me as she shook her head slowly, her face falling. Without another word she turned around and left, closing the door quietly behind her.

"Goddammit!" I swore, driving my fist into the bed. Just when it seemed like we were starting to get somewhere, I was back to step zero again. Who was I kidding? She would never see me as anything less than a freak, one with his lips wrapped around a bottle no less. I looked at the bag held tightly in my hand. I could throw it in the lake, or toss it in the old cast iron wood-burning fireplace in the corner. I overturned the bag, and the snow globe dropped into my hands. The raised black lettering on the back had faded but was still legible – *Produit de France.*

Turning it over in my hands, I examined it closely, inch by inch. My fingers caressed the smooth surface of its watery depths. I implored it to reveal its secrets, as if it were a Magic Eight Ball. Half an hour later I set it down, defeated. I had risked my life for a snow globe. I was struck by the absurdity of stealing such a cheap trinket in the first place. Had I lost my mind? Was this just another pathetic manifestation of my grief over losing Celeste? That was 5 years ago for Christ's sake! I felt foolish for hiding it from Penelope, and for thinking it could help me somehow.

What about the dream.

Bullshit. That's all it had been, a dream.

What about the voice in your bedroom?

Hearing things was nothing new for me.

A sudden surge of anger rose up within me. I shook it violently before my face. "Show me something!" I cursed. "What do you want from me?" The snowstorm, fueled by my rage, swirled violently within, the island city stoically weathering the tempest, unaffected.

"Fuck you then!" I yelled and dashed the globe upon the concrete floor at my feet. The dome cracked, and a spray of white flecked water gushed out like a miniature geyser. I had killed it. *Good.* I stared at it in satisfaction for a minute, and then bent down to clean up the mess. As I picked it up, the plastic base fell off and something dropped out.

"Hey Buddy."

My heart jumped at the sound of Eric's voice behind me. How long had it been since I'd heard him snoring? How much had he seen?

"Everything cool?" he continued, taking a step around the cot.

I quickly snatched the cloth wrapped object from the wet floor and stuck it between my legs on the bed.

"You ever hear of knocking? Almost gave me a grabber just now," I said, trying to sound irritated.

He sat down in a chair across from me, resting the Remington across his legs like Jed Clampett.

"Heard something," he said, as I eyed the gun, "It used to take a lot to wake me up." He glanced at the wet floor and then at me.

"I'm sorry about Justin," he said looking down, "I got scared."

I knew it wasn't easy for him to say those words.

"Anyone would have done the same thing in your position," I answered.

He looked up and then smiled, and just like that everything was cool between us again. I love that about guys, shit gets smoothed over and then it's like it never happened. You moved on.

"Hey, I've been wondering about something," he said, "Why didn't you ever ask Justin for help with your condition? I mean, if he was an expert at supernatural stuff maybe he could have helped you somehow."

"I did ask him," I said. "And he told me that there actually is a cure."

"Really?" he asked, perking up. "What is it?"

"Chopping my head off for starters," I answered. "Or burning me alive. A bazooka would probably do the trick too."

"You jerk," he frowned. "I was actually getting my hopes up for a second there."

I sighed. "Justin said that in all the books he'd read there was a clear consensus. The curse is permanent."

Eric nodded his head as if to say *Yeah I guess you are fucked after all.* "So what's the deal with this mess?" he asked. I was glad he'd changed the subject, only I wished it had been to something else.

Keep it safe Thomas.

A burst of anger flashed through me. *What exactly was I supposed to be keeping safe? And from whom? The only friend I had left?*

All else aside, Eric had probably saved my life tonight, and not for the first time. If I couldn't trust him, who could I trust?

I pushed aside the voice in my head. "I think I may know why the German, and maybe this black demon, are both after me." My throat felt dry as the desert. A cold beer would've helped.

"I'm all ears," he said, leaning forward. So I told him about my crazy gambit to retrieve the snow globe from my apartment.

"I'm not sure what I've found though." *But Celeste sure as hell felt it was important enough to risk her life over and then hide from everyone, including me.*

I slowly opened my hand. It certainly didn't look impressive – just a rag tied around something with a piece of string.

I pulled the string and it disintegrated.

"Wait a minute!" Eric exclaimed. "What if it's dangerous or something?"

"I have to know." My words carried an inflection of desperation I didn't like, but I'd made up my mind. With trembling hands I carefully unfolded the cloth, and gasped. I held in my hands a star. A red giant.

"Holy mother of God in heaven," Eric whispered.

So this is what she had sought after that night in the woods. Small wonder they wanted it back. It spanned the length of my finger and the width of two, with three distinct planes, one smooth and polished while the other two were jagged and looked sharp enough to cut. A cold fire flashed within its crystalline depths.

"It's colored, Ramsey." Eric said, still whispering. "Do you have any idea how rare it must be?"

I couldn't speak. I'd heard of colored diamonds, but never one this large. It was like a dragon's eye. It captured the light, refracting it back in a thousand facets across the walls and ceiling.

"It must be 100 if it's a carat." Eric whispered reverently.

"Oh!"

I started at the voice and looked behind me to see Penelope, her features slack with wonder, staring at the massive diamond in the palm of my hand.

How many people were going to get the drop on me tonight?

* * * *

My hands shook as I brought the steaming mug to my lips and took a sip, the bitter liquid burning a molten trail down my throat. I'm not a tea drinker by principle (unless it's spiked), but at least it was hot and strong. I set it down and looked across the table. Eric and Penelope both had that million mile stare, their eyes tracking some point between spaces.

"Well," I said cracking my knuckles and pursing my lips.

"Yep," Eric replied, his eyes still vacant.

"Mmmm," Penelope hummed, taking a sip out of a cup with *World's Best Gay Dad!* emblazoned across it in rainbow-colored bubble letters.

On the table before me, its magnificence muted once more within its sodden remnant of cloth, lay the thing that had hidden within the snow globe, like an impossible prize waiting at the bottom of a Cracker Jack box. The desire to gaze upon it again was powerful.

"I'm not sure what I've gotten myself, or us, into," I began. "But I do know one thing. As long as I have this, we're all in danger, and a lot of it."

"Maybe we could, you know, find someone to buy it," Eric said, licking his lips.

"Great idea. I'll just take it to Lonnie's Pawn in Bronzeville and see what I can get for it." I could see him bristle at the sarcasm in my voice. "Seriously Eric, this thing may not even have a price. Who the hell would I even approach, Christie's? It would be all the over the internet before you could say viral. A huge red diamond popping up out of nowhere won't go unnoticed."

"Ben's right." Penelope said, reaching out a hand towards it and then quickly pulling it back. "It'll draw the whole world's attention. How can we possibly explain how we came to possess it?"

Eric slammed his fist onto the table with a crash, drawing an uncharacteristic squeal from Penelope, and causing most of the tea to slosh out of my mug.

"I can't believe what I'm hearing!" he shouted, eyes bulging with anger. "We just won the fucking lottery and you're both acting like the world has ended! This could change everything. Can't you see that?" he pleaded, looking wildly from Penelope to me.

What had gotten into him? I'd never seen him this furious.

"Don't you see what this means?" he went on. "No more scraping together leftover equipment and huddling in this damn dungeon waiting for the power to get shut off again." He looked to me. "We could put a proper lab together! A real state-of-the-art facility where maybe, just maybe, we could make some progress towards a real cure instead of fumbling in the fucking dark!" He made a visible effort to calm himself and reached out with his hands, imploring. "This…this could be the break we've been looking for, can't you please at least consider that possibility?"

I looked to Penelope for support, but she was busy chewing her nails, her eyes vacant and unfocused.

"I need some time to wrap my head around this," I said.

"Fine," Eric said his arms crossed. "But if you're right about this black thing, and it's on its way here, time isn't something we have in spades at the moment."

I didn't reply. What else was there to say? Eric got up and stalked away. We sat there listening to his angry steps going up the stairs, across the floor, and with a slam of the door he was gone.

"He'll be alright, he just needs to cool down," I said. I wasn't sure whom I was trying to convince.

"Can I …can I see it again?" she asked casually, but the longing in her voice betrayed her.

As if I could deny her anything.

I picked up the cloth bundle and then gently taking her hand, I dropped the fiery jewel into her palm.

Put it away! Cover it up!

It was not Celeste's voice in my head, but my own this time. I looked at Penelope and recoiled at the sudden transformation that had come over her. In the weird ruby light of the massive gem, she appeared to have aged. The smooth skin on her face stretched across cheeks that were thin and sallow, while deep lines furrowed her forehead. Her lips were moving. *Was she talking to herself?* Her eyes were terrible. I lunged across the table and wrenched the diamond from her grasp. She gave a small cry and flailed after it. For a moment I felt certain she meant to attack me, nails ready to slash at my face. I hastily covered it once more, extinguishing its malignant light. She gasped, her hands flying to her face as if I'd slapped her.

"Penelope?"

She didn't speak for a long time. She just sat there, slowly rubbing her arms, cradling herself as if trying to ward off a chill. I waited, giving her time to pull herself together. After a while, being who I am, I fished around for a stray can of beer at my feet and my hand brushed something else—Justin's pack of smokes, lying somehow miraculously intact under my chair. I lit one and when I looked up her eyes were on me.

"Ben?"

"Yes Penelope."
"Do you care for me?"
"More than I'd like to, frankly."
"Then swear you'll never show it to me again."

CHAPTER THIRTY

Acutely aware of the hard bulge in the front pocket of my jeans, I looked out the frosted window of the 88 CTA bus. *Is that a giant diamond in your pants, or are you just glad to see me?* The thought brought a snuffle of laughter to my lips, but at the suspicious glare from an elderly black woman I suppressed it and assumed *the face*. It's one that riders of public transportation everywhere don to discourage the potential threat of having to speak to one another.

Before leaving the mansion, I made a show of opening an old lockbox we'd acquired for some forgotten reason, sticking my hand inside and saying "best to leave it here." I hated lying to them, but Penelope's behavior had me worried and Eric wasn't exactly himself either. Usually cool and collected, his emotions seemed to be overriding his reason. I'd also seen the effect the diamond had had on Penelope. Who knew what influence it could have over Eric's mind? It might have done so already. I never would have been able to justify taking it with me, and I felt certain he would have insisted on accompanying me.

There was also the matter of the black thing and its attraction to me. I had to hope they would be safer without me around. I patted my front coat pocket, my hand tracing the outline of the iPhone. Penelope had reluctantly surrendered it to me, and I was determined to surprise her by returning it unmolested.

I jumped when it suddenly rang and struggled for a moment to free it from my pocket. Putting it to my ear I heard, "He's not picking up, you're sure he called earlier about my article?"

"Hello!" I said enthusiastically. "Is this Bret, I mean is this Mr. Shelby?"

There was a pause, and a voice that had been savaged by a 1000 cigarettes said, "*Brent* Shelby, who's this?"

"Mr. Shelby, this is…"

Dumbass! Don't give him your name!

"…someone that has some information regarding the incident at Washington Park."

"Listen buddy, the CPD is still taking tips on this. The hotline is 773…"

"No, no, no. Listen to me," I told him. "The cops have no idea what they're dealing with. I can't go to them. You're the only one I can talk to."

There was another pause, followed by Shelby clearing his throat. It sounded like a spoon stuck in a garbage disposal.

"Listen Mister…"

"Black."

"Right. Mister *Black*, I have a lot on my plate right now and I simply don't have the time or the resources to devote to this. I'm sorry."

"Sir, please. I think I can finger the attacker that killed those people. All I want is a few minutes of your time."

Another pause. I swore I heard the snick of a lighter. Did they still let them smoke at their desks?

"Alright, let me understand this."

Before he could continue someone else in the room yelled, *"Goddammit Shelby, the Fire Marshall is going to fine us into the Stone Age. Put it out!"*

I liked this guy.

"Things ain't what they used to be," he muttered, "Anyway, how do I know you're not making this up and wasting my time?" he asked. I could tell I'd piqued his interest. I just had to reel him in a little further.

"Because I know what you left out of your story. The bodies. They were partially eaten, weren't they?"

It was silent for a moment. "Meet me at the Palace Grill in an hour," and the line went dead.

* * * *

I had just ordered a cup of coffee when the phone rang again.

"Ramsey's Retrieval Service," I answered out of habit.

"Ramsey huh? Sounds like a real nice name," Shelby said on the other end.

"My mom thought so," I replied and punched the air. No wonder I'd failed as a private dick.

"A change of plans Ramsey. I'm sure your mom's a real sweet lady who'd trust you with her life, but I don't. I won't be meeting you for coffee. Here's what I want you to do."

"I'm all ears."

"There's a blue line stop two blocks east. Take the steps down to the station and pay, but don't get on. When you get to the platform walk through the tunnel to the Chicago Avenue exit one block south. There's a Greek Place across the street. Go to the alley behind it and wait there." *Click*. Either Shelby had watched too many espionage flicks, or he had a good reason to be cautious. With everything I'd been through lately I couldn't really fault him.

I palmed some money onto the counter and hurried outside. Stepping through the door I collided with a stick-thin man in a shabby suit, knocking him to the ground. Helping him back to his feet, I started to apologize, but the words died in my throat as he raised his face to mine, his eyes bright with madness. The smell of sour sweat clung to his slight frame, and the collar of his once-white shirt was creased with grime. I backed away but his hand shot out, grasping my wrist with surprising strength.

"He comes," he whispered, his voice raspy but urgent.

I tried to extract my hand but his fingers were locked tight.

"Prepare!" he shouted, startling me.

Religious wackos always had to get the last word in. Recovering from my shock, I tore my arm free and tried to push past him, but he stepped in front of me again.

"Prepare for his coming!" he screamed, spittle flying from his chapped lips. I straight armed him, knocking him off his feet. I stepped around him and was halfway down the sidewalk when he started screaming.

"He comes for you! You can't hide, Thomas!" I whirled around to see him calmly stand up, brush himself off, and step into the oncoming path of a city bus. A woman exiting the restaurant screamed as his body folded and rolled under the tires like a human scarecrow. I ran, my shoes slapping loudly against the pavement, and my heart pounding in my chest as I bounded down the stairs of the subway entrance.

He comes for you.

What the hell was happening? Had I finally lost it for good? He hadn't really called out to me by my real name. *He was just a crazy bum, that's all, just a bat-shit crazy bum. Just a bum…*

I kept repeating it to myself like a mantra, until I looked around and saw that I was at the alley where Shelby said to meet. He wasn't there yet. I stood blowing into my hands and wishing I'd gotten my crappy diner coffee to go.

I didn't have long to wait. After a few minutes he appeared. Although we'd never met, I knew it was him. He looked just like I imagined he would. His hands were jammed into the pockets of a charcoal-gray overcoat buttoned all the way up. The smoke from his cigarette trailed from a hard and heavily lined face. Staring out from under the stingy brim of a crisp fedora were eyes that carried a warning; *fools take heed.*

He stopped and held out a hand. I took it and winced. For a man who wrote for a living he had a handshake like a steel worker.

"Military?" I asked.

"Navy, 17 years," He replied and jabbed another filterless Pall Mall into his mouth. No wonder he sounded like a gravel truck.

"Sorry bout' the cat and mouse," he said, scanning the alley. "I've been doing this job since before you were born kid, but lately every shadow seems circumspect."

A chill rose on my skin. *Had he encountered the black thing?* Not likely, he wouldn't be here if he had.

"Enough with the pleasantries, what did you want to tell me Ramsey?" He fixed me with a look that said I better have something good.

"I have to know something first." It was time to act on my hunch. I desperately hoped I was right. "What did the survivor tell you?" I asked. He was a newsman. No way would he pass up a chance to get an eyewitness account. Even if it meant bribing or lying his way into an intensive care unit. I looked at him and waited. For a second I had the crazy feeling he might run.

"Survivor?" he exhaled and a great quantity of grey smoke momentarily obscured his head. "She croaked before I could talk to her."

He was lying. Even in the cold air, it had a signature, like a gallon of milk two weeks past its expiration date. I decided to go for broke.

"What happened to those people in the park was no random burglary gone awry."

His eyes narrowed. "If you know so much about it, why don't you tell me what it was then?" he growled.

"Do you mind?" I asked, gesturing with my hand. He frowned but then jerked a smoke out of the pack. I inhaled and winced. It was like wrapping your lips around an exhaust pipe.

"It wasn't a man Mr. Shelby," I croaked. "In fact, it wasn't a person at all."

He didn't say anything so I plowed ahead, painfully aware of how crazy I sounded.

"The thing in the park that night was something right out of a kid's nightmare. It was something that could rip your head off as easily as twisting the cap off a beer. It wasn't a man, not fully a man anyway. It was a *wolf*-man. A real, honest-to-god werewolf."

And by the way, maybe it was me. Now watch while he does run.

But he didn't run. He cleared his throat loudly and spat. He was silent for a moment before saying as clear as day, "I thought you were going to tell me something new, Ramsey."

I almost fell over.

"You know what?" he continued. "I'm too old to be freezing my ass off out here. Meet me at Twin Anchors tonight and we'll take it from there. By the way, you're buying." Without a second look he was three strides down the alley.

"How did you know?" I yelled after him.

"Because she told me," he said still walking, "just before she died."

I knew it.

"Did she say what he looked like?" I yelled again.

Just when I was sure he wasn't going to answer, he stopped. Without turning around he said over his shoulder, "She said he had piercing blue eyes. She figured he must have a thing for blondes, because unlike the rest, he only took her leg off."

"His hair, did she say what color his hair was?" I shouted, but he was already out of sight. *Damn. How did he move that fast?* I'd only had one of his smokes and I felt like renting an iron lung. *Piercing blue eyes.* That narrowed it down – to either me or the German. *Shit.* Oh well, I had to play along for now. At least, he wanted to meet again. Either that or the cops would be waiting for me at Twin Anchors. But my nose told me he was on the up and up. I hoped so anyway. They hadn't been staking out my apartment to ask me on a date. Either the word had come down to lock someone up, or…

Or you had yourself a little snack in the park that night.

I shivered and pushed it from my mind. I refused to accept it. Yet.

At least he'd chosen a decent place to rendezvous. Twin Anchors had some damn good ribs. Sinatra used to go there back in the day just to get a rack. As for me, I'd never met a rack of ribs I didn't like.

* * * *

Back on the 66 bus, Penelope's phone started ringing again. I picked it up and heard a voice I'd hoped never to hear again.

"You are more resourceful than I thought, my young friend," the voice purred before a fit of coughing ensued. The German sounded like shit.

"You sound like shit Hans. Got a touch of the black flu?" I said, trying to sound nonchalant. Inside I felt like throwing up.

"My name is Klaus, you mongrel, and I would not make the mistake of underestimating me again. I very much doubt you would survive another encounter."

"I thought our mutual acquaintance had resolved that for both of us."

"I am not so easily indisposed."

"Too bad."

"I want what I came for."

"Now that I know what it is, I don't have it anymore."

"Someone says differently, perhaps you'd like to talk to her?"

My heart dropped into my stomach when I heard her voice.

"Ben! He was waiting outside the house and, *oh*!"

"Enough prattling, I assume you get the idea."

The phone felt like a hot coal against my ear. "You fucking touch her..."

"She is in perfect health and will continue to be as long as you cooperate fully. Now listen closely and do exactly as I say."

I listened closely alright, and when I'd taken the phone away from my ear, a plan was already taking shape. I quickly dialed Eric's cell. Considering the circumstances, I prayed that he was still in one piece. The recent spat between us aside, I'd still trust him with my life, and had many times before. He was the Watson to my Holmes, and Watson was loyal to a fault if he was anything. Without him my plan was doomed. I exhaled with relief when I heard his panicked voice pick up on the other end.

"Nells? Nells, is it you? Jesus tell me you're OK or ..."

"Eric, it's me. I have her phone. Are you OK?"

"Ramsey! He's taken her. He wants it. He wants the diamond!"

"I know," I answered. "I just talked to him."

A homeless man pushing an empty shopping cart edged around the corner of the alley and stopped to lift the lid of a dumpster. He glanced my way, and I got a brief glimpse of a filthy beard and a face lived too long out in the elements. I lowered my voice and continued.

"What happened? How did he get her?" I turned my back to the bum and started walking towards the street. "Never mind, right now there's only one thing that matters, getting her back. But we can't let him have the rock, it's the only thing keeping her alive."

"Jesus Ramsey. I don't like this. Why don't we just give him what he wants?" he said, hysteria edging his voice.

"Because once he has it, he'll kill her anyway and then finish us off too. I've met this motherfucker before—he'd do it without even blinking and then go out for a steak dinner afterwards. Trust me, killing is something he enjoys. We'll get her back. I have a plan."

There was a pause. "Alright, I'm yours, just tell me what you need me to do,"

That's why I loved Eric. He'd throw himself on a grenade to help his friends.

"Good," I said. "Now listen closely and do exactly as I say."

* * * *

He pretended to dig through the trash as he watched his prey. The human didn't look like much of a threat, but he had learned long ago that appearances meant less than nothing; his current disguise a case in point.

He could feel it. The boy had it with him, concealed on his person. It thrummed with a bone-deep vibration like a plucked string, the sustain infinite. He felt a powerful urge to take it by force right there, but it was not yet time. More than 800 years of existence (*life* was a word that belonged to others) had taught him that brash acts often had unintended, even fatal consequences, such being the nature of his own so-called birth.

The boy ended his conversation, and looked one last time in his direction before exiting the alley. As their eyes met he felt the other's hard appraisal, and wondered if perhaps he had sensed something. He affected a sudden preoccupation with the zipper of his pants until the boy walked away.

He waited a few moments to be certain and then took his true form once more. Where a bedraggled miscreant had been a moment earlier, there stood a distinguished looking gentleman of middle age with a neatly trimmed beard and an academic, regal bearing.

A sound brought him quickly around. Had he underestimated the youth after all? But no, it was only another denizen of the street, making his daily rounds to the very dumpster he had been feigning to plumb moments ago. One look told him that the man had seen everything. Who would believe him? And yet, the smallest thread could unravel the finest of tapestries.

The man turned and ran, and he flowed after him like the shadow of a cloud skidding across the water. There was no scream. In the morning the wheels of a garbage truck would roll unnoticed over the small pile of tattered clothes that had once been a man.

CHAPTER THIRTY ONE

I hated to stand up the one person that could possibly clear my name.

Or implicate me as the murderer.

Whatever the outcome, Shelby had information that I desperately needed. Blowing him off was not going to help my cause one bit. Perhaps he had a softer side, and that grizzled exterior sheltered a great big forgiving heart.

Not likely.

The German's parting words echoed in my ears.

Don't underestimate me a second time.

I didn't plan to. If I'd had a bazooka, it would have been slung over my shoulder. Despite my tendency to screw most things up, I didn't go out of my way looking for trouble. It just had a way of finding me first.

The German could not have picked a more obscure setting for our rendezvous. Little did I know that Chicago, once an enormous festering swamp, still had one. A shabby forgettable bridge marked its eastern boundary, its long gray wall of Jersey barrier curb blocking the view from passing cars. From the omniscient perspective of Google Earth, it looked like any other abandoned industrial area, overgrown and forgotten. Who would have guessed that among the shuttered warehouses sat an ecological diamond in the rough.

Meet me at Hegewishe Marsh at midnight. Be sure to…

Wait, did you say marsh?

Yes, meet me at…

Are you cracked? This is Chicago not the bayou.

Twenty mosquito infested acres remained from what had once been an area the size of Rhode Island. It was far from an unspoiled tract of wilderness though. Thousands of tons of toxic slag and flue ash had been dumped there fifty years ago, back when America still shipped its steel to the world.

But nature endures. According to the *Friends of Hegewishe Marsh* website, foxes, beavers, and muskrats, were showing their hairy faces there again.

I had to give the Kraut some credit. Finding a clandestine place to meet in a city of three million people was no small feat. Whatever happened tonight, there would be no witnesses, or unwanted intrusions. No one would know we were there, or that there even was a "there" there.

An abandoned rail line leads to the old switching yard. Wait for me there. Bring it with you and I will bring her. Come alone, or I swear you will watch while I devour her, one pretty piece at a time.

I stopped midway across the bridge and leaned over the crumbling concrete barrier, peering into the darkness below. Back when the fires from the massive blast furnaces had burned day and night, this place must have looked like a scene out of Dante's Inferno. Now, it sat dark and silent as a crypt, the wind whispering through the long marsh grasses was the only sound. To ordinary eyes, the marsh below would appear to be impenetrable, a vast and featureless opaque expanse. But not to me. It had been 40 years since the last shipment of steel, but an oily stench still clung to the air. The marsh had reclaimed most of the rail line, but I could still discern small segments rising up from the tangle of vegetation and black water.

I stood on the tips of my toes, straining to see the yard and any landmarks. After a moment of searching I found it. Among the ruins of collapsed structures, a low squat brick building still stood. Using it as a backdrop, Eric should be able to see enough to have a clean shot. Even then it would be one hell of a shot. If anyone could pull it off, he could. He'd plugged me once with a tranquilizer dart at a full run from 300 yards.

I walked to the other end of the bridge and stopped before a metal door (locked!). It led to a metal staircase enclosed with chain link on all sides, so someone wouldn't be able to edge along the outside of the bridge to shimmy around the door. The door was covered with ivy and patches of rust. It didn't look like it had been used in ten years. A faded sign hung lopsided above the door showing the figure of a man being impaled by a giant bolt of electricity. I looked at my watch, ten minutes left. Not enough time to search for another way down.

I pried a chunk of concrete loose from the wall and used it to smash the door knob. It made an impressive sound, but failed to do more than scratch the steel. I walked over to the bridge again and looked down at the light playing on the silent black water below. I was tempted to jump, but the notion of leaping over the side when I didn't know the depth of the water, and what might lay beneath waiting to impale me, dissuaded me.

I waited for a car to pass and then swung my legs over the railing and onto the thin edge there. Leaning back, I stretched out a foot and touched the base of the chain link partition alongside the stairway landing, but try as I might I couldn't get a foothold. I'd have to jump from the bridge, grab hold of the fence with both hands and jam the tips of my shoes into the gaps in the links. From there I could gradually climb down along the outside to the ground. No problem. *Then why was my heart pounding?* I visualized myself successfully grabbing the railing with both hands, said a silent prayer, and jumped. The cold night air whispered in my ears and then the fingers of both hands curled around the links in the fence and my shoes popped snugly into two gaps.

I let out a "woohoo!" in appreciation at my own feat of daring. "I can do this," I said to myself and pulled the toe of one shoe out right as a jarring screech rent the air. I held my breath as a section of fencing shuddered once in protest.

Shit--

SPROING!

With a lurch it pulled free from its moorings, plunging me into into the swirling mists below.

CHAPTER THIRTY TWO

My fears regarding the depth of the marsh were unfortunately justified. Bruised and wet, but still alive, I crawled out from the frigid water onto the hard mud of the bank nearby.

Tightrope walking a half-submerged railroad track in the dark hadn't factored into my original plans, but after climbing out of the water, I realized that it was my only hope of crossing the marsh without drowning or becoming entrapped in the freezing muck. The steel beams still appeared to be whole, though they were draped in marsh grasses and dipped below the surface at times to reappear further ahead, like the undulating spine of a sea serpent. I squared my shoulders and set off into the marsh. By the time I reached the other side my clothes were heavy and slick with an odorous black swamp funk.

I hobbled over to the side of a rotting wooden shed and braced myself with one hand against the mossy boards, while I grasped each pant leg with the other and gave it a firm shake. As I bent down to go to work on my shoes, a voice boomed from behind me.

"I can see you opted for the scenic route," The German said as he emerged from behind a hoary old cottonwood tree. Although diminished somewhat by the dreariness of our surroundings, he was still something to behold, a tight fist of masculinity, his broad shoulders and chest straining at the thin fabric of the trench coat cinched tightly around his waist. He moved gingerly, walking as if he'd been astride a saddle too long, his steps small and measured. A quick study of his face confirmed the strain reflected there. He was still suffering from his injuries, though he was trying to hide it.

"I hope for your sake and that of your whore, that the crystal is not lying buried at the bottom of this swamp." The casual tone he affected belied the underlying threat of violence in his voice.

I noticed that the other hand was still pressed against the tree. Was he using it to support his weight? Just how badly was he hurt? *Please God let him be really hurt.*

"It could be tucked up my ass for all you know, but a rock that big would leave one hell of a mark," I answered.

He took a step towards me, his hands closing into fists.

"I have it hidden safely close by, and if you lay one meaty finger on me or Penelope, I promise that hidden it will remain."

He stopped, his eyes murderous, before shuffling back to glare at me, his hand on the tree once more.

I stood up and flapped my arms, a spray of muck splattering against the ground. I jammed them in my pockets so he wouldn't see them shaking. I could feel the diamond pressing against my breast, tucked into the vest pocket of my jacket. Under any other circumstance, I probably would have broken into a sweat, but it's hard to sweat when you're standing in sodden clothes in a frigid swamp at night, even for someone with my enhanced metabolism.

As I stood there, face-to-face with a trained supernatural killer in a swamp at night, my original plan seemed a bit thin. The German coughed again and spat. It looked black, but it was impossible to tell in that light if it was bloody or not. After he wiped his mouth with the back of his hand he did something very scary. He began to softly laugh.

"Why do I get the feeling you're stalling?" The mirth didn't reach his eyes; they were as empty as my bank account.

What could I say? A fear had taken root in me from the moment I'd looked down into the darkness from the bridge. I was on the verge of losing my nerve – of losing control. I had to act quickly, or I would never leave this swamp alive and neither would Penelope.

"You're the one that's stalling, asshole," I said with as much venom as I could muster. His face became somehow even more murderous-looking.

"Where is she?" I continued before I lost my nerve. "Choke me again for all you like, but that fucking diamond is gone if I don't see her *right now*!"

I was panting when I finished, from fear or actual rage I wasn't sure.

He looked at me, his face hard as stone. I prayed that I hadn't just sealed our death warrants.

"Fine. We'll do it your way. Wait here." He said, and disappeared back behind the cottonwood. He returned a moment later, a gagged and bound Penelope grasped in one arm. I nearly collapsed with relief. She must have been there all along, listening to everything. She didn't appear hurt. Terrified maybe, but not injured. I wanted nothing more than to wrap her in my arms and run.

"Ok. Let's do this then," I said. "Let her go and it's yours."

"I don't think so," he said, and the hand holding her was suddenly covered in coarse hair. I knew from experience what the claws were capable of.

"Give it to me now or she loses the arm."

His yellow eyes shone in the dark. Penelope shuddered and moaned in fear but did not faint.

I'd been afraid something like this might happen. Penelope was too close to him and could easily become the target if Eric's shot went awry. I pictured him leaning over the bridge, steadying the rifle against the rail, his finger slowly inching the trigger back.

"Take it easy Hans, just take it easy," I said and reached into my shirt pocket.

"My name is…never mind! I knew you were bluffing little cub," he sneered.

I pulled out the lighter, praying it wouldn't be too wet to spark. I took some satisfaction at seeing the smile on his face fall away.

"I'm not stupid. I buried it here right before you showed up."

I knelt, pretending to scan the ground. I flicked the lighter once.

Snick.

Come on baby.

Snick.

Please God.

Snick!

A blue flame wavered in the air. I made as if to lower it towards the muddy ground and then thrust it triumphantly above my head.

He looked confused for a second and then I saw his canines pop as he figured it out. Penelope wrenched her arm from his grasp and fell to the ground as two darts took him squarely in the chest, the impact nudging him back a step. He snarled and then collapsed like a marionette with its strings cut.

The smile froze on my face as a dart suddenly sprouted from Penelope's thigh and she too crumpled to the ground. I took a step towards her and jerked as a bee sting lanced into my back just under the shoulder blade.

The next thing I knew there was mud in my mouth. It tasted exactly like it looked. I tried to spit it out but my lips wouldn't work. Neither would my legs. I managed to roll onto my back as the night sky rushed down to cover me like a shroud.

CHAPTER THIRTY THREE

"Ben?"

Someone had cracked open my head and filled it with sand and broken glass.

Go Away.

Ben is temporarily unavailable.

He's tied up, out of the office, on vacation.

Actually Ben is dead, so sorry. Now please go away.

"Ben. Can you hear me?"

You again? I told you already.

He's checked out, left the building, bought the farm, taken the last train.

Thank you and fuck off.

"You've got to wake up honey. Please, wake up."

Honey?

Someone shook me gently. I opened one eye the width of a hair and winced as the light stabbed through.

"Turn them off" I managed to whisper.

"Oh, I'm so sorry. Eric, could you?"

I stiffened at the name. The light behind my eyelids dimmed from an angry red to a muted orange, and I heard the soft slap of shoes against the concrete as someone approached the bed. I managed to half-open both eyes and look around.

I lay on a gurney in the lab, my feet sticking out from beneath a hospital gown. The familiar sight of an I.V. trailed from my left arm to a bag of sodium nitrate. Penelope sat in a chair to my left holding my hand. I smiled at her and then shifted to look at the person sitting on my other side.

"How you feeling buddy? We thought we might have really lost you this time." Eric said, his face full of concern and worry.

I smiled at him in return, and then I was flying out of bed, the I.V. ripping painfully out of my arm. I wrapped my hands around his throat, bearing him to the floor and pinning his arms with my knees.

He tried to speak, but it's hard to talk when you're being strangled. I should know. I could feel Penelope wrap her arms around my chest and try to pull me off. I chose to ignore her.

"Wait!" he managed to wheeze.

My fingers clenched tighter, sealing off his esophagus.

"It wasn't ..." that was all he could get out. His face was starting to turn a pretty shade of chartreuse.

Penelope had changed tactics, and was now beating ineffectually at my back with her small adorable doctor hands. His eyes began to roll back into his head.

Something slammed into the side of my head with enough force to knock me sprawling onto the floor next to Eric. The room did a slow spin as I looked up to see Penelope holding the shotgun like a baseball bat. Next to me Eric had managed to sit up and was retching for air.

I put my back against the wall, holding my throbbing head in both hands.

Penelope moved to set the gun down and then apparently thought better of it. "I'll get a couple ice packs," she said and left the room.

"Why Eric? Why did you do it?" I moaned.

He rubbed his throat and tried to speak, but only a squeak came out. He coughed and then tried again. It sounded painful.

"It wasn't me!"

* * * *

The plan had been simple, highly dangerous, and carried very little chance of success. Eric would use the last of the serum (he'd tried in vain to talk me out of it) to take out the German. It was the only way to be sure. We would free Penelope and neutralize our enemy in one decisive strike. After that we'd lock him up in the safe room where even his terrible strength couldn't free him (or so we hoped). Then he would answer our questions or rot there for all I cared. That had been the plan anyway, until everything had gone to hell.

I looked at Eric again. For the first time things were switched up. My human intuition told me he was lying while the wolf sensed nothing. He was either telling the truth or was a phenomenally gifted liar. The only way to pull that off entailed accomplishing the impossible - convincing yourself you weren't lying. If the first scenario held true, I'd just attacked and savagely choked my most trusted friend and companion. If it were the latter, he was far less than the friend I'd thought he was, and had certainly lied to me in the past.

"Ben, you ..." he stopped to clear his throat again "you *have* to believe me.

The use of my first name caught me off guard. In all the time we'd known each other, he'd never referred to me as anything other than Ramsey.

"I thought you were going to kill me."

So did I pal. So did I.

He mistook my silence for capitulation and gave me a playful shove. "Just give me a warning before you start choking me next time, like howling or growing a tail or something."

His laughter sounded forced. I couldn't blame him. I still didn't know which part of me to trust.

"So tell me something that makes me not want to choke you again," I said.

He righted the chair I'd knocked him out of and sat back down in it again. Penelope returned with two smack packs and soon Eric and I were both nursing our throbbing extremities with shared sighs of relief. After a bit, he began.

"I got there late, dammit if I didn't! I thought I knew where the scope was and then when I went to look for it, well, I left later than I should have."

I certainly couldn't stand in judgment on that one. I could hardly be relied upon to catch a stray house pet. He swallowed and continued, "So I'm racing there, at least as fast as that excuse for a vehicle can go that you're driving these days." He smiled but I couldn't. The van reminded me of Justin, and you just couldn't make light of someone getting their head blown off.

"When I got set-up on the bridge, the first thing I saw through the scope was you kneeling on the ground. I almost started shooting right there. A minute later you held up the lighter and I took aim."

"Hell of a shot too," I interrupted.

"Thanks, but ..." he stopped and looked up at me with haunted eyes, "I didn't make that shot. " The last came out in a whisper. "Something else did. I took a breath to steady myself before the shot and the blood turned to ice in my veins. I've never been so cold in my life. Something... went *inside* me, and took control, like I was a puppet. I was still there but I couldn't move, blink, anything. I could feel it inside of me. I could feel what it was feeling," his voice rose, wavering, "and it was enjoying it Ramsey." He was unable to continue. Penelope rushed to his side and put an arm around his shoulders. After a moment he continued.

"I thought it was going to empty the whole clip, but for some reason it stopped. One second I was a marionette and the next, my fat old self again."

I could see how it must have unfolded. Eric, with the German in his sights, when from out of the shadows a black mist arises. All at once it rushes towards the still figure, streaming up into his nose, his eyes, his ears and mouth as he convulses in shock, helpless to even scream. After the last tendril of smoke disappears within him, the Eric-thing raises the rifle and takes a perfect shot, followed by two more. The gun falls from his hands and he drops to ground as the smoke exits violently in a torrent and disappears.

"After I was certain it was gone, I stumbled to the gate, but it was locked. So I got back in the car and tried to find another way in." He looked beseechingly at me. "I kept thinking about how in God's name I was gonna get you both out. There was no way I could make it across that swamp carrying even one of you. But I eventually found a street about a quarter mile around that led in a ways. A scarier fucking neighborhood you can't imagine – outside of Gary, Indiana anyway. The road was in pretty rough shape, but it got me within 100 yards. The funny thing is, when I went to pick Penelope up, she didn't even need my help. Seems the dart didn't deliver its full payload, thank God," he said looking at Penelope. I frowned. Something he'd said made me do a double take.

"Wait, did you just say that you dragged *everyone* back?"

He turned to me and a grin split his face from ear to ear.

"Where is he?"

"In the safe room, nice and cozy," Eric replied. "And boy is he pissed."

My smile turned to stone when I caught sight of my filthy mud-caked clothes and jacket laying in a pile next to the bed. Trying not to panic, I reached out a hand and grabbed my jacket. Miraculously, I felt the hard lump still inside and moved to take it out, but then stopped.

Keep it hidden.

I tried to convince myself that my intentions were pure. I merely wanted to protect my friends. But deep down I knew that was a lie, and it shamed me to admit it. I just couldn't quite trust them yet.

So I decided to lie some more. Muttering loudly to myself, I said "It has to be in here somewhere!" I grabbed the lump and shook the jacket, harder and harder. I felt the pockets again, turned it inside out, and then dropped it into my lap and hung my head, my hands wringing my hair.

Before either of them could say a word, I leapt up and flipped the chair over to crash against the floor. "Dammit!" I screamed.

Eric looked to me and then at Penelope in confusion. I saw her figure it out first, her hands flying up to her mouth. Eric frowned, not comprehending, and his eyes grew huge as understanding finally dawned on him.

"You brought it with you?" he whispered, his voice incredulous. He slowly lowered his head into his hands, and then for the first time in my life I saw Eric cry.

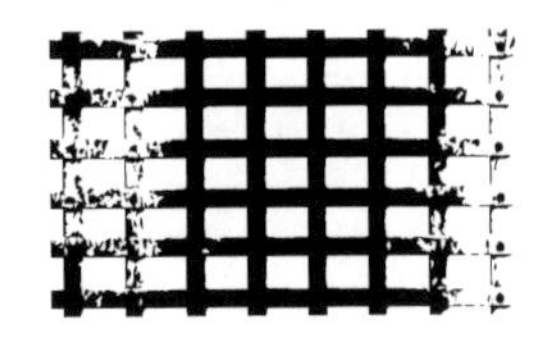

CHAPTER THIRTY FOUR

A word about werewolves.

When they're tearing after you through some foreign stretch of woods in the dead of night, they can be pretty terrifying. They're in their element, and chasing down helpless prey with no chance of escape is what they excel at. But when they're on the other end of a camera mounted to the wall of a concrete cell, with 3-inch steel doors able to withstand a direct hit from an RPG, they just don't make quite the same impression.

The German certainly fit the definition of a caged animal – pacing and panting from one corner of the tiny cube to the other, never still, even in his diminished state. The limp was prominent now, as were a series of blue-black bruises encircling his torso where the black thing had constricted him. I'd mistaken the marks on his face for shadows in the dusk of the swamp. The poor quality of the camera feed lent a grainy, washed-out look to the scene. It reminded me of the undercover footage I'd seen on television of a drug bust, or prostitute sting. Even looking at him with my own eyes, it defied belief that we had really captured him. Now that we had, what the hell were we going to do with him?

"If it can hold me..." I said, my eyes on the screen.

I could still remember the feel of his hands around my throat, my feet rising up off the floor. Could we hope to contain such a thing? It pained me to imagine myself in his place with Penelope and Eric watching. What had gone through their minds?

"He's not going anywhere," Eric said as he stepped into the room and kicked the door closed behind him, "Trust me." As if to confirm he'd been reading my mind, he added, "More than once, me and Nells asked ourselves the same thing about you."

Eric plunked an orange plastic five gallon bucket full of beer and ice down on the floor between us and dropped into the chair next to mine. We tapped our bottles together and tipped them back in unison.

"Sorry about--"

"Forget it amigo," he said, cutting me off. "I would have been pretty upset too if it'd been me down there. I hope this bastard is worth it though."

"Worth what?"

"Using the last of the magic juice."

"Does Penelope know?"

"She hasn't heard it from me. I like my face the way it is."

I reached into the bucket. "It's going to be a long night."

"Yep. Too bad about the rock," he said looking at the floor.

"What?" I said pretending not to hear.

Can I trust you ol' buddy? Can I?

"Guess we should get started," I said.

"Yeah." He didn't exactly sound eager about the prospect. I didn't feel too excited about it myself.

"You sure he can hear us in there?" I asked, picking up the microphone.

"Yep."

I drained the beer and turned the switch on, letting loose with a belch that must have reverberated like a jackhammer off the concrete inside the safe room. The German stopped and stood still for the first time in hours.

"Season's Greetings Hans. This is Santa Claus. I'm afraid you've been a very naughty boy this year and won't be getting that American Girl doll you wrote to me about."

Eric whipped his head to the side to keep from spraying the screen with beer.

I heard the door open behind us and Penelope entered the room. She walked over to stand behind us and simultaneously slapped the backs of both of our heads.

"Goddammit Nells!" Eric said while rubbing his head.

"How could you do something like that without consulting me first!" she cried. "That was years of work, MY work! It can't be replaced! Oh Ben, why?"

Eric rubbed his head and muttered something about women and hormones.

I stood up and looked into her anguished, beautiful face.

"Penelope, I can stand to lose the only shot we have at a cure, but what I cannot, what I *will not* stand for, is the thought of losing you."

I'm not sure who moved first. Her mouth pressed hungrily against mine, and a spark of arousal awoke within me. I wanted her. I always had. Her desire fed my own, fanning it into a bright flame. I pulled away, breathing a little too heavily. It was too risky.

"This could get dangerous," I said, gesturing to the monitor behind me. She knew I wasn't speaking only of the German. I had to protect her, even if I was the one she needed protecting from. "I'm staying," She said suddenly, grabbing a beer out of the bucket. "And don't you dare try to talk me out of it." The look of surprise on Eric's face was priceless. Penelope never drank.

"Alright then," I said and picked up the microphone again. Before I spoke, Penelope leaned down and whispered in my ear. "According to Wikipedia, a golem is a creature created out of clay or stone, anything inanimate." Her lips and breath in my ear were driving me crazy. "In Jewish folklore, a Rabbi would conjure a golem to protect the Village from an invading army, and when it was over, he would return it back into what he had made it from." I had no idea what to make of that information. Had the garden gnome flubbed his message? What had Jonesy been trying to warn me of?

"Jesus, get a room," Eric said, a look of disgust on his face as Penelope stood back up and winked at him. I tried to act like my heart wasn't beating a mile a minute. As Justin would have said, I was way out over my skis. I still couldn't believe that he was dead. When I looked back at the monitor I nearly dropped the microphone. The German was gone. In his place stood an upright wolf at least 8 feet tall, his muzzle smashed up close to the camera. He was desperately trying to reach it, tearing at the protective metal cage with his teeth and claws.

"It's gonna be a lot harder to do this if he gets that off the wall," Eric said.

I decided to change tactics and drop the taunting, although it had been fun while it lasted.

"I have it with me Hans," I announced.

Eric looked over at me, a questioning look on his face. I winked at him and continued.

"The thing is, I don't care much for jewelry myself. I'm sure someone else would, especially when it concerns a giant red diamond. Imagine what something like that would fetch on the open market? As you can see for yourself, my accommodations could use an upgrade."

The massive head pulled away from the camera, yellow eyes staring at us with an intelligence that no animal should possess. It shook its head once as if to dispel a bothersome fly and then the German stood in its place once more.

How did he do that? I couldn't help feeling envious. And then like a million light bulbs going off at once, I knew what I wanted from him. I needed a teacher, a mentor to help me master the wolf. Of course! A golden opportunity lay before me, a chance to learn from a true master. It was the next best thing to a cure. I only had to convince him to agree to it.

"I already know that you have it," he said, handling the shredded remains of his clothes with a look of regret. "I can sense its presence. You will not trick me again."

My heart jumped, but I didn't dare look at Eric or Penelope.

"It is priceless, my young friend." He spoke in a calm and measured tone, as if he hadn't just been a hideous monster moments ago. "There is no auction house in this world that could adequately ascertain its true value. But I happen to know certain individuals that would reward you most handsomely for the return of such a treasure."

Now we were talking.

"I don't want the money," I said. After a few minutes he took the bait.

"So what it is that you want Ramsey?"

I made him wait while I chugged another beer. And then I told him.

CHAPTER THIRTY FIVE

It hovered before him in the night air, an inkblot sprung to life from a psychoanalyst's flash card, moving fluidly from one abstract shape to the next. It radiated agitation and something approaching anger, although not truly, for that was a decidedly human emotion.

He had underestimated the strength of the Tracker. To reduce one of the *Cythraul* to an incorporeal state required an enormous exertion of power.

Interrrfeeered.

The word whispered inside his head. He watched as its shape solidified into the whelp's helper, Eric, and then dissolved back into smoke.

He felt a modicum of anger rise within him in response. The thing had forgotten its place.

"My dear, loyal Praxus," he began. It had chosen the name for itself eons past: they all had in the misguided hope that it would lend some measure of legitimacy to their false existence. "You have lost your way, old friend. I must now take these matters upon myself to resolve. The crystal will be recovered, but by my hand alone. You have served well. Your time here is ended. Go now and return to the others."

The shifting shape paused but then began anew, accelerating to a fantastic rate of speed. The shapes blurred before him seamlessly as Praxus appeared intent on imitating all that it had witnessed in the joyless eons it had spent on Earth. An owl morphed into a tree that dissolved into a butterfly, which then became a murder of crows and on and on. Faster and faster the shapes spun until at last there stood floating before him the first, their father, their jailor, their god – Merlin. He looked upon a black mirror of his own reflection.

It was forbidden for any but himself, the first of their kind, to take the maker's form. The shadow raised its staff high as if to smite him. The air around them crackled with energy as he gathered his power, the essence of all that he possessed, drawing it to a point within his being no larger than the tip of a sparrow's tongue.

He was the first and he would be obeyed.

As the staff descended he released it. All of it. The glass windows in each of the adjoining buildings bowed outward and then exploded, raining glass down upon the alley. The shock wave fell upon the false Merlin like a tidal wave upon a sandcastle, and it was no more.

He dropped to one knee as the world before him wavered. He looked at his arm and saw that it had begun to break apart, sifting into the air like ash.

NO

His work was not yet complete. He would finish what he had come to do. Marshalling what strength he had left, he pulled at the far flung expanses of himself, calling the motes back to once again take the shape he had been cast from so long ago.

Moments later police cruisers screeched to a halt at the entrance to the alley. The officers failed to notice the regal older man walking in the opposite direction down the street, his head bowed against the cold and dark.

CHAPTER THIRTY SIX

"Personally, I don't care much for this prick," Eric said, his face buried in a dog-eared *Penthouse* from 1987, "But he's persistent. I'll give him that."

I nodded as I watched the German try again to get at the camera. He had chipped several teeth in previous assaults and his muzzle was flecked with bloody spittle. He had also spent the better part of an hour spitting bloody phlegm at the lens. I kept checking the irrational urge to wipe it from the screen with my hand, like a fogged over windshield.

"He'll get tired of this eventually," I said. He had to. No one could exert this much naked aggression and hostility without succumbing to exhaustion at some point. He hadn't reacted well to my proffered exchange and had flown into a rage more terrifying than any before.

The safe room had been one of the main reasons we'd chosen the mansion to be the base of our operations in the first place. Someone very wealthy and even more paranoid had once lived there, outfitting it with a panic room constructed for the sole purpose of keeping anything and everything out. Once you were inside, it was virtually impenetrable from the outside. It must have cost a small fortune to procure the thick steel plates that had then been bolted to the stone foundation. With a few adjustments, we had repurposed it, turning it from an unassailable refuge to an inescapable prison. If Eric and Penelope had ever harbored any doubts regarding its integrity, they had been put to rest.

"Ramsey."

The tone in Eric's voice made me look up. I had been unconsciously rubbing the fabric of my jacket where the diamond lay concealed. I stopped as I looked at the screen. The German, in human form once more, sat cross-legged on the bare metal floor.

"It appears my choices are somewhat limited at present," he said calmly. "Congratulations on capturing me. You'll be pleased to know you are the first ones to do so, and I have been roaming this earth since the reign of Genghis Khan."

My jaw dropped. If it had fallen off I wouldn't have noticed.

"Did he say…?" Penelope stammered. "I think that's over 700 years" Eric added, looking like someone had just told him Darth Vader really was his father.

"If I agree to this thing that you ask, I have your word you will relinquish the crystal?" he asked.

"Yes," I replied after a moment, still in shock from his admission. "I'll hand it over with my own two hands." I wasn't telling a lie, not technically anyway. After teaching me all he knew, I would gladly hand it over, right after I'd killed him. With my own two hands.

"Then let's get started!" he said with obvious mock enthusiasm. Standing up, he slapped his bare ass with both hands. "I don't suppose it would be too much to ask for some assistance with my wardrobe?"

* * * *

Once we had struck a deal, he wasted no time in demonstrating why the Germans have the well-earned reputation of being the most industrious of their European brethren. He seemed wholeheartedly dedicated to the task of tutoring me and even appeared to be enjoying himself. For the first time in my life, I had another person who, although knowing next to nothing about me, understood me more intimately than perhaps anyone. I began to feel the seeds of hope take root within me – that I could live a life of moderate predictability again, free from the ever-present fear that I might kill anyone for any reason at any time. I conveniently chose to ignore (for the time being at least) the fact that he had brutally murdered my first love.

"You first must unlearn everything you think you know, because you know nothing. Your mind and spirit have become polluted with the foul drugs you willingly swallow." I listened intently to his words while trying not to look at him. Eric swore the "Don't Mess with Texas" sweater and plaid polyester men's slacks were all he'd been able to find in his size at the Family Thrift.

"I'm curious about something," I said, speaking into the microphone, "Why Jim Morrison's Headstone? It seems a bit melodramatic wouldn't you say?"

"Isn't it obvious?" he answered. "He was one of us, of course. The headstone seemed like the perfect place to hide the crystal, until the vandalism heaped upon it reached a level that made us fear for its safety." He closed his eyes then and began to chant.

Lift your hoary breast to my ruby lips mother
And let me run down your shattered hall of
yesterday's mirrors

"He wrote that?" I asked. "I've never heard of it."

"The archives of The Brotherhood are filled with reams of his words," he said, and then added, "Sadly, he gave up the pen for the bottle. Like you he had a weakness for it. We are extraordinarily hard to kill, but we are not immortal. When we found him, his blood contained enough heroin to kill 100 men. The wolf will not tolerate being drugged and sedated like some domesticated mongrel."

"It worked pretty well with you," I countered.

"And it is fortunate for you that it did," he said, a malicious grin unpleasantly twisting his mouth. "My point is that like any drug, the effects are fleeting and ultimately unfulfilling."

I couldn't argue with that. As much as I loved beer it didn't love me back nearly as much, especially in the morning. Unless you had another beer, that is.

"Okay Hans, I get it, but assuming that I do what you say and give up the happy pills, how can I keep from sprouting a rug every time someone upsets my apple cart?"

He smiled and there were fangs everywhere in his mouth. "It's quite simple, Thomas."

I stiffened and whispered fiercely into the mike "I told you not to use that fucking name!"

I had asked Eric and Penelope to leave so I could talk with him alone, but what if they were eavesdropping from the other side of the door? But they wouldn't do that. They were my friends, right?

"It's simple, *my friend,*" he continued. "When the wolf is outside, there is only one thing to do. I'm afraid it also happens to be the one thing you do not wish to do."

He couldn't be serious. What he was suggesting was insane.

"That's pure crazy," I said.

He stood there silently, looking into the camera.

Seconds dragged into minutes.

"Let it in," I sighed, conceding.

The German smiled, beaming like a proud parent.

* * * *

"This is without a doubt the worst idea you've ever had," Eric said, shaking his head in disbelief. "And you've had some really bad ones."

"Are you going to help me or not?"

He sighed, and nodded his head. "If he eats you, I get dibs on your stuff. Oh, but I forgot--you're broke and everything you own has been impounded. Well, it's been nice knowing you, I guess."

"I told you," I said, putting my hand on his shoulder. "He thinks we still have it. He won't do anything to jeopardize that. Not to mention all the other bullshit we fed him."

"Filling the room with poison gas?" Eric laughed. "I don't know where you come up with this stuff."

I laughed with him but my heart was in my shoes. Getting eaten remained a distinct possibility if things went wrong.

"Tell me when he's in position," I said and moved to stand before the door to the safe room.

No number of threats had been enough to dissuade the German. He insisted that I needed to be physically in the room with him. A part of me had known all along that it would come to that.

"One can learn to hack an iPhone, or make a tuna casserole from YouTube," he'd said, "But no one has ever mastered the violin, or learned to paint like the Dutch Masters from looking at a screen. It is the only way."

"He's coming in." Eric said. "You sure you're sure about this, compadre?"

I nodded and looked back at the screen. "OK, he's in position."

The best we could come up with was to have him turn around with his back towards the door, legs spread apart, both hands on the wall before him. Having seen firsthand how fast he could move, I knew it would still be a close shave if he decided to try anything. Eric loaded three fresh shells into the shotgun, pumped the action, and eased the safety free. He moved to stand behind me. I swallowed and pressed the red button on the panel outside the door. There was a series of metallic clicks and the door swung partially outward. I slipped hurriedly through the gap, and pushed it shut behind me. I gagged at the stench inside. It smelled like an alley in mid-July during a garbage strike.

The German turned around to look at me and I could feel the walls pressing in from all sides. I already wanted to leave.

"Everything ok buddy?" squawked Eric's voice, fuzzy and distorted over the single speaker mounted onto the camera.

I nodded once, and then gave an exaggerated thumbs up when I remembered how compromised the quality of the video feed had become.

The German stretched his hands above his head, his knuckles brushing against the low ceiling, and then he closed the short distance between us in a flash, his fist connecting solidly with my jaw.

Eric screamed my name, his voice ricocheting off the bare metal floor and walls.

I shakily regained my feet with the aid of the German's hand.

"I'm OK. I'm OK." I said and held up a hand, waving to the camera.

"Goddammit. You could have warned me," I said angrily, rubbing my sore jaw.

He stepped back and studied me. "It has begun. I can sense it awakening."

I could sense it too. His punch had been crude but effective. The wolf was stirring. Without thinking I reflexively began to measure my breaths, trying to slow the beating of my heart.

He slapped me hard across the face.

I could taste blood on my lips.

"You're starting to piss me off."

"Not nearly enough," he said, driving his fist into my stomach. I had been ready for another slap and it drove me to my knees.

Eric started screaming again, and I managed to hold up a hand to show him I was alright.

A familiar heat began to build in my chest.

The German looked pleased. I braced myself for another punch, slap or even a kick, but he just stood there, an expectant look on his face.

"It comes," he said reverently and put a hand on my shoulder, staring hard into my eyes. "You must not show fear. Open yourself to it. Greet it as a friend, a brother. Let it in." He leaned closer and whispered into my ear, his breath hot on my flesh, "Let it in, *Thomas*."

"What are you doing?" I asked as he chose a spot near the wall and sat down.

"Preparing to meet my brother."

I shut my eyes tight and wrinkled my nose at the smell of my own sweat, sour with trepidation. I closed my eyes and focused on the rhythmic pounding of my heart. Soon the room no longer smelled terrible. It smelled familiar. The German was right. A wolf *was* at the door. All these years I'd been putting up walls to try and protect myself from the monster within. That had been my first mistake, I could see that now. My walls had been built from nothing more than my own fears. A scratch sounded at the door.

Let it in.

The German's voice cut through my fear like a steadying hand on my shoulder. The door shuddered as a great weight was thrown against it. I reached out a hand, how odd that it did not shake, and turned the knob. It swung slowly open, revealing a hulking shape, cloaked in shadow on the threshold. I opened my arms wide as it leapt, bearing us both down into darkness.

CHAPTER THIRTY SEVEN

Hunting during the day went against every instinct, but a ravenous hunger had disturbed my dreams and driven me from the den. Creeping silently from the warm crush of slumbering bodies, I left my mate and cubs to go in search of prey. Out in the woods I tested the air, nostrils flaring at the thick odor of a musk ox – a large male from the potency of the scent. It grazed nearby, many times my weight but slow and stupid. I looked back at the entrance to the den and a low whine rose in my throat as I nosed the earth, reluctant to leave. The urge to piss was strong. The wind shifted, and the scent enveloped me. A killing song filled my head, and I padded forward. Its flesh would fill my belly and those of my family.

I ran under a cloudless sky to where the trees gave way to long grasses. Slipping within the cloak of their gently swaying embrace, I crept forward until a warning snort sounded from ahead. The male had sensed my presence. My muscles tightened with anticipation as I rose up on my haunches to get a glimpse of it. It stood ten yards away in the shallow reeds lining the edge of a lake, the water lapping at its shaggy underbelly. Larger than any I'd hunted before, it nearly equaled its larger brothers whose curved white spears could disembowel with a shrug of their massive heads. I could be killed attempting a lone strike on such a bull. It snorted again, blaring a challenge through the night air. It did not fear me.

I rose to my full height, offering a challenge of my own. It rotated its great head towards me and we stood, neither one moving. It shifted its weight and a small winged lizard hiding in the grass took flight, squawking loudly. It spooked him and he bolted, tearing through the muck, spraying water and mud in great gouts behind him. I howled my joy to the sky and gave chase.

The speed of his gait belied his massive size, but he soon began to tire under the strain of the sucking mud and his own sodden bulk. I checked the speed of my pursuit and waited for the moment to strike. He had no choice but to make for the firmer, drier ground of the surrounding plain and grasslands, where his hooves would find better purchase and perhaps even permit him to outdistance me with time. I was ready when he suddenly lurched away from the lake, and I leapt roaring to bury my jaws in…empty air. My momentum carried me well past him to roll over and over before coming to a rest on my side, wet and aching.

I rose to my feet, but he had put too much distance between us to pursue now. Confusion and shame warred within me as I made my way back towards the woods, eager to return to the den. As I stopped to worry at a twig wedged between the pads of one paw, a fledging great white owl dropped to the ground before me from the treetops above. It flapped its ungainly wings, hopping into the air with little success. I would kill after all. I leapt at it, saliva spraying from my mouth, but it somehow evaded me. Again I pounced, my jaws again closing on nothing but air. After a dozen failed attempts I lay down panting and watched as it flopped noisily away. The desire to kill was eclipsed by the immediate need to rest. I dropped my snout and pawed at the thick and spongy undergrowth, intent on creating a crude den of my own making. Soon, my powerful legs were spraying soil, a hole opening below me. I yelped as my claws scored something hard and cold. I stopped and sniffed, the hair on my back standing up as I jumped back and then returned to the hole. I tentatively pawed at it once more and saw the cold black surface of a frozen lake underneath. It didn't smell like water though. So cold and unyielding…what was it…

Steel.

I shook my head. I should leave the hole and go back to…

It's steel, Thomas.

I whipped my head from side to side searching for the origin of the sound.

You are not in the woods.

I touched the *steel* again. It burned like winter ice.

You're here in the vault.

Look at your hand

What was a hand?

Look down.

I looked down. My paw had disappeared.

NO!

My thick coat had fallen away revealing pink skin bare to the cold night air. My paw had become –

A hand.

A hand?

I was no longer a wolf. I stood on my hind legs as the woods began to spin. I cried out as they swirled faster and faster, blurring into a thousand colors: the magnificent blue of her eyes to the red flush of her skin after we'd made love, to the scarlet trail that led from my bed to the basement of my father's house, to the muted grey of the winter sky as I knelt over the body of the dog I'd killed with my bare hands, to the cold blue steel of the cell I was trapped in. Trapped with a monster that was my only true family.

I cried out in despair as I opened my eyes to see the German before me.

"You are neither the wolf, nor are you the man," He said, his eyes holding mine. I couldn't look away from him. "What are you?"

"I—"

He struck me then, not a playful slap as before, but a real blow. My head snapped back and I would have fallen if he had not grabbed me and pulled me forward.

"Show me!"

I saw him cock his arm back.

You are not a man.

His knuckles popped as he closed his hand.

You are not a wolf.

His fist flashed forward.

You are both.

"*NO.*"

His fist connected with my jaw, only it did not, because my own hand was there to stop it. A hand covered in hair.

NO.

With my other fist I threw a punch that sent the German airborne, flying back to slam off the metal wall and crash to the floor.

He rose to his feet and wiped the blood from his lips, smiling.

"Willkommen," he said, and held a dripping red palm outwards in a salutation. "Welcome to the Brotherhood."

CHAPTER THIRTY EIGHT

I threw back my head and howled in triumph. Strength flowed like a swollen river of fire through my veins. The German had spoken the truth. Neither wolf nor man, I had become both, but more. Much more. I could feel the raw, wild energy of the beast surging within me, pulsing with every heartbeat. Where it would have overwhelmed me before, I now wielded the control to harness its fury, not as a master but as a keeper, an equal. And I knew that I could use it as my will dictated. I looked at my mentor. My brother. In spite of what I knew about him I wanted to believe his words.

Welcome to the Brotherhood.

Joining them offered the chance to have something my human existence had always denied me – a family. A place where I could belong. A home.

"How did you do that?" I asked, "How did you get inside my head?"

"We all share a common ancestor, connecting us each to one another through generations beyond counting," he waved his arm to encompass the world outside our cell. "It is a bond stronger than blood. Stronger than death. It transcends the barriers of the flesh, opening a pathway between the present and past. I will show you. Look at my face. Concentrate only on me and tell me what you see," he finished.

Drunk on my newfound power, I did as he commanded and looked foolishly into his eyes. A whisper rose within the room, filling the empty space with a soft keening music. I strained to hear more, and as I did it grew, erupting with a roar. Screams of anguish and pain battered my ears. Images of men and women, bloody and broken, came unbidden to my mind: thousands of souls in torment, their cries of agony and pleas for mercy shrieking inside my skull.

"Enough!" I screamed.

The awful images and sounds fled as quickly as they had appeared. Understanding dawned cold within me. For a brief moment I had been inside the German's head. I wished above all else never to go there again. His face betrayed nothing, but his eyes shone with arousal. He had enjoyed sharing it with me. I shuddered and looked away.

"I am made to kill," he said. "As are you. Look within yourself and tell me I'm wrong."

I held a hand up and turned it slowly before me, flexing my fingers. Human in shape, yes, but the claws! I looked down the length of my torso. I was covered in a fine mane of black tawny fur. My thighs were bowed and my legs appeared slightly convex, as if I would be at home on all fours or standing on two. I turned my shoulder to look behind me. No tail. I was struck by how utterly surreal everything had become. I was a motherfucking wolfman.

"If you are done admiring yourself," he quipped, "we do have a small matter to attend to."

I looked at him. What had I become to barter with such a monster? He had boasted openly of murdering my first love. In gaining a view into his twisted mind, I had glimpsed the countless victims he'd tortured and killed throughout his long reign of terror on this planet. Surely he deserved to die. Nonetheless, I felt a stab of doubt. Killing him would end any conceivable chance I had of joining the Brotherhood. I would be an outsider once again - alone and isolated. If I simply gave him what he wanted I would be accepted and embraced as a confidant, as a brother. I had only to tell Eric to bring my jacket to the door.

"I need to know something first," I said, "Did you kill those people in the park?"

"What do you care?"

"The police seem to care a great deal. Enough to arrest me and then stake out my apartment," I answered.

"Ah yes, of course," he replied with a grin," Well, I am sorry to disappoint you. I had nothing to do with it unfortunately. As I was taking you back to your apartment we happened to pass them on the path. The Rohypnol I'd dropped in your beer must have set off the transformation. In the bloody chaos that ensued you managed to escape."

My heart sank. It *had* been me after all then. I had murdered them all in cold blood.

"If I may give a last bit of advice *mein freund*, you'll discover that people will continue to find themselves in the wrong place at the wrong time when they cross your path. Call it an occupational hazard. Your *occupation* being the hazard they encounter. Get used to it."

"But who...*what* are we? How is this even possible?" I said, gesturing at my impossible anatomy.

"To find the answer to that brother, you must return with me to London," he said.

"Ben!" Eric's voice suddenly cut in, squawking harshly over the intercom. "Something weird is going on out here." I gave the German a sharp look, but he shrugged.

"The controls," he continued. "They seem to be, uh how do I say this, they're frozen or something. There's like ice crystals on the screen, man."

Ice crystals? Oh shit.

"It's here," the German said. "The Demon has found us!"

CHAPTER THIRTY NINE

The shadow. The black assassin. The thing that Justin said couldn't be killed. The picture of the Mage with the staff and his dark twin. What was the connection? What did it want from me?

What if it was never about me at all?

The diamond still lay hidden in my jacket pocket in the observation room.

"Eric!" I screamed, pounding on the door, "Open the door, you're in danger! Open the fucking door!" There was no response. I lowered my shoulder and rammed the door, but it didn't move so much as a hair.

"Your friend is already dead," said the German from behind me.

I threw myself at the door again, "You don't know that!" I grunted, hitting it a third time.

"Tell me where you have it hidden and I will lend my strength to yours. Together we may force it open."

"It's in the room with both of them!" I shouted.

The German cursed and leveled a venomous look at me.

"I thought you killed it!" I yelled, hammering on the door again.

"Fool!" he spat. "You cannot kill what has never lived! They can only be weakened for a time until they restore their chosen form once more."

"Weakened?" I said, the memory of the door being ripped from the van flashing through my mind.

God help us.

He moved to stand next to me. "On three!"

The door may as well have been set into the base of a mountain.

"Again!"

Even rippling with muscle and covered in thick fur, my bones shook from the blow.

"Again!"

The door gave a small groan. I was panting.

"Again, with everything you have!" he cried.

The door exploded outward, banging across the floor of the room as if C4 had been set to its hinges.

I leaped through the opening, followed immediately by the German. Eric huddled in the corner, the shotgun propped against the wall near the monitor, much too far away for him to reach. He must have gotten cold because he was wearing my jacket.

A figure stood before him, its back to us. It did not appear to be made of smoke. It wasn't even black. It turned to face us and I found myself looking at an older man, handsomely attired in a vest and matching sports jacket. A cane with a polished brass handle in the shape of a dragon was cradled in his hand. He looked every bit the gentleman out for a stroll. I began to wonder if there had been some sort of mistake, until the German spoke.

"It's been a long time," he said, his voice dripping venom.

The man grinned coldly in return, "Yes Klaus, quite a long time indeed. 56 years if I'm not mistaken, and I'm never mistaken."

"Your minion seemed intent on taking my life."

"Regrettably, his instructions were simply to locate the crystal and kill the wolf that possessed it. Praxus fulfilled the first but there was one more wolf in Chicago than I'd anticipated," his grin evaporated. "I hope he wasn't too hard on you. He can be a bit single-minded."

The German sneered, "It takes longer to heal from one of you black bastards, but I will be whole again at the next cycle of the moon. It doesn't matter. I don't need to be at my full power. There are two of us here." The German clapped my shoulder, squeezing it. "That's right, devil, he's one of us now."

The man, or whatever he was, looked at me. His eyes carried untold hidden depths within them, like an underground waterfall spilling down to the center of the Earth.

"Is it true, Thomas? Are you a member of the esteemed Brotherhood now?" the man asked. One of his fingers thrust out at the German. "What fine company you keep. Klaus is one of the better ones. He kills helpless women and children in the name of science. The others do it solely for sport."

The German growled in response.

"Yes, my young wolf cub, this one has been known by many names over the centuries. They all have. Perhaps you've heard of Josef Mengele? Your *brother* here was one of his most devoted pupils. Quite disturbing, the things they did to those children in Auschwitz. The others soon learned not to take the proffered sweets when the good doctor came calling."

"It lies!" The German howled, "It's not even human!"

I couldn't detect if it was lying. It gave off a smell like old embers in a fireplace. I couldn't assess the German either. Perhaps my internal lie detector only worked on mortals. It didn't matter either way. I had seen inside the German's soul, hadn't I? I knew the countless depravities he'd joyfully indulged in. I felt nauseous that I had actually contemplated joining such a twisted sociopath.

The German leaned close and whispered fiercely in my ear, "Don't believe him! He only wants the crystal!"

"It belongs with me, *with us*." The old man said, his voice still calm but his eyes dangerous. "Sabine, or Celeste as you knew her, was charged with bringing it to me before she was most foully murdered by your *friend* here." He said, looking at the German.

And then it struck me. "You were the one she was talking about," I said as the night in the woods came flooding back into my memory.

"Of course," he replied. "I'd known for some time that the beasts had it hidden, incorporating it in some fashion into their annual midnight rituals. The same location was never used twice. Sabine was my best hope of discovering it. But winning their trust had a cost."

"Me," I said angrily. "I was the cost."

"When I took her off the streets, she was half-dead, whoring her body for heroine, an orphan. It was a simple matter to make her believe that the Brotherhood was responsible. To avenge the death of her family, who in fact perished in a tenement fire, she became a willing disciple. That is until she decided to inexplicably save your life, and keep the crystal."

My poor Celeste, used and misunderstood by everyone, including me.

"It belongs to the Twelve!" The German growled next to me. "We found it, it's ours!"

"Indeed?" the gentlemen said, lifting an eyebrow. "I suppose that is true, if massacring a crew of archeology interns qualifies as a claim to ownership."

Klaus started to protest again, but the man turned to me, ignoring him. "They were on a field outing exploring the remains of a Bronze Age metal mine at Llanymynech Hill on the Shropshire border. It's quite depressing even by Welsh standards, a desolate place of rock and scrub, although it wasn't always so." His eyes seemed to turn briefly inward but then snapped back into focus. "I imagine they were hoping to unearth some remnant of a mining implement, but they found far more. How puzzled and overjoyed they must have been. Until they were slaughtered to the last. It was merely a case of bad luck on their part, but camping in the Highlands on the night of a full moon does take some courage. Before their blood was cold, the crystal had already cast its spell on the beasts' leader," he turned to Klaus, "*Bartos*, that was what he called himself I believe?"

I thought of Penelope's face when she'd held the crystal and shuddered.

"May his name be cursed for all eternity," spat Klaus.

"Bartos wasted no time in forming his own *brotherhood*, until his untimely death along with every single one of his followers."

"It can't be controlled!" snarled Klaus. "It destroyed them all!" He turned to me, "We must keep it hidden and protected. Forever."

I looked at the old man. "What would you do with it?" I asked.

"It will be used...to set certain things to right once more," he said cryptically.

"Who...What are you?" I asked.

"Have you not deduced it yet?" he said with a smirk, "You're a clever one I can see. What am I, Thomas?"

I thought back to Penelope's whispered words and of the picture from Justin's book. *An old man in a robe with a long walking stick in his hands, thrust out before him towards a mirror image of himself.*

He was right. I did know what he was. "You're nothing," I said, and watched as his face darkened. "You're a shadow, a golem, created by Merlin and sent to do his bidding. Only when he tried to send you back, you killed him. No wonder you want the crystal." I finished. "It's your God, your creator."

"And I know something else," I continued, "If Klaus failed to kill even one of your kind, and I'm not at all certain you *can* be killed, then what chance do any of us have of getting out of this room alive?" The man, *the golem*, had gone absolutely still, his eyes locked on mine, the intent in their inky depths unknowable.

"If I give it to you, I need your word that you'll take it and leave us unharmed."

I held my breath. I could sense him sizing me up.

He dipped his head a fraction. My internal lie detector was useless around him, but good old fashioned intuition told me he would kill us all the second he had the crystal. There was no doubt in my mind about it.

"You can't! I forbid it!" raged Klaus.

I looked at Klaus and he shrunk away from what he saw blazing in my eyes. "I could kill you in your weakened state, and we both know it. You're fortunate I'm letting you leave this room alive, you murdering scum."

I pointed at Eric. "It's in my jacket," I said, and all eyes went to him. As he looked at me in disbelief, I gave a barely perceptible shake of my head. His eyes widened and he swallowed, nodding once in return.

Eric started to take the jacket off, and then pivoted, running for the door.

For a split second everyone stood motionless, and then chaos descended. The German launched his body into the air after Eric, claws outstretched, fangs bared, murderous intent rippling through his muscles. As I watched, the old man moved without moving. One moment his body occupied one space in the room and the next he stood blocking the door, transporting his body a dozen feet in the blink of an eye. I leapt, not in the direction of the door but towards the shotgun, turning back into my human form as I did so. Claws weren't very helpful for what I had planned.

"Eric! Down!" I screamed. Raising the stock to my shoulder, I pulled the trigger. The recoil of the blast slammed me back into the screen behind me, shattering it in an implosion of glass.

At such close range, a hole the size of a cantaloupe opened in the side of the German's back, but not before he'd taken what would be his last and perhaps best blow at his old adversary. His claws razored through the air, catching the old man directly across the neck, severing his head clean from his shoulders. A look of surprise registered on his face as it bounced off the wall and rolled to a stop, the eyes staring sightless up at the ceiling. The body swayed for a second before toppling to the floor next to Eric who, although covered in the German's gore, appeared unharmed as he scrambled away.

My back felt warm where I'd hit the screen and when I touched it my hand came away red. The German gave a wet cough and then vomited up a great gout of blood onto the floor. He managed to drag himself over to the wall and collapse against it, a shaking hand wiping vainly at the blood from his mouth.

"Clever." He said, a large pool of blood spreading outward from his body across the floor. His body shrunk before my eyes until a mortal wounded man lay dying. "If I had not been impaired…no matter." His head began to dip, his body slumping. "Y-young wolf…retrieve the remaining shards …and you may yet survive."

"Wait!" I cried, "What other shards? What are you talking about?" His head dropped to his chest. He was gone.

I set the gun down and approached Eric.

"Are you alright?"

"I don't think I ever will be again," he said, "Who's Thomas?"

I frowned and then let out a deep sigh. "There are some things I haven't been completely truthful about. I'll explain it all later, I swear." I held out a hand, but instead of accepting it, his eyes widened in fear.

"Look man, I know it's going to be hard to trust me, but--" I realized he wasn't looking at me, but behind me.

Oh, hell.

I spun around to see the body of the old man thrashing on the floor as if riddled with invisible bullets. Thin fingers of smoke began to seep from its skin. They writhed as if alive, gathering into a small storm cloud near the ceiling.

Too late, I wished I'd asked the German how he had managed to escape the other black thing, the minion. The old man had referred to it as Praxus. How could I possibly hope to succeed where he had failed? A wild and desperate thought seized me. If it wanted the crystal so badly, maybe I could still force some kind of parlay.

"Eric, give me the diamond!" I screamed turning back to where he'd been sitting, but the space was empty.

Instead I saw him scrabbling towards the door, backing away from the body of the old man, doing a sort of terrified crab walk.

I screamed at him again and his head snapped towards mine. "The diamond, Eric! It wants the diamond! It'll kill us both. Throw it to me! Now!"

I was afraid he was beyond reason, so stark was the terror on his face, but then he thrust his hand into the inner lining of the jacket, and pulled out the diamond. It released a single brilliant burst of light as he cocked his hand back and threw it. I watched it sail through the air, as the temperature of the air around me plummeted. The light began to dim as the smoke thickened above me. The diamond spun, its facets catching, and redirecting the light, scattering it across the walls. I strained to reach it, willing it into my hand. In the second before its surface brushed the tips of my outstretched fingers, the light in the room snuffed out and a legion of black worms fell upon me.

My mouth split wide in a scream of silent agony as they poured past my lips in one wriggling inky mass down my throat, filling my belly. Wracked with convulsions I felt my body descend into shock. My fist involuntarily closed around the diamond and a burst of light lit the room like a flash grenade. The light expanded into a red giant, encompassing everything in its fire.

My legs gave out and I collapsed to the floor. The worms ceased their ravenous feeding. I slowly opened my hand and stared in wonder at the red star in my hand, the entire room awash in its ruby brilliance. I was wracked anew by a fresh attack of spasms as a black torrent exploded in a grotesque flood from my mouth, returning to the living smoke that had once been the figure of a man. I gaped at it, a thick string of black drool hanging from my lips as it fled, flushing under the door in a rush of air. The light faded until I held a mere diamond once more. I was a shell, emptied of everything but the involuntary will to continue breathing. I don't know how long I lay there. When I finally managed to open my eyes and lift my head, Eric was standing over me, wearing a strange look on his face. I raised my hand to him and watched as he swung the barrel of shotgun around.

"Alright Ben Ramsey, or Thomas – or whoever the hell you are," he said and pumped the action once. "I think I'll be taking that diamond now."

CHAPTER FORTY

"I can explain," I said, wincing at the raw redness of my throat and lips.

"Explain what?" he said angrily. "That you've been lying your ass off to me, the chump that's been backing you up for the last 5 years?" He shook his head. "I'm done being your wet nurse. All the times I've risked my life saving your ass, and you don't even trust me enough to tell me your real name!" He looked at me suspiciously, his eyes studying my face. "What is your name anyway?"

I sighed. "Thomas. Thomas Spell."

"Yeah? Well I like Ben better."

"So do I."

"And you're not from Chicago either?"

"Kansas. Just outside of Abilene."

"Kansas!" he laughed. "Jesus fucking Christ!"

He lowered the shotgun slightly, but brought it back up fast when I raised a hand towards him.

"Eric, I only did what I had to do to protect you, both of you."

He snorted in contempt.

"You're the only family I have." It was the truth, sadly enough. "When I got back from London I was lost, alone and on the run. She was supposed to come back with me but…"

"She?"

"Celeste, a girl I met in Paris." I said, and then it all came out in one big rush. "She nursed me back to health after I was attacked, although I didn't know then what had really happened to me. I thought I'd been attacked by some deranged maniac that night in the forest. She told me she'd infiltrated this cult that preyed on foreigners. As an initiation she'd been told to bring someone to them, a sacrifice. She cried a lot and kept apologizing - told me she only did it to find out where they performed their rituals so she could stop them. She said she was looking for something they had, something valuable. Thanks to me, we found it right before they showed up.

"She said a lot of things, but I was in bad shape. I only remember bits and pieces. The night she left, she mentioned a loose end she had to tie up, and then we could be together, and we would be safe. Two days passed. I could still barely get out bed. I went through her things, looking for a clue, anything that might tell me where she'd gone. All I found was a key with a number on it inside an envelope in her purse. It looked like it might fit one of those lockers you can rent at the airport."

I stopped to spit a black gob onto the floor. I wondered if any permanent damage had been done to my insides. I cleared my throat and continued, "I didn't know what to do. I was all alone and I didn't know anyone in London. The next morning on the news …." I paused, not wanting to relive those memories. "My French sucked, but I didn't need to understand what the news anchor was saying when they pulled the body out of the Seine. I knew. They blurred her face, but I recognized the hair, jacket, and boots. It was her. I wept. I loved her, and maybe she loved me too. The next day I set out on my own because there was nothing else to do. I showed the key to a taxi driver, and he took me to the Charles De Gaulle airport. As it turned out that key did fit a locker, and inside was a backpack with a change of clothes for both of us, some money, and two passports, only the names inside weren't our real names. There was one other item she'd packed in there too. I always thought she put it in there for sentimental reasons. She had a great sense of humor, you know. I think you can probably guess what it was."

"The diamond."

"Yeah. Hiding right under my nose in that stupid snow globe all these years. But it's not a diamond, Eric."

"Oh really?" he said a sneer twisting his face, "It sure as hell looks like one to me. I think I'll take a closer look and decide for myself."

I hurried on, "It's got some sort of power. It saved me just now. I'm not sure how, but it did."

"Well, that should make it even more valuable then, shouldn't it?" he said.

I looked at him and realized in that moment that I didn't really know him at all.

"So that's it? After all we've been through, this is how it ends?"

His face reddened. "I'm done cleaning up after you, sitting in the shadows as you take all the glory."

I was dumbfounded. "Glory?"

"You get to do whatever you want, you selfish prick!" he raged. With each word, his face grew darker, his voice shaking with anger. "You're a murdering fucking drunk that can't even hold down a job flipping burgers! You're a train wreck of monumental proportions! I have a masters degree in Chemistry, but what am I to you? Just a pusher, nothing else." He jabbed the muzzle forward until it was touching my forehead. "And the most ridiculous thing of all is that she's in love with you and you don't even know it!"

"What?"

"Don't fucking play with me!"

The muzzle was a blur, knocking me to the floor as he brought it across my face in a vicious sweep. There was blood in my mouth. I tried to push myself back up, but before I could he drove the heavy wooden stock of the shotgun into my back, knocking me back down. I gritted my teeth and decided to stay down rather than encourage another blow. The Wolf wanted to tear his head off, but I controlled it now. Whatever the German's faults I owed him that much.

"I've earned this," he resumed in a calmer, more triumphant tone. "I knew that if I stuck around long enough something would come my way. I was ready to burn this place to the ground too if I had to."

What?

I lifted my head. "No, I don't believe it."

"Kind of a coincidence wasn't it?" he laughed. "That fucking fire alarm caught me off guard though. Just bad luck that Nells had put it up the night before."

"But you were burned," I said, not willing to believe what I was hearing.

"Yeah, I had to make it look good, a little too good. That Kerosene was more flammable than I thought. I'd splashed some on my shirt sleeve when I was spreading it around and whoosh!"

"But why? Why would you do that to me?" I cried. "My whole life burned up in that fire!"

"Shut up!" he prodded me with barrel again. "The bitch was getting too close! Never in my wildest fantasies did I dream she'd actually find a cure! But then she came running out of the lab, all wild-eyed and yelling about a break-through and I knew what I had to do. I had to set her back. What was going to happen to me, if she succeeded? Did you ever think of that? Once you were cured and everything was hunky dory, what would happen to *my life*? I'll tell you exactly what would have happened. I'd be right back to filling prescriptions for high blood pressure and foot fungus at the drugstore every day, and watching *Family Guy* reruns at night. Back to my sorry-ass boring life. I wasn't going to let that happen. I was part of a team! I was the right hand man of a werewolf, for Christ's sake! I mattered for the first time in my life. And I knew, *I knew*! That if I was patient and bided my time, something would come along. And here it is."

My mind raced. I turned over and looked into his flushed face.

"And the swamp? The black smoke?"

"You're the one that told me about it in the first place!" he laughed. "The rest just took a little imagination. After I found the lock-box empty," he grinned even wider at my puzzled look, "You never thought there might be two keys? Anyway, the dart that hit that little ice queen was a dud. When I came down to get you she was wide awake. I couldn't very well start rummaging through your pockets. A good plan spoiled by shitty luck."

"So it's all about money?"

"No *Thomas*, it's all about a shit-load of money!" His glee sickened me. "This has been fun, but it's time to bid you a fond adieu. Hand it over old buddy."

Maybe I could have transformed and finished him off before he had time to shoot me. Maybe. Probably. But I didn't. I couldn't bring myself to do it, even after the betrayal. He was, or had been, my best friend. I felt empty. Without another word, I flipped it to him.

He caught it with one hand, still training the shotgun on me with the other.

"Don't try and follow me, Ramsey."

"My name's Thomas."

"Whatever."

"And I won't have to," I said, as the door behind him swung open.

His confident smirk slipped an inch. He tried to swing the gun around but it was far too late. I'd never known Penelope to shoot anything before, but at this range it didn't matter. The rifle recoiled twice and Eric's head jerked to the side, a hand to his neck. He managed to pull one dart out and then crumpled to the floor.

"You're not the only one with a surprise up your sleeve, asshole," she said.

The diamond was still clasped in Eric's hand. I thought I saw it pulse once, but when I looked again it lay muted and silent.

And then who should come padding into the room behind Penelope, but Duke. He looked like a wounded soldier with half of his head wrapped in white gauze, but his step was as spry as ever. He trotted over to where Eric lay, sniffed once, and then lifted his leg before either of us could stop him.

"Duke, no!" she scolded, trying not to laugh. I couldn't help but join her. At the sound of my laughter her eyes flashed towards me, cold and piercing. She had never looked more fiercely beautiful than in that moment. As our eyes met, she adjusted her grip on the rifle.

"You've got some explaining to do, Thomas," she said.

"Yes," I said, careful not make any sudden movements. "Yes I do."

CHAPTER FORTY ONE

Detective Michael Hannity had a headache. A bad one. It had subtly announced itself two days ago with a slight throb behind his left eye. That same day one of the new beat cops, a big clean-cut Southside Irish kid fresh from the academy, had rapped on his door and then stood nervously outside his office for permission to enter. It had struck Hannity as pretty damn humorous considering the kid could probably bench press him without breaking a sweat.

You were intimidated by Detectives too at one time, he reminded himself.

He sighed and lowered the lid of his laptop, nodding at him to come in.

"Sorry to disturb you sir, but I thought you'd want to hear this."

Probably some bullshit dead end lead on another home invasion. Feigning interest he said, "I'm all ears Flaherty, lay it on me."

"It just came over the radio, shots have been fired at the suspect's apartment sir," Flaherty blurted out.

He looked at the kid, waiting for more, but when he continued to just stand there looking at him, his good humor soured, "Which suspect Officer? DB Cooper? The Unabomber? I need a little more to go on here."

Flaherty cleared his throat and plowed ahead, "Your suspect, sir. The Washington Park slasher, Ramsey."

That was when the throbbing had started. And no amount of Advil since had managed to put a dent in it. He still couldn't believe that someone, maybe Ramsey maybe not, had managed to sneak into the apartment, overpower two seasoned officers, and make a clean getaway. And for what? That was what he couldn't figure out. The place had already been picked over by half a dozen cops and a K-9. If the murder weapon was there they would have found it. So why? It didn't make any sense.

Two days had passed since then and still no leads. Ramsey was probably halfway to Guadalajara by now. The mayor would not be a happy camper when he found out.

He flinched as a fresh bolt of pain erupted behind his left eye.

Jesus, this fucking headache!

Knowing it wouldn't do any good, he opened his top drawer and pulled the half-empty bottle of Advil out anyway. He shook four out into his hand, and then thinking better of it added another two. He washed it all down with the dregs from a cold coffee cup, grimacing at the chalky bitterness. When he looked up, all he could think was "*I'm having déjà vu.*" There was Flaherty again, standing outside his office. Through the fog of his throbbing skull he watched him raise a hand to knock.

"Just come in for Christ's Sake!" he barked, startling Flaherty, who adjusted his hat before opening the door.

"I'm sorry to bother you sir," he began.

"Just spit it out officer, I'm not in the mood for 27 questions right now." He knew he was being a jerk, but he couldn't help himself. The pounding in his head grew stronger, as if anticipating what the kid was going to say.

"You'll have to come see this for yourself sir."

Hannity grimaced and stood up.

I should have been a firefighter like my old man.

He walked numbly past the rows of cubes, mostly empty, out to the front door of the station. There were lights flashing and the sounds of voices, ones he recognized. He was surprised to see most of the station standing outside. There were squad cars blocking off the street on either end of the block. A tight knot of officers were crowded around something on the ground. As he approached them, they parted to reveal what lay on the pavement.

He could tell right away the person was dead. There's a certain way that corpses lie, like marionettes with their strings cut, arms and legs askew at odd angles. The corpse had been wrapped in a fleece blanket, one of those massive bedsheet sized ones they sell at stands on the side of the road, emblazoned with Sponge Bob or Elvis or maybe a snarling jaguar. This one happened to sport a garish neon zebra-stripe pattern. Whoever dumped the body hadn't bothered to secure the blanket with any rope or twine so it had rolled free to sprawl naked at the front steps. Lights were on in some of the homes across the street. Maybe someone had gotten a look at the vehicle's plates, but the late hour and cold would have kept most people inside, not looking out their front windows for a corpse to drop. To make matters worse, the planned installation of a camera outside the station had been delayed again due to budget cuts.

Hannity sighed and kneeled down to examine the body. The John was a huge specimen of a man, one who'd obviously lifted weights judging by the armor of muscle covering his broad chest and arms. It hadn't saved him. Judging by the ragged softball size hole in his ribs, he'd been shot by something powerful and at a very close range, most likely a 12 gauge.

Whoever snuffed him was smart enough not to use their own blanket or sheets, which probably meant no prints. As he bent over the body he noticed something attached to the skin with a safety pin, rustling in the night air, a handwritten note on a sheet of office paper.

Pulling a pen from his pocket he carefully flipped the folded end over, and his headache suddenly vanished.

It read, "Dear Detective Hannity, Merry X-mas. DNA doesn't lie. This jerk is the Washington Park slasher. You're welcome asshole."

CHAPTER FORTY TWO

I pulled the van over to the curb and killed the engine.

"How did you know?" Penelope asked.

I looked at her, my eyebrows raised. She was rubbing her eyes and yawning. We were both wiped out.

"That you weren't going to shoot me?"

"No, stupid. How did you know he was lying–that he was the one who murdered the people in the park?"

"It was something that he said to me right after he took the necklace from me – the one that Celeste had always worn. He said that sometimes he would keep something, a memento from his victims. At the time I didn't think about it. I just went crazy after he admitted killing her..." I stopped and shook my head in shame. I had been ready to forgive the cold-blooded murderer of my first true love, simply because he'd welcomed me into his club.

I buried the feeling and went on, "Afterwards his words kept coming back to me, nagging at me, but it wasn't until I went through the contents of his satchel that it struck me." There was nothing unusual inside it at first glance, just ordinary things you might expect someone to tote around – a tin of mints, half a pack of smokes (that I pocketed), his passport, a pack of gum, and best of all, money. He'd been carrying a little under 3,000 in Euros, more money than I'd hoped to see in a long time. "When I turned his bag upside down and shook it, something clattered to the floor -- a gold wedding band with B.C. engraved on the inside." I looked at her to see if she'd figured it out yet, but she just nodded impatiently for me to continue.

"Those initials sparked something in my memory and my meeting with the reporter, Brent. The blonde he'd talked with, the one that died in the hospital, what had he said her name was? He hadn't. But he'd put it in his article – the one I'd stuffed in my pocket after my place was tossed. I went through my pockets and found the page from the paper. There were the names of the victims – Darren Copeland, Anya Czacki, Duncan Freeley, and Bridget Cler: B.C.

Penelope shook her head, "But why did he kill them? What did they have to do with anything?" I shrugged, "Knowing him it could have just been for the fun of it. Or more likely it was just bad luck on their part."

People will continue to find themselves in the wrong place at the wrong time when they cross your path.

He had been an efficient killer if nothing else.

But with the German dead, how would I ever be able to clear my name? Who would believe me? Penelope had surprised me with her straight-faced suggestion that we simply deliver the German to the cops and let them do the rest.

"I guess I owe him in a way," I said. "Without him I don't think I ever would have been able to gain control of it on my own."

"So you don't need them, the pills I mean, anymore?" she asked.

"I'm not absolutely sure, but I don't think so." I could feel the wolf stir as the words left my mouth. I knew that it would always be watching, circling, looking for an opportunity to break free.

"Who would have guessed that surrendering was the key to beating it? I feel like I'm walking around with a lion on a leash, but it's better than looking over my shoulder, waiting for it to ambush me."

"That still leaves…" she didn't need to finish.

I could feel its weight in my vest pocket, but it was just a rock again. It seemed to have gone back to sleep for the time being.

"I don't know what it is and I don't know why Celeste wanted it in the first place, or why it means so much to the Brotherhood and whatever the hell those other black things are. But what I do know is that it's not done with us yet. It still has a role to play somehow or somewhere. I can feel it in my bones."

I licked my lips and went for it. It was now or never.

"Penelope?"

"Yes?" she said a little warily.

"Do you like fish and chips?"

"What?" she said, and then laughed. "Yes, actually. Why?"

"Because I think it's time to take it home," I said.

"Take *what* home, the diamond?"

"It's not a diamond. It's a Crystal from Merlin's Staff."

I waited for her to laugh at me, but she didn't.

I plowed ahead. "They won't stop looking for me – for it. One way or another this has to end. Penelope, will you go with me to London?"

She looked at the floor for a moment and then back up at me. "Go to London with a bona fide werewolf? To the power center of a thousand-year-old secret society that tried to kill you in order to possess the one thing you'll be bringing directly to them? Not to mention, that black shadow-thing, and the possibility that there may be more of them there?"

"Well, when you put it that way," I said.

"I'd love to."

"I knew it was a stupid – wait! You will?"

She leaned in close and nipped my lower lip softly with her teeth.

"An entire Brotherhood of wolves couldn't keep me away. *Thomas*."

I smiled and closed the short distance between us, but then stopped short, "There's one last thing I need to take care of before we leave, though," I said.

"I have something of my own to take care of," she said and pulled me in.

The wolf growled and bared his fangs.

Down boy.

Down.

CHAPTER FORTY THREE

"Would you care for a beverage sir?" asked the pretty young flight attendant as she bent over, a single strand from her long blonde tresses floating weightless on the air between them. Chanel No. 5 and Listerine mingled not unpleasantly about her, but failed to mask the two vodka martinis she'd had for lunch. His lips curled in amusement.

Naughty girl.

He'd always preferred brunettes, but then again, he was no gentleman. He favored her with a wide smile. His perfect white teeth were strangely luminescent in spite of the sunlight shining in through the small port window next to him. Handsome in a roguish kind of way, she found herself unable to deny him a smile in return, one usually reserved for cute guys at the bar after work. His eyes held hers in a gaze that seemed to promise something. A spark of desire ignited deep within her and she discovered that the first two buttons of her blouse had somehow come undone. As she moved to fix herself, one of his long fingers reached out, drawing a lazy "S" down the nape of her neck. A low moan escaped from her lips.

What's happening to me?

She found she didn't care. Her eyes fluttered and closed, as he bent closer to whisper something softly in her ear like a lover. When she opened them again, his face filled her vision, and she gasped, taking an unsteady step backwards, upsetting the ginger ale in the hand of the passenger behind her.

"Hey! Watch what you're doing!"

But she was already gone, hurrying, *no running,* down the aisle, nearly tripping in her haste to escape. That night she would awake screaming in her hotel room, and in the morning she would tell herself that it was just a trick of the light and too many double shifts. She hadn't really seen his mouth filled with long jagged teeth, sharpened to points like miniature daggers, the entire side of his face a melted horror of scar tissue.

The following week she would quit, citing nervous exhaustion, and overdose on sleeping pills, unable to stand the nameless gnawing fear that no amount of therapy or intoxication could free her from.

The human mind was so weak. So suggestible.

He pondered this idly not for the first time. It was no wonder that the herd of humanity was oblivious to the wolves roaming freely among them. He took a sip from the small Waterford rocks glass on the tray before him and sighed contentedly.

Unfashionable perhaps, but he still preferred the lightly sweetened Old Tom Gin from better days past. Bordeaux, once his one and only passion, now carried with it the bitter aftertaste of betrayal – another gift *she* had given him. Refilling his glass from the pewter flask in his coat pocket, he stifled a yawn.

He tapped his long fingernails on the tray before him, his thoughts returning to the business at hand, and this *was* a business trip, by God. Although one couldn't begrudge oneself a bit of play now and again. The image of the girl's terrified eyes as she fled down the aisle brought an unpleasant smile to his lips. There were still unfinished matters to attend to and he would enjoy seeing them brought to a decisive and satisfying *denouement.*

Never again would he question his instincts. It had been a critical error in judgment to trust the Shade in the first place, one that he now intended to remedy with his own personal intervention. It had sworn it could control the rest of the horde. How they managed to cling to some semblance of humanity was a mystery.

The Cythraul had turned out to be far stronger than he had surmised. He'd thought their power had been diminished from hiding in the shadows all these years.

Shadows within shadows

They'd merely been biding their time, waiting for the right opportunity to strike. And the tracker had made a bloody mess of things. To his core he'd remained nothing more than a brute killer. If something stood in his way he dispatched it with no hesitation or regard for consequences. He had even let the police get involved.

Careless.

There lay an important distinction between the display of power and its employ. At times it could be just as effective to show your enemy the sword as to use it. The Tracker had fought when he should have exercised restraint, and lay dead now as a result.

The power of the Twelve was undeniable. But they had become complacent, secure in the belief that they were no longer beholden to the physical laws of nature, Gods walking among men, beyond death. And yet they had been "The Hundred" once. But that was long ago. The world had changed. The Mage had been right; all were cursed to forget.

The man with the Ruby Rings knew that he was neither the strongest nor the oldest of his kind, but he had something far more useful: patience. That and the will to act as the circumstances demanded, no matter the price.

The captain's voice informed him that they would be landing at Heathrow shortly. From there it was a quick hop to Paris, barely enough time for a gentleman to enjoy a drink.

He poured the last of the gin and held his glass before him, toasting the empty air. It had become a ritual of his these years past, a way to honor the memory and grieve a loss in his own cheerless fashion. "To you my dear, my most promising student, and gravest disappointment, my darling, Celeste." And then under his breath, "Bloody harlot." He drained the glass and closed his eyes. The liquor warmed his blood, but made the massive purple scar that spread over the left side of his face burn with a slow, hot itch. Another gift from *her*. He had survived, just as he always would, and now it was within his grasp at last. He looked down at his hands. The plane dropped a wing, and the rings flashed once in the lights from the city below, briefly painting the cabin about him in a brilliant crimson palette. He closed his eyes and began to hum a song from an age long past. An aspiring young bard had sung it for him one night on the road after they'd shared several flasks of wine. He liked it so much that he'd decided to take it, along with the man's beating heart.

To the city ere I go good man to make my fortune true
For in the market there tis bound to be a fool or two
Mine sole possession be this blade and it hath done me well
Both pockets they be empty and I've clothe nor fowl to sell

It matters little my good man, I'll send them all to hell
I'll send them all to hell

Four rows up, a young man shared a laugh with the dark haired beauty next to him. As they kissed, the man with the ruby rings grinned in anticipation. The sacrifice would still be given, he would see to it personally. He smiled contentedly as the landing gear dropped open. "To the city ere I go…" he said with a smile.

* * * *

On the west side of Chicago, a young man sighed heavily as he bent to lift the metal rolling security gate in front of the store where he worked. He sighed yet again as he opened the door and flipped a switch on the wall, bathing the drab aisles and shelves in the washed out light of the overhead fluorescent panels. A long monotonous day of filling prescriptions lay before him as he shrugged into his white lab coat and straightened the label pinned to his pocket that read, "Eric Evans, Assistant Pharmacist."

* * * *

In another part of the city a little girl awoke in her bed to the sound of paws padding across the floor. She was certain it was just another dream, until the familiar feel of a wet tongue eagerly licked her face. "Mommy!" She cried, hugging the small body fiercely to her own. "Mommy! He's home! Duke is home!"